THE GOD HUNTERS:

WHERE THE LAND MEETS THE SKY

MARK REED

authorHOUSE®

AuthorHouse™
1663 Liberty Drive
Bloomington, IN 47403
www.authorhouse.com
Phone: 1 (800) 839-8640

Published by AuthorHouse 11/18/2016

ISBN: 978-1-5246-5133-6 (sc)
ISBN: 978-1-5246-5131-2 (hc)
ISBN: 978-1-5246-5132-9 (e)

Library of Congress Control Number: 2016919357

Print information available on the last page.

This book is printed on acid-free paper.

Prologue

Dean, a small alien male with dark-blue skin, made his way carefully through the rounded white corridors of the Masters of Science and Technology (MST) spaceship known as the *Nortahn*. At every corner he would crouch and stall for a moment before moving cautiously ahead. He listened for distant footsteps, a sign of any fellow soldiers moving about. Fortunately, he heard nothing while sneaking through the corridors. The vessel was unusually quiet for some strange reason.

Step by step, creeping through more of the ship's hallways, he eventually made his way closer to the bridge. Only a few more decks to go and he'd be able to contact the high council and let them know about the mutiny on board.

Just hours ago, most of the four hundred crew members had renounced their affiliation with the MST. The crew had secretly joined the band of rogue agents—those individuals who would stop at nothing to ensure they maintained a dominant hold over all races living within the Expanse. Security forces on the ship had tried their best to control the situation, but several serious fights had broken out. In the end, none of the original security crew, which included the ship's captain, had survived.

"C'mon. C'mon," Dean quietly fussed at himself. "You're almost there. Stop stalling."

He was covered from neck to toe in a black armored bodysuit with boots, and a holstered handgun was strapped around his thigh in case he had to deal with any unexpected problems.

With his back pressed flat against a white steel wall, he quickly peeked around the corner down a long, wide hallway. Bright lights shone through silvery metal grates overhead, reflecting upon the polished floors below.

Again, there were no sounds.

After a much-needed sigh of relief to calm his nerves, Dean brushed his hand over his short black hair, then crouched down a bit before he hurried down the hallway, making sure every boot step fell as quietly as possible.

The huge main door to the bridge stood ahead, and he smiled knowing he had managed to get this far without grabbing anyone's attention.

Proximity sensors detected his approach. The thick, dark steel door split in two with a hiss and slid into the surrounding walls. Dean slipped through the slow-growing gap without hesitation or heed. When he turned around, he gasped in shock at the sight before him on the spacious bridge.

"About time you join us," said an extremely tall and burly alien male. His name was Rhynor, and he was a longtime acquaintance of Dean's. He stood before the roomy captain's chair that sat atop a three-tiered platform with steps built around its outer edges.

Rhynor was dressed in an identical armored suit but had his zipper open to show off his powerful chest. He came from a race of demons having charcoal-colored skin and large, spiraled brown horns just above both temples. He was bald with a rough and tough-looking face. His race was known for their resilience and impressive anatomy, which included formidable musculature and height.

The bridge design was a typical MST layout, composed of a substantial round area with numerous workstations positioned throughout. A movie theater–size view screen covered the front wall. Short staircases linked the different levels together, and overall it was very easy to get around from one level to the next.

Dozens of officers stood around staring at Dean, and all of them sported a look of familiarity, of friendship. However, they clearly showed signs of uncertainty as to whether or not Dean could be trusted. Each gave him a questionable glance with a brow raised.

"Why have you seized control of the ship?" Dean asked, turning to face his old friend. "So many worlds are opposing the MST right now, along with the media, who are painting such a bad image of us. Entire star systems are armed with fleets of ships ready to destroy any MST vessels that show up. Whatever you've got planned, you're just going to add to the problem and get a *lot* of innocent people killed."

With a mild laugh, Rhynor shook his head and walked down the three steps from the captain's chair. Close to seven feet tall, a mix of powerfully built and stocky, he dwarfed Dean when he stopped in front of him and stood with his hands clasped on his waist.

"I don't intend on getting any of *my* people killed," Rhynor boldly stated. "But I can't promise the same thing for anyone who stands against our goal."

"Your goal?" Dean stared curiously into Rhynor's eyes. He sounded out of breath, nervous, and confused. "What are you planning?"

Rhynor laughed as he turned away and walked over to a workstation occupied by a small female alien from a reptilian race. Her short and stubby lizard tail whipped from side to side through the back opening of her chair. Her emerald scales glimmered in the bright lights shining from above. She had no hair, her scales covering her entire head too.

Rhynor leaned over and tapped several holographic buttons floating above the workstation's smooth and glassy black top.

"The quickest way to kill a person is to stab them straight through the heart," he stated matter-of-factly. "So that's exactly what we intend to do."

On the main screen at the front of the bridge appeared a zoomed-out image of the Citadel hovering in the Field of Gods.

Dean let out a mild laugh riddled with a hefty amount of doubt and surprise. "You're going after the Keeper of the Citadel," he said. "With all those Bear Paw ships swarming around it? You're going to get yourself killed."

Rhynor rolled his eyes while shaking his head. "You sound like you don't have much confidence in me or my troops."

Now Dean shook *his* head. "You've read the reports, the stories published in the *Transgalactic Press*," Dean reminded his friend. "The Keeper will destroy every ship you send there. It's a futile attempt. Not to mention completely stupid. He's remarkably powerful. Haven't you read the reports about all the spirits he can summon? They will rip this ship apart and you along with it."

Rhynor ignored the remarks and focused on activating a few more glowing buttons floating over the workstation. Feeling confident in his plan, he reached up and stroked one of his enormous brown horns. "Maybe, maybe not," he answered in a haughty tone. "We've recently upgraded our weapons and our defensive systems, so I'm sure we'll be more of a challenge than before."

He paused for a moment, then returned to fiddling with some switches. "You may not be aware that we are able to mechanically reproduce some of the supernatural dispersion effects Ahzoul used against summoned spirits. Our methods are not as fine-tuned as his were, by any means, but they should still present an unexpected surprise during our attack. The Keeper won't be able to call forth any of his support creatures."

Dean crossed his arms over his chest. He doubted any type of assault on the Citadel would work, especially since he had witnessed in person the shredding of several MST spacecraft over the past few months. He knew exactly how powerful the Keeper of the Citadel was.

After he finished tapping buttons, Rhynor stood straight up, then turned around to face his friend. "But before we begin any crusade to restore the MST's position of dominance," he said, "we need to figure out what to do with you."

"Me?" Dean sounded surprised and somewhat confused, but he faintly smiled as he asked, "Do you feel threatened by me?"

Rhynor chuckled. "Not at all," he said. "It's just that I don't want to leave any loose ends lurking around here that could present a problem for us in the future."

Dean lowered his arms to his sides. He stared into his friend's dark eyes with growing concern. He thought of joking with his old buddy, recalling good times from their past, but then suddenly changed his mind. He wasn't here to play around. He only wanted to get word out of what was happening.

The main screen changed to a view of space as more officers moved around the bridge, all of them focused on various tasks, standard operating procedure.

"So I guess you're going to kill me then, huh?" Dean said bluntly.

Rhynor pulled his bulky handgun from the holster strapped around his thigh and pointed it right at Dean's face. "I think that would be a prudent course of action... Wouldn't you agree?"

Not surprised in the slightest, Dean took a deep breath and narrowed his gaze. He showed only a fraction of contempt considering the situation. Best to play it humble for now. "*Or* I could remain on board and help you," Dean offered with an easygoing smile.

Rhynor tilted his head with a questioning glance at his friend. "Why should I trust you when you seem so utterly opposed to what we want?"

In a bold move, Dean stepped closer to his friend, so that the tip of the gun stood only inches away from his forehead.

"If you wanted me dead," Dean said, "I think you would have fired by now."

Both of them paused for a moment before grinning at each other. Memories of their long-term friendship rolled around in each of their minds—the good times and bad, the headaches and laughs, the numerous missions they had completed together.

"You need me," Dean happily told his friend. He knew in his heart that he would never fully support any vengeful agenda by these rogue agents, but hopefully he could coerce his way into their gang. "With my decryption expertise and years of experience, you'd be foolish not to take me along on your mission. I can hack any ship's computer system, and you know it."

Rhynor gave considerable thought to Dean's proposal. After a long moment, he slowly lowered his gun and slipped it back into its

Truth be told, I missed our home. It had proven to be comforting for both me and Doug, especially being there together and having a place where we could simply relax and walk around naked without any worries. I remembered waking up to morning sunlight shining in through the sheer white drapes of our bedroom. Now I opened my eyes to thousands of glimmering stars or sometimes the occasional planet or swirling nebula saturated in vibrant colors.

"What are you thinking about, Little Bear?" Doug brushed his hand along my arm in the dim light of our bedroom.

We both had just woken up and were still in bed, both naked, the sheets a mess, covering half of my legs and neither of his feet. My tough guy lay curled alongside me with one side of his bearded face pressed upon my hairy chest. He softly rubbed his hand back and forth over my stomach. From his position, he could easily glance into my eyes, and I gathered he could tell I was lost in thought.

"You okay, sweetie?" he asked with a mild pat on my stomach.

I somewhat laughed while rubbing my hand back and forth across the defined muscles of his back. I loved the fact Doug didn't shave any part of his body. His shoulders and sides had a nice amount of hair covering them. A thicker area covered his butt crack, especially at the top.

I cradled the back of his head, slowly opening and closing my hand, moving my fingers over his short, smooth, dark hair that I enjoyed so much. "Yeah, I'm good," I told my sexy man with a sweet smile aimed his way. "Just remembering our house and how much fun we had there. You think we should try to get another one, or should we wait awhile?"

Doug took a deep breath, then let it out slowly. In the stillness of the moment, he moved his fingertips as lightly as he could over my stomach and chest. "Nothing would make me happier," he confessed with a trace of sadness in his voice. "That day hit me really hard, sweetie. And I don't blame you for what happened by any means. You know that."

I gave him a few consoling pats on his back. "I know you don't," I said. "But with that in mind, maybe after I get done with my meetings and some Bear Paw stuff, we could shift on over to Kakadu and see what kind of homes are available in the city. Does that sound like a plan?"

He covered my nipple with a soft, wet kiss. "I'd like that a lot," he said with a smile. "What time is your meeting with the high council?"

I glanced over at my pdPhone lying on the bedside table. A small holographic display of a digital clock floated just above it, no bigger than a paper check.

"I've got to be there in about two hours," I told Doug as he glanced into my eyes.

"You want me to come with you?"

I nodded. "You're more than welcome to. Plus, I think it would only strengthen our relationship with Admiral Rohn. At least I would hope so. He's been pretty cooperative during the transition and end of the MST's control. I'm still surprised the high council agreed to let the Bear Paw take over."

Doug laughed. His stomach and chest jiggled against mine. "I don't think you left them much of a choice with the recent ass kicking you put them through," he reminded me.

I rolled both of us over, placing Doug on his back so I could lie on top of him and enjoy his hairy, muscular chest. I let my body collapse against him, and he gave me a warm, tender hug, wrapping both of his arms around me with his beard pressed along my neck. A trace of his cologne tickled my nose, and I took a deep breath followed by a comfortable and contented sigh. Doug always smelled fantastic, and that included his sexy feet and socks after wearing a pair of leather cowboy boots. The sight of both always left me drooling and anxious to place a ton of kisses over them.

"I guess we need to get up soon and get our day started, huh?" I brushed my hand down his hairy arm.

Doug smiled at me. He tightened his hug and then, with a sweet and playful sway from side to side, kissed my cheek. "Yeah, the Keeper of the Citadel needs to get his tight little butt moving," he said. "Things aren't gonna change themselves."

That was for sure.

"Speaking of changes," I reminded him as I playfully drummed my hand against his chest, "isn't James getting the ship's engines upgraded today?"

"Oh, crap! I think you're right." Doug gently bounced his body beneath mine, flexing and moving his beefy legs up and down along with his hips as he kept both of his feet braced against the mattress. "I'm guessing Shake and Finger Pop will probably be here soon, if they're not already. We'll have to get some clothes on. Doubt they want to see us naked."

"Probably not," I agreed with a smile. "Although sometimes I do pick up a gay vibe from Finger Pop. You know how flamboyant he can be. He might actually enjoy seeing you naked. You never know."

Doug rolled his eyes with a shake of his head.

I pressed my hairy chest against his as we shared a few more kisses. He grabbed hold of my behind with both hands, then rubbed and massaged both cheeks slowly with a nice firm grip. Doug was a well-known ass man, without any doubt. He loved mine and tended to comment about it whenever possible.

As we crawled out of bed, I asked out of curiosity, "Did James fill you in on the details about the upgrade?"

Both of us were standing in front of our long mahogany dresser sifting through our drawers for socks and underwear. A huge mirror sat on top of it, connected with bolts.

"Nope," he answered with a shake of his head. "I mean, James already has shifting engines. Can't imagine what more Shake and Finger Pop would be bringing for him."

Doug selected a sexy pair of red-and-black over-the-calf socks without any underwear, since he preferred to go commando. A pair of blue-and-yellow crew-length socks caught my eye, and along with them I grabbed a favorite pair of boxer briefs covered in white and blue vertical stripes.

We walked into our bathroom and sat our undergarments on the white marble countertop in front of the huge mirror mounted on the wall above it. James had graciously provided us with a few minor upgrades to our room, just as he had done to his own quarters. Now, we had two sinks instead of one, and his highly skilled maintenance team (consisting of Kurt, Reese, and Amp) had widened the bathroom and made the shower about twice the size it had originally been.

I reached in and turned the silver handle halfway around to activate the water. Completely programmable, the shower shot warm water out of three overhead jets at a preset temperature.

Nearby, attached to the shower wall, was a two-foot-long shelf molded from the same ceramic tiles covering the shower walls. It provided a convenient spot for our bottles of bodywash and our bath sponges.

Doug and I always enjoyed washing each other. It proved fun getting my playful man all covered in soap, especially his boys and floppy weenie. And of course, he always spent several long moments working a soapy sponge between my cheeks. He usually also managed to work his fingers deep between them too. He just couldn't resist.

I could have stayed in the shower all day with him, but right now I felt kind of anxious to see what Shake and Finger Pop were going to offer to James. His ship upgrades really had me intrigued. Honestly, I couldn't imagine anything else they could do.

I stepped out of the shower first, dried off, and then slipped on my socks and underwear. Doug followed me right after he shut off the water. He stood in front of me with his hands on his waist, acting like he needed my help with putting his socks on.

Truth be told, pulling a pair of socks up Doug's legs was almost as arousing as taking them off of him. His calves, which were covered in dark hair, were so sexy.

I placed a kiss on his impressive wiener as he leaned back and wiggled his behind up onto the bathroom counter. He flashed me a twisted grin, sitting with his legs spread apart, his feet and toes dangling in the air. How could I refuse such a tempting invitation?

"You need some help there, big guy?" I reached up and gently tweaked his nipple.

He gave me a flirty wink but kept quiet the entire time as he lifted his right leg and handed me one of his socks. I leaned over and gave him a kiss on top of his foot. I bunched up the sock, slipped it over

5

his toes, pulled it up his outstretched foot, and then slowly worked it along his leg to where it stopped about three inches from his knee.

"You look sexy as hell in those," I told him.

After I helped put his other sock on, I glided my hands down the length of his legs and savored the feel of the cottony fabric. The socks had red feet with black toes, and both legs were completely black save for two red horizontal stripes around their tops.

My handsome man jumped down from the counter and gave me a kiss on the top of my head. "Thanks, sweetie," he said. "I enjoyed that."

As an added reward, he reached up and held my chin with one hand before he gave me a passionate kiss. He then held me close as he wiggled us back and forth together in a quick and happy dance.

Back in our bedroom, Doug's pdPhone chirped with a text message while we were getting dressed. It was a message from James. His two guests had arrived. "You guys *are* coming down to the engine room, right?"

Doug laughed. "We'd better get moving. Don't want to piss off James."

I put on a blue T-shirt with a pair of dark-blue jeans. Doug chose dark-brown jeans and a gray tank top with a black tattoo design printed on the front. He loved showing off his big biceps and muscular arms, and I didn't mind staring at them. I slipped on my black-and-white high-top sneakers, and he put on his hefty brown boots with steel toes and thick soles.

"Ready to roll!" I stood up from the edge of bed where I had sat down to tie my shoes.

Doug walked over to me and then reached down and rubbed his hand over my head. With his skull-cracking boots on, he stood a lot taller. He was already a smidge over six feet in height, but now with the added thickness of those boots, his manly frame seriously dwarfed my five feet seven inches.

I made my way to the bedroom door leading out into the hallway. Doug quickly moved past me with a grin on his face as he added some playful tickles along my side.

The white metal pocket doors separated and slid into the walls.

I shook my finger at Doug. "You'd better behave in front of our guests."

He laughed before glancing at me like I was crazy. "Me?" he said with a giggle. "I'm always a perfect gentleman. You know that."

I couldn't stop myself from laughing along with him.

We walked out into the pristine white hallway of the ship, our bedroom door closing behind us.

As we headed down the corridor, I leaned to the side and nudged my arm against Doug's. "Well, just to be on the safe side," I told him, "I'll keep my ass pointed away from you while we're down in the engine room."

He blew out a doubtful laugh. "Yeah, like *that's* going to stop me from touching it."

I raced ahead of him and opened the elevator door at the end of the hallway. "After you," I said with a courteous gesture of my opened arm, signaling for him to enter.

As soon as Doug stepped inside, I followed him, and we held hands while riding down to engineering.

2

Surprisingly, I had only been to the engine room twice despite so many visits to the ship *and* living on board. Two gigantic, tall cylindrical structures, the cores, sat beside each other at the far end of the fairly large area. These clear vessels were the primary components that powered the ship, and both glimmered similar to a glass of water and glitter that had just been stirred.

At the center of the room sat a semicircular setup of workstations with dozens of glowing, colorful holographic readouts and displays floating above their flat, glossy surfaces. James, Shake, and Finger Pop were standing there fingering all types of controls. There were even a few cords attached to the stomach of Shake's mechanized black bodysuit. It looked like one machine interfacing with another, from what I could tell.

The three maintenance guys were here too, two humans, one alien. Each kept busy with some sort of hands-on task. Also, the three Devil Bunnies we had met before seemed to be assisting them. I could only imagine how the much the maintenance guys loved the Devil Bunnies, especially since they were scantly clad and had very curvaceous bodies.

We walked right up and stopped behind James, who was my height and about the same build.

Doug tapped his little brother a few times on the shoulder. "How's it going?"

James turned around and actually smiled, which was a bit surprising considering James seldom showed a happy expression.

He tended to be serious and direct in most situations. But I shouldn't be so negative toward him. Now that he had a boyfriend, he surely had a lot of reasons to smile.

James was dressed in his usual garb of black pants tucked into knee-high leather boots with a tank top and a holstered gun strapped around his thigh. He always looked ready to fight or defend.

"It's going *very* well," James replied with a mild laugh. "We've got Shake hooked up to the mainframe, and he's installing a pretty awesome upgrade to the ship's systems."

Doug looked about as curious as I felt.

"Oh, my boys," Finger Pop said with dramatic flair after he'd spun around to face us. He flung his arms wide open as he walked over to greet me and Doug. A huge smile covered his small demon face. He was a very short guy, and his gray skin and the stubby horns on his head were always an interesting sight. He was wearing tiny black pants and jacket with matching leather boots.

"How have you two been?" he asked us. "I feel like I haven't seen either of you in forever." He rolled his eyes and flashed a lighthearted wink and smile toward James, a bit of friendly teasing aimed toward our captain.

In my opinion, Finger Pop had always seemed like one of those happy drunks who would smile, laugh, and bat their hand through the air while drifting from one subject to the next with no concern at all. His counterpart was a complex machine, essentially a black bodysuit with helmet that walked and supported his tiny friend in many ways. Theirs was a unique relationship, and they mostly dealt in the armament trade.

"We're doing just fine," I told Finger Pop. "Some minor hiccups here and there, but I think we're finally getting our goals accomplished."

Finger Pop's small and dark demon eyes opened wide. He acted pleasantly surprised. "Well I am *very* glad to hear that," he said. "Maybe I should hire you two to help me with some business issues since you're so good at solving problems."

Doug and I both chuckled, and mechanical Shake let out a reply that sounded like a car's engine trying to start. I had no idea what he had said, but it made Finger Pop grin excitedly.

"So what's this amazing upgrade?" Doug sounded eager to know the details.

Finger Pop gestured for us to step closer before he turned back around and moved forward to tap a few controls at one of the workstation consoles.

"This particular upgrade," he explained, "will lift James right up to the same level as the MST, just like he should have always been."

High in the air one of the orange-and-green displays showed a scaled-down version of the Expanse with James's crab-shaped ship positioned in the center of it. Then to the side, another universe appeared, and slowly James's ship moved from one to the other.

"They're reprogramming my shifting engines so that I can actually take my ship out of the Expanse." James paused for a short moment. I could hear the excitement in his voice. "I'll be able to travel anywhere!"

The captivated and speechless stare on Doug's face must have matched mine perfectly.

"So anywhere the MST goes, James can follow," Finger Pop added with an excited bounce.

"Why would you need to do that, though?" Doug asked.

"Yeah," I added. "And please don't forget outer space in other universes is lethal. Make sure you don't leave the cargo bay doors or any windows open before you shift all around."

James lowered his head and eyeballed both of us with a "whatever" sort of look. "I'm not a total idiot, you two."

Willie, James's towering half-bear, half-human boyfriend, had walked up from behind us. He patted my back, then reached around me to give Doug a friendly shove on his shoulder.

He stopped beside James. "Plus I recently heard a rumor that a lot of MST and rogue agents are fleeing the Expanse, since so many worlds and races are opposing them right now and hunting them down. I'm surprised your journalist friend didn't call and tell you anything about that yet."

Interesting point. I hadn't heard from my reporter friend, Fred, for about ten days now. But I guessed with so much shit happening everywhere he was probably completely and utterly swamped with articles to write and interviews to cover.

Doug slung his arm across my shoulders and pulled me close. "I guess you'll have to give him a buzz and get the latest scoop, sweetie."

"I definitely need to," I answered.

Finger Pop tapped a few more controls. "Once everything gets uploaded from Shake, you should be able to scan your destination area and shift right to it. That'll allow you to start collecting coordinates for various places. And, James, I'm *sure* with David's help you'll be able to select several favorites right off the bat!"

I smiled. "I'll take you to *my* Earth, where Wyler and Josh live."

James nodded happily, clearly liking the sound of my suggestion.

"So how is everything going with integrating the Bear Paw into their new position?" James asked me.

I took a deep breath, then blew it out slowly through partially closed lips. "Well, I've got a meeting that Doug and I need to get to in a few minutes. The MST is supposed to be allowing several high-ranking bears into their council area today, as well as appointing a bunch of them to key positions on several worlds. It might actually turn into a long and exhausting day for us."

"So are any Bear Paw members meeting you two at the high council?" Willie sported a curious look. He was dressed in a pair of brown cargo shorts, absolutely huge sneakers since his feet were like size seventeen, and a sleeveless shirt he had left halfway unbuttoned, showcasing his hairy, humanlike chest.

From the enticed glances James kept flashing at his boyfriend, I imagined the captain of our ship was bogged down with various dirty thoughts rolling around inside his head.

I nodded in response to Willie's question. "Yeah, I told one of the captains we'd meet him on his bridge and then go down to the council meeting together so I could smooth over the introductions." I looked into Doug's eyes. "In fact, we probably need to get going."

Doug pulled me closer and rubbed his strong hand over my shoulder and then down my arm. He added a kiss on my head. "Let's go meet your bear captain."

The captain's name was Mah'garam Atlex, and I had met him a few times before, so I possessed his signature. Clearly, James and his companions were all consumed with the installation process, so the two of us leaving right now worked out perfectly.

"Well," I announced, "I guess we'll take off so you guys can finish up your work."

Willie paused for a moment from tapping buttons and turned to face me. He gave me a furry thumbs-up, along with a contented smile. "My people greatly appreciate all you've done for us, Keeper," he said in his gruff voice. "All growda ha'tars are thankful for your determination and your care for their well-being. And it means a great deal to me too."

I gave Willie an appreciative nod and smile. "More than happy to help," I assured him. "We've still got several issues to deal with, but we're definitely getting closer to the goal. Your race will be the caretakers of the Expanse. You have my word."

"Just be careful," James told us while he slid his fingers over a few controls. "The MST are notorious liars. Kick them in their asses to get things moving along if you have to."

Doug laughed as he reached down and patted my rear. "You're talking to the butt master, James. We've got it all under control. Trust me."

Amused, I shook my head with a minor roll of my eyes. I'd known a reference to my behind would enter the conversation sooner or later.

"All right," I said with a playful tap against Doug's stomach, "we're out of here."

I focused for a brief moment and then shifted us away.

Doug and I appeared at the center of a Bear Paw spaceship's bridge, which was somewhat like an office environment. Furry male and female bears were busy working at their posts, seated behind oversize workstations since all of them stood between ten and thirteen feet tall, with muscular, beefy bodies to match. Multiple doors surrounded the bridge's square shape, along with workstations positioned in groups of three with a few large chairs positioned nearby.

"Keeper," Atlex happily said as he walked over to greet us. A smile had grown along his short, thick snout. He wore only a black leather vest with matching knee-length shorts, along with black boots decorated with silver metal accents along their sides and around the fronts of the toes. One of the biggest bears here, Atlex positively dwarfed me *and* Doug.

We shook hands with our captain, who was covered in rich black fur with some touches of gray. With my remote-viewing ability, I sensed an overwhelming positive energy coursing throughout the ship's crew. Willie had hit the nail on the head. It pleased me to see them all happy for a change, versus agitated or degraded in one way or another.

"We have fifteen heavy cruisers in orbit of the planet Kallex," Atlex informed us, "and several shuttles are ready to take the new council members down to the central chamber room."

"Good," I told him. "I can shift us down to Admiral Rohn to get things started before the rest of your associates arrive."

Atlex held up his huge, furry paw for a second to pause our conversation. "However, despite the MST giving in to your demands," he said, "we are prepared to fight if needed. After years of seeing how untrustworthy they are, I've planned for the worst to happen."

Doug and I both found his prudence amusing.

"I don't blame you one bit," my handsome man said with a smile. "I'd do the exact same thing."

I pulled my pdPhone out of my pocket and tapped my finger over its screen to send Admiral Rohn a confirmation text to let him know I was ready to appear. After a few minutes of watching the bears doing their jobs and the impressive view of the Bear Paw fleet on the main view screen, the admiral returned my text message with a friendly invitation. I slipped my phone back into my pants pocket.

"I guess we're ready to go," I announced.

Doug patted my back in a consoling gesture as four barefoot bears, three males and one female, walked over and stood beside their captain. They were all dressed in shorts and armed with holstered handguns strapped around their impressive thighs.

I seriously hoped a firefight wasn't about to break out. I didn't need any more headaches or bloodshed right now.

I focused and shifted the seven of us to the admiral's signature. We appeared in a huge Romanesque room, complete with a grand balcony that overlooked a vast valley of green hills and tall trees as well as a shimmering lake beneath a pale-blue afternoon sky. Tall ornate marble columns lined the beautiful room, and story-telling mosaics covered the fluted ceilings. Overall, it was a very attractive and relaxing venue. Plenty of space for a few dozen bears.

MST soldiers lined the room, and all had dressed in their signature bodysuits with rifles holstered across their backs. I guessed neither side fully trusted the other. Entirely understandable, though.

"Keeper," Admiral Rohn greeted me pleasantly as he approached us.

All the council members were dressed in identical white suits with matching shirts and shoes. There was a variety of races included within their ranks. I stopped counting after I reached a couple dozen different races.

"Admiral," I acknowledged him in return. He shook hands with me and Doug and then Captain Atlex, which surprised me. But seeing them amiable with one another also calmed my nerves. Maybe this swap of authority would go more smoothly than I had originally anticipated.

"Are more Bear Paw coming?" Admiral Rohn was an older human male with gray hair and some extra weight around his stomach and legs. Noticeable wrinkles surrounded his mouth and eyes.

"Yes," Atlex answered. "They should be here shortly."

The admiral nodded as he turned and outstretched his arm in an invitation for us to follow him. He led us toward the balcony with its decorative stone banister made of small vertical columns topped with a smooth and pristine marble handrail.

Two other council members joined us near the edge of the balcony. They were from the same alien race, and both were older-looking females with dark-green skin and flowing, stylish black hairdos.

The three council members faced us with their backs toward the beautiful world outside. I could sense how unsettled each of them felt with the five towers of fur staring down at them with suspicious looks.

"Keeper," the admiral said with considerable sorrow and humility in his voice, "we acknowledge our actions have been damaging toward many of the races throughout the Expanse, and after much deliberation the MST has decided to fully accept your demands. The Bear Paw will be the new protectors of the Expanse, and we will gladly aid them with anything needed as they establish themselves into their new position."

Interesting, I thought. *I guess when an entire universe rises up against your organization it doesn't really leave you with much of a choice, does it?*

"On behalf of the Bear Paw and *all* growda ha'tars," Atlex said as he stepped forward and offered Admiral Rohn a handshake, "we graciously accept your assistance."

As they both shook hands—or, more accurately, as Atlex wrapped his enormous paw around the admiral's entire forearm—I felt a rapidly growing sense of satisfaction. The growda ha'tar race had been the pawns of the MST for thousands of years. They'd sacrificed their lives many times over and always been treated as second-class citizens. But now they had finally achieved their goal. Time and persistence had paid off, not to mention how many lives over the ages had been sacrificed.

Admiral Rohn took a deep breath, then let it out in a frustrated huff. "Unfortunately, with so many rogue agents on the loose, this transition may not go as smoothly as we had hoped," he explained. "They are determined to keep a hold over the Expanse. Entire ships' crews are rushing to their side. Hundreds of MST vessels have been hijacked by their forces."

3

I shifted Doug and myself back to our quarters on James's ship with the intent of making a few phone calls. As I paced around checking the messages I had received while we were in our meeting, Doug sat along the edge of our bed. The second I was in range he playfully grabbed hold of me, locking his hands around my waist and pulling me close, so that I was standing between his opened legs.

He took my phone and set it on the bed. Then he raised my shirt and placed several kisses all over my stomach. I absolutely loved feeling his beard brush over my skin. His affection always soothed me. It calmed my heart, taking me to a better place every time.

"What's on your mind, sweetie?" he asked. Being so tall, he could mostly look straight into my eyes even while sitting on the bed.

I leaned forward to give my tough guy a quick kiss on his forehead. "Well," I said, "I've got sort of a crazy idea that might help us deal with all these rogue agents. But first I need to run it by Jay E Jay. And apparently he's with Kirill and Aldis on New Cardall at their recently opened Bear Paw headquarters."

Doug pursed his lips, a slightly puzzled yet intrigued look on his face. "Then why don't we jump on over there and see what's going on," he said.

"My thoughts exactly."

I then followed up with a gentle pinch of his nipple beneath his shirt. Before business, I wanted to keep my happy feeling going strong, so I pushed him back onto the bed and crawled on top of him, straddling his body with my thighs.

Doug reached around below my waist and kept busy squeezing my behind while I took my turn and raised his shirt so I could kiss his hairy chest and then suck on his nipples. Both of them perked up fast and stood firm.

"Oh," I sighed happily, "I can never get enough of your wonderful chest."

He slipped one of his hands down the back of my pants so he could run his fingers through my crack. He gently pulled on bunches of the hairs, playing with them, enjoying himself immensely.

I braced my hands against the bed, pushed myself up a few inches, and then moved along his defined body until our lips met and we eased our tongues into each other's mouths. A few minutes passed before I let myself collapse against him. I always savored the feel of our bodies pressed together. I took in a soothing deep breath, then let it out as slowly as possible.

"You're the best thing to ever happen in my life," I told Doug. "I love you so much."

He tenderly massaged my back, pressing his fingers against my body. He used his broad palms against my shoulders and then rubbed the tips of his thumbs along my spine.

"I love you too, Little Bear. You mean the world to me, sweetie. There's nothing I wouldn't do for you."

Doug gave me a firm hug, and then I sat up and patted my hands on his shapely chest.

"Is there anything you need to do before we head out?" I asked.

He laughed, then thrust his hips up and down a few times, bouncing me against his legs. "I can think of something I'd like to do to you, David. But I don't think we have that much time right now."

I nodded happily yet frowned a little too. "Yeah, some hot and heavy sex with you right now would be amazing. But you're right. We need to get moving."

Both of us got up off the bed and shared a few kisses. I couldn't resist massaging his impressive crotch for a short time. And since he wasn't wearing underwear, I could feel every bit of him beneath his jeans. We then headed downstairs to our kitchen, where we each grabbed a glass of orange juice.

I called Jay, and he answered after a few rings.

"How's everything going?" I asked my big bear friend.

"Things are going very good, Keeper," Jay answered in his deep voice. "Many Bear Paw troops are here, and they've integrated well with the ornighs and humans throughout the city. Several more vessels have just come into orbit too."

"Sounds like you're handling your new position like a pro, Jay."

He let out a deep and robust laugh into his phone. "I certainly hope so."

"Well, Doug and I plan on swinging by to see you. Do you have some time to talk for a few minutes?"

"I do," Jay said with enthusiasm. "I'll see you in a few, Keeper."

Doug walked over to me, rubbed my shoulder, and then wrapped his arms around me before giving me a kiss on my head. "I'm proud of you, David. You're really making a huge difference throughout the Expanse. And you're changing so many lives."

With my face pressed against his chest, I mumbled from the corner of my mouth, "You're just *now* seeing how awesome I am?"

Unfortunately my joke started a serious round of tickling. Doug kept one arm locked around my waist while he tickled me along my side and under my armpit. In between laughing hysterically, I tried my best to tickle him in return. After a few minutes both of us were hunched over laughing and crying from sharing such an enjoyable moment. It always warmed my heart to know he and I could exchange such simple pleasures. Doug was the man of my dreams, in many ways.

I took a moment to readjust my shirt before we headed out.

"We haven't heard from Bryan and Seth lately," I said. "You think we should pop in on them and see what they're up to?"

Doug read between the lines. I could sense he knew where I was going with my question. "Oh, I'm sure both of them are enjoying their new abilities." He also straightened his shirt and then adjusted his crotch and his belt. "But I think you're right. We should probably visit them sometime soon. Bryan sent me a text yesterday. He and Seth came across a few MST ships lurking around K Field." Seth and Bryan lived out in the wilderness in a village with Seth's people, and K Field was very close to them.

I had a sudden sick feeling in the pit of my stomach. I sighed and rubbed my forehead. "Did they destroy them?"

Doug shook his head with a mild chuckle. "Believe it or not," he said, "but they behaved themselves. And apparently so did the MST."

I stepped closer to him, quickly reached up, and then massaged his beard fairly hard. "Don't freak me out like that, you goofball."

We both laughed before he snared me within another warm hug.

"I'm sorry, sweetie," he apologized with a kiss. "Nothing happened, so I didn't want to worry you for no reason." He rubbed his hands lovingly along my back, pausing, pressing tenderly. "Bryan and Seth are behaving just like you told them to. But I know for a fact they'd appreciate some intense action. So whatever idea you plan on sharing with Jay E Jay, you might want to include my filthy brother and his boyfriend too."

I leaned back and flashed Doug a smile while gazing into his pretty blue eyes. "That actually sounds like a nice plan," I told him.

He scrunched up his face with his eyes narrowed. "So what exactly *is* this idea of yours?" He sounded so intrigued.

I laughed and softly tapped his cheek with my fingers before I slipped out of his arms and shot him a playful look and wink. "I guess we need to go meet Jay, and then you'll find out all about it, sexy butt."

After a few minutes of some good-humored poking and groping in all the right spots, I shifted us to Jay's signature.

"Hey!" I blurted out as I turned around and looked at all the great work they'd done. "You guys are really making some progress."

Kirill walked up and gave me and Doug each a hug. Big green Aldis wasn't far behind, and I saw Jay standing over near the new construction. Wearing a sleeveless shirt and camouflage cargo shorts, Aldis locked his massive arms around me and then lifted me up within a huge bear hug. He and Doug did a much more macho greeting and simply exchanged a fist bump, followed by some manly flexing of their biceps in comparison to one another. Aldis's biceps greatly dwarfed Doug's. How butch of them. I couldn't stop from giggling.

"Glad you like it," Kirill said with a wide and proud smile. He had on jeans and boots, with an opened sleeveless jacket. Kirill loved to show off all his great tattoos and his Mohawk hairdo. "Our bear friends don't play around when it comes to getting things done," he added.

The Bear Paw headquarters here on New Cardall were located further within the heart of the city than Kirill's tattoo parlor and our favorite restaurant. Several workstations already sat along the plaster walls and near the tall arched windows, where a nice view of the city streets could be seen. There'd be plenty of space for a large gathering of towering bears, muscular green ornighs, and determined humans. It looked like an amazing start toward their partnership.

"Are those fucktards cooperating with you?" Aldis wasn't about to hold back his hatred for the MST, and I really couldn't blame him. He even let out a bitter-sounding growl, showcasing his two pointed lower teeth that pressed against his upper lip.

I sort of laughed at his outburst but then nodded. "So far Admiral Rohn and his subordinates have done everything I've told them to do."

Doug swooped in from behind and slung his arms around me. He rested his chin over my shoulder, then drummed his hands against my chest as he gave me an overzealous kiss on my cheek. "And those fucktards are doing what my Little Bear here says because they don't want their asses whipped again."

All the bears chuckled. So did Aldis and Kirill, who looked quite short in comparison standing next to Aldis.

Doug straightened himself but kept his body pressed against my back as I looked at Jay.

"Unfortunately," I told Jay, "the MST did emphasize how the rogue agents were taking over their ships and quickly expanding their ranks, which is why I'm here."

He stared at me curiously. "What do you have in mind, Keeper?"

"I think it's time for some of your troops to be upgraded," I explained. "And then you can assign small groups of them to watch over specific galaxies. That way the rogue agents won't stand a chance, and we'll maintain our hold over the Expanse."

"What sort of upgrades do you plan on giving them?" Jay asked me.

I could sense everyone's overflowing amounts of curiosity, including the bears who kept working hard at installing various components around the room.

Doug rubbed his hand against my back in an affectionate sign of support. I couldn't have asked for more support from my tough and sweet man.

"Well," I told Jay, "I'd like to gift the ability of flight, spirit calling, and shifting to about four hundred of your best warriors. Then after they're trained, they'll be able to shred hostile ships and knock down any forces just like I do."

Everyone stopped and stared at me. Kirill's mouth hung open in surprise, while Aldis nodded over and over again looking absolutely thrilled by my suggestion. Despite everyone else in the room, it was Jay's feelings I focused on. I could sense his excitement, his worries, and his thoughts of which bears to choose.

As I stared into Jay's dark eyes, at his furry face and snout, I held up my hand to stop him before he spoke. "Now I'm not trying to freak you out," I kindly told him, "but the sooner you choose, the better off all the races throughout the Expanse will be. We don't have a lot of time to spare."

Jay took a deep breath as Doug moved beside him and sympathetically patted his long, furry arm. Our towering bear commander then slowly let his breath out. He nodded. He smiled. He paused for a moment to gather his thoughts. And then Jay spoke. "Keeper, give me until later today, and I will have your candidates ready. You honor my people with such abundant generosity."

Jay and I stepped toward each other, and he wrapped his enormous hand around my entire forearm in a typical growda ha'tar–style handshake.

"It is *you* who honor me with your devotion and strength," I said to Jay. "I couldn't change the Expanse without the Bear Paw backing me up."

I could tell my furry buddy felt much better, more relaxed after this compliment. His associates did too.

As I stood there soaking up everyone's emotional states, Doug approached me from behind and rubbed his hand over my back before giving me a kiss on my head. Kirill and Aldis happily held hands and glanced into each other's eyes. Both of them smiled and then stared at me. They felt contentment, which not only showed on their faces but in their hearts, more so than I had seen in a long time.

From the corner of my eye a figure caught my attention, and I turned to see Sanvean floating several inches above the floor across the room. In her flowing, sheer gown and contrasted by her long cobalt-blue hair, her pale-blue skin had seriously caught my attention. I was certain only I could see my spirit guide. She nodded a single time to me with a pleased smile before gazing straight into my eyes for the longest time.

Soon I heard her voice inside my head. Her words came to me as clearly as if she stood beside me, whispering directly into my ear. "Keeper of the Citadel," she said in her soft, sweet voice, "your destiny is at hand."

4

As the image of Sanvean vanished before my eyes, Doug's phone beeped a few times with a text message. After he checked it, my handsome man gazed at me. "It's from Ellet. He said Nheyja wants us to stop by her house to discuss some things."

Considering how Nheyja felt about me, I was surprised she'd actually extend an invitation. She absolutely adored Doug. Me, however, not so much. But I wouldn't disappoint Doug by refusing to go. In his heart he wanted to. I could feel it. Plus, it was always nice to see the city of Anourish.

"Sure," I gladly answered him, with some quick and playful tickling along his side. "I'm kind of curious to see what she has to say."

Doug nodded. "Me too, sweetie."

A couple of bears had walked over to Jay with questions about where to place certain components for a few of the workstations. Everything had been powered up. Only a few last-minute tweaks needed to be completed.

"Just call me when you're ready," I told Jay.

"I will," he promised. He then quickly glanced over the large tablet-shaped notepads both bears had handed him.

"Taking off already?" Kirill took a few steps closer, then nudged his bare shoulder against mine. He looked so different in jeans and a T-shirt, as opposed to his swashbuckling attire. Kirill had never been a pirate, and he usually dressed in that type of style. It was nice to see him wearing casual clothes for a change. However, he'd never get rid of his spiky Mohawk or his stylized mustache and pointed sideburns. In my opinion, those particular features made him look quite appealing.

I sighed with some noticeable disappointment. "Yeah," I mumbled, "I guess we need to get going."

Huge green Aldis wasted no time. He moved right in and gave me another all-consuming hug, holding me so incredibly tight against his beefy, muscular body. There was no way I'd ever get my arms around him, so I just patted him along his sides.

Kirill hugged me, and we both rubbed each other's backs a little. He even slipped in a quick kiss on my cheek.

"Thanks for everything," he said while glancing into my eyes.

I let out the tiniest of laughs. "Well, I'm determined to make life the best it can be for you two. I promise."

Doug gave Aldis and Mr. Pirate Adventure a pair of warm embraces. No fist bumping this time, which surprisingly left me feeling a bit disappointed. I always got a kick out of watching them show off and act so rough and tough.

"Okay," I said loud enough so everyone in the room could hear. I took a moment to glance at Jay, who did the same at me. "We'll be back."

I recalled Ellet's signature, and in the blink of an eye Doug and I shifted to the main foyer of Nheyja's elaborate Romanesque home, where we appeared maybe ten feet from barefoot Ellet. Afternoon sunlight poured in through the tall, decorative windows with an almost blinding intensity. The light filled the round entrance hall and made Ellet's pale-blue, silvery skin seem even lighter. Ellet stood no taller than me and was slightly thinner than I was. He wore only a delicate powder-blue wrap around his hips. It had a fancy, decorative silk edge but was extremely short and gave us a view of the silvery hairs all along his thighs and what few were on his chest. He let his garment hang at an angle, and I imagined if he had to bend over to pick something up, we'd probably get an unexpected view of his butt.

"It is so good to see you both again." Sporting a wide smile, Ellet couldn't have looked any happier.

Doug and I both shook hands with him, and I took a brief moment to look down at his bare feet upon the pristine marble floor. The last time Doug and I had been here all the towering glass windows had been broken. Shattered glass had lain in piles all around us. But since then all the damage had been repaired, and there was no sign of it now. Everything—the tiled floors, the mosaics on the high ceiling, the decorative bits of glass, and the tall statues upon their fancy pedestals—looked as flawless as always.

"How's Nheyja doing?" Doug asked.

"Much better," Ellet answered. "She came back home the following day after her injury and then hired a large crew to repair all the damage. We still get a few minor skirmishes throughout the city, but overall, any major conflicts seem to have settled down."

"Well, that's good to hear," Doug said. "Anourish always gets knocked around for no reason, which I've never understood."

Ellet laughed and shrugged his shoulders. "Everyone does seem to bring their problems to our city for one reason or another."

"Hopefully those days are over." Doug smiled, then gave Ellet a few pats on his bare shoulder.

"If you two are ready, I can take you upstairs?"

Doug and I both nodded.

Ellet turned around and started up the broad and grand marble staircase one step at a time while occasionally running his hand along the ornate metal handrail, which was made of spiraled metal leaves and what resembled vines. We were headed to the long hallway above that led to the main chamber room of the house.

As we headed up the stairs, I glanced down at a bathroom off to our left, beside a huge stone statue of birds in flight. I'd come out of there several months ago and bumped into Doug before we'd known each other, and that was when he had referred to me as "Little Bear" for the first time. I would hold that memory close to my heart forever and ever. Lost in such a delightful thought, I took hold of Doug's hand. He glanced down at me and smiled the entire time as I rubbed my fingers against his.

Soon, we turned the corner at the top of the stairs and entered the main room. As I expected, Nheyja stood beside the spacious reflecting pool at the center of her beloved room, with its high fluted ceilings covered in mosaics, marble floors and walls, and statues of ancient veeri warriors posed atop huge pedestals. The entire pool sat about two feet above the ground, surrounded by a round marble retaining wall, and a small fountain rained down upon the water's surface.

Again, everything looked flawless, including Nheyja.

"Doug," she said in a humble voice. "And David," she added with a smile. "Please come in. I feel as though I haven't seen you two in forever." Nheyja gestured with a few flaps of her hand for us to come closer toward the pool. Beyond her lay a wide terrace, complete with white marble posts topped by a thin metal banister.

Dressed in as little as always, she wore only a loose-fitting bikini top that fastened in the front (just enough to cover her breasts) with a matching minimal wrap similar to Ellet's dangling loosely around her hips. Her silvery skin appeared flawless. There were no blemishes at all. And her grayish-blue hair sat piled upon her head with delicate metal vines and leaves interwoven throughout its strands.

"The last time we were here you didn't seem too keen about having us in your house," Doug pointed out. He spoke politely yet blended it with some mild bitterness. I couldn't blame him for feeling the way he did. He and Nheyja had been close friends for many years. There was no need for them to be bitter toward one another.

Nheyja bowed her head slightly, and I could sense legitimate guilt and regret churning inside her. "I apologize for my actions and for what I said that day," she said. "I value you as my friend, Doug Colt. And to push you out of my life would be a regrettable decision that would torment me forever."

She moved closer, working her way around the knee-high edge of the pool. Her bare feet lightly tapped against the marble floor. Doug did the same until they stood close enough to share a hug. She was dwarfed while standing in front of him, wrapped in his arms like a child.

It wasn't long before Nheyja glanced over at me. She slipped away from Doug and approached me. A decorative bracelet hung around her ankle, its tiny, shiny baubles quietly chiming as they struck together. She stopped a few inches from me.

"Forgive me, David." Nheyja had the beginnings of tears in her eyes. "I allowed my feelings to influence my judgment. I see now that you are a benefit to the Expanse and not a threat. Please accept my apology for everything I said."

She opened her arms and invited me closer. How could I refuse after hearing her admission of guilt, after sensing her feelings, and with Doug and Ellet watching with hopeful looks? We exchanged a hug. I patted her back. She did the same to me.

"Don't beat yourself up too hard," I told her as I stepped back a bit. "You're not the only person who fell for the MST's bullshit and lies. I'm just glad the truth has finally come out."

She nodded and wiped away a tear before it rolled down her silvery cheek.

Doug came over and stood beside me. He rubbed his hand over my back a few times as Ellet moved closer too.

"Then I take it the MST is cooperating with you?" Nheyja asked.

"More than you can imagine." Doug chuckled. Then he reached lower and tapped me a single time just above my behind.

Speaking of taps, I could have sworn I felt a few quick tremors move through the floor. I looked around the room and listened intently. I scrutinized Nheyja's home and stared outside beyond the terrace at this particular tier of the city.

"What's going on, David?" Doug asked, rubbing my shoulder.

"Did you guys just feel the floor shake a little?" Maybe from being a shifter I was more aware of such minor occurrences. Although with those two being barefoot, I figured they would have noticed something out of the ordinary.

Ellet nodded and quickly came closer to us. "I think I did feel something." He sounded nervous.

"Hopefully it's not any more—" Doug's observation was cut short by a powerful tremor that shook the entire house with the force of a major earthquake.

Nheyja squatted and held on to the pool's short marble wall as Ellet rushed in to assist her in anyway he could. Doug planted his boots firmly against the ground and jiggled in place. I flew into the air and raced over to one of the enormous statues that was about to topple over. I grabbed hold of the figure's massive shoulder and somewhat stabilized it. Unfortunately, two other statues across the room fell over with a thunderous crash. They shattered a huge area of the marble floor, leaving large indents and thick cracks all beneath the rubble.

"They must be attacking the city again!" Nheyja shouted out in a frustrated voice. I could sense her growing hatred of the MST, of problems throughout the city, of her home being devastated on an almost-daily basis.

After the shaking had stopped, Doug raced over to check on Ellet and Nheyja. "Are you two okay?" His voice was rattled with concern, with fear.

"We're fine," Nheyja said as she and Ellet both stood up with angry looks on their faces.

I floated down beside them and grabbed hold of Doug's arm for a brief second. "We can go see what the hell is going on," I explained real fast. "Will you two be safe here while we run out to the city streets?"

"We'll be fine." Nheyja swiped her hand through the air to clear a cloud of dust away from her face. "Use your gifts to stop them," she told me.

It pleased me immensely to finally hear her support, her acceptance of my role as a protector of life. I nodded and gave them both a reassuring smile as I swooped Doug up into my arms and then instantly shifted us into the sky, high above the city, to see what had happened.

The damage stood out like a sore thumb, and both of us gasped in shock. A mountain-size chunk of Anourish had broken off from the side of the main island and was in the process of drifting away, moving outward through the clouds and air. I assumed any piece of the land would float through the sky, since that was exactly what all the main island did, literally defying gravity.

Docked spaceships all along the edge of the city had been damaged, and some were on fire. Three of the lowest tiers of the city had been affected too. Homes, businesses, and streets had been cut off or damaged. Entire avenues had fallen over the edge. Bits and pieces of pavement and stones plummeted down through the sky, through the puffy clouds.

"There!" Doug pointed at a small fleet of crafts from within the safety of my arms. "More rogue agents, I bet."

Twelve spaceships in a variety of shapes and sizes hovered near the damaged edge of Anourish. Some were black and chunky with forward-mounted weapons. Others looked sleek and shiny, fast and highly maneuverable. Each vessel held its position as several small shuttle crafts shot out from their cargo holds and raced toward the city, where they landed upon the streets. There were several tiers to the city of Anourish, and the rogue shuttles seemed to be making their way mostly around the lower ones. The lowest level was primarily shipyards and docking ports.

"I'm so sick of this crap." I sighed miserably.

Doug gave me a supportive pat along my back. "Let's go fuck 'em up, Little Bear!"

After I gave my man a quick yet tender kiss on his cheek, I flew us down to the city, zooming through what few clouds there were until I landed not too far away from the shuttles.

Doug jumped down from my arms and planted his feet firmly on the old cobblestone pavement. He had a hateful scowl on his face as we both stared at rogue troops pouring out onto the streets.

More than a dozen soldiers stopped and stared curiously at me and Doug. They had their rifles pointed at us. They looked uncertain of who we were and why we were standing here in their way.

But all of that was about to change.

I wasted no time summoning nine of my oversize bear spirits, each half the size of a bus. All were transparent yet glowed with outlined hues of blue and white. One raced a few steps forward, lowered itself, and then forced its head between Doug's legs until he sat on top of it, mounted on its back like a rider on a horse. My tough guy grabbed hold of a huge amount of ghostly fur on the bear's back, and I silently commanded my group of spirits to charge toward the rogue troops as I rose into the air.

Shots rang out. Bolts of white energy rocketed through the air, but my ethereal beasts reflected every deadly pulse. And Doug resisted any rounds that hit him, thanks to the supernatural enhancements I'd gifted onto him. Gunfire would feel no different against his body than if he had been struck by a dozen sticks of butter.

With furious growls, my bears trampled any troops stupid enough to not move out of their way and ripped apart shuttlecraft with their fearsome teeth and savage claws. Chunks of metal flew all around the street. Sparks shot forth with sizzling and popping sounds as piles of shredded steel grew taller and taller around us.

"Die!" one of the masked agents shouted as he fired directly at a bear's face.

My spirit beast rushed forward and let out a loud, angry growl before trampling the rogue agent to the ground. It knocked him out cold, shattering his rifle into pieces with paws the size of a car's tire.

The commandeered MST ships were slowly moving closer, and as I started to summon several large alien whale spirits to break each one apart, a powerful strike landed against my back. The extreme force of it hurled me through the air and launched me down the street. I hit the cobblestone, shattering the stones into dozens of pieces and leaving an indent in the ground considerably larger than my body. I braced my hands hard against the ground and raised myself up to look at who I *knew* had struck me.

"Kroma M8," I mumbled hatefully. *Well isn't this just fucking wonderful.*

Several of the genetically engineered giants stood before me. The stinky, filthy, muscle-clad wrestlers looked like they had grown up on overdoses of steroids and were completely naked. Their matted, greasy black hair and dirty grayish bodies were all too familiar to me. Bastards.

Faster than a fired bullet, I flew toward the one who had hit me and slammed my fist against his jaw with all my gifted strength. My attack sent him flying backward, knocking his hateful ass flat onto his back.

A huge hand grabbed hold of my ankle as I hovered above the street, and another of the freaks pulled me down and slammed my entire body against the street like a stuffed animal in an angry child's hand. Bam! Bam! Bam! My body shattered more of the street, leaving an even bigger crater than before.

Right after the Kroma M8 let go of me, I rose back into the air and summoned spirits to help me out—a team of gigantic ostrich-type creatures with long arms and vicious-looking claws in addition to flapping wings and munching beaks full of sharp teeth.

Another freak came for me, but I pulled a Bryan-inspired move. I launched a sort of roundhouse kick with my leg and foot, striking the Kroma M8 against the side of his head. My attack didn't do as much as I had hoped for, but it did send him stumbling to the side.

I glanced over at Doug. He was still sitting on top of the bear spirit, still leading the assault on the shuttles. Honestly, there wasn't very much left of them. My bears could shred metal as easily as tissue paper. And all but a few of the rogue troops had been knocked out or disarmed or had their high-tech black bodysuits mostly ripped away from their bodies.

"I'm fine!" Doug shouted to me before he quickly pointed over my shoulder. "There's one behind you, David!"

I spun around and came face-to-face with another Kroma M8. He grabbed hold of me with his massive, dirty hands and tried his best to crush me. He snarled at me, and I could smell his rotted garbage-can breath and the stink rolling off his filthy body. His grimacing face was dark gray and covered with dirt; his eyes black and lifeless; and his long, dark hair matted and greasy.

My right arm hung free, but his hands were getting tighter and tighter around me, and surprisingly the pressure started to affect my breathing. The Kroma M8 were a smidge stronger than me and more durable too. Could he crush me? That was definitely possible.

I panicked. I wasn't about to get killed by this asshole.

As hard as I could I struck his face repeatedly with my free hand, but he took every punch like a pro and only squeezed his hands harder around my torso.

In a slow-motion sort of moment, I watched as Doug and the bear he rode on raced over to help me, but more of the Kroma M8 freaks rushed in and stopped him in his tracks. My spirits could resist their attacks; that had been proven before. But the thought of Doug getting hurt or killed started to seriously piss me off.

"You son of a bitch!" I struck the Kroma M8 over and over again against the side of his ugly face, against his thick jaw and forehead. I didn't know if these freaks came with different degrees of resistance and strength or what, but this one was putting up a good fight!

Then, from out of the blue, a sudden rush of peace and calmness came over me. I felt the influence of my spirit guide, her gentle touch and kindness. Sanvean's words from long ago came to me as if she was standing beside me. *Your touch will convey your will. Speak... and you will make them strong.*

I placed my right hand against the freak's bulging bicep and held on as tightly as I could. Chills raced up and down my back as I bonded with this engineered creature's anger. There was an unbelievable amount of it, to say the least. Could I change him? Could the Keeper of the Citadel take away his pain and suffering or change his thoughts?

I focused only on good things, on the need to help others, to take charge and stand against anyone who desired to cause harm to the innocent. "Free yourself," I whispered as his grip around my chest and stomach tightened even more.

I could barely breathe. I squirmed within his hold. I stared into his eyes while keeping my hand upon his arm. "You are no longer a slave to their demands," I said. "There is a higher destination for all of us. *You* are an individual. Stand with us... and make a difference."

His grip loosened considerably as he stared off into the distance. Did he feel the heat from my hand, the influx of my gifts as his mind awakened?

The look on his face had changed from one of hatred to one of realization, of awareness, and through my touch I could feel his mind coming alive with new thoughts and desires, with feelings of care, warmth, and need.

Suddenly he released me, and I floated in the air before him. My breathing became much easier. Doug had jumped down from his bear and stood before all the other Kroma M8. I could sense each one of them had changed in this moment. No more feelings of hatred or desires to kill and destroy everything in sight came from any of them. But how? I had only touched one of them. Had my influence changed them all? Could all of them changing have something to do with them being genetically identical to one another?

"David!" Doug yelled as he stepped closer with his fists ready to strike. "You okay?"

I glanced at him and then quickly turned my head back to face the towering beast standing in front of me. The Kroma M8 raised his sweaty, dirt-covered arm and rested his massive hand on my shoulder. I stared up into his dark eyes, not really sure what to expect.

"Keeper of the Citadel," he uttered in a deep and gruff voice yet with a kind and bewildered look to match. Several strands of his long, greasy black hair hung over his eyes and covered his ears. "We see... *so* much more." He stepped back and showed his gratitude with a single nod.

All the other Kroma M8 turned to face the one who stood before me. He stood as straight as an arrow and said in a loud and commanding voice, "Protect the city."

Within seconds, all of them bolted away from me and Doug. They raced after the few rogue agents who had slipped by my spirits and made their way farther down the streets of Anourish. With the shuttles torn apart, that only left the huge cruisers to deal with.

I lowered myself to the ground. Doug hurried over to me and took a few moments to run his hands along my body, inspecting me for blood or any other signs of injuries.

"I'm fine, I'm fine," I reassured him as we gave each other a loose, quick hug.

"What the hell did you do to that freak?"

"I opened up his mind, freed him from whatever hold the MST had over him," I said. "But it somehow changed the others too, from what I can sense."

Doug looked absolutely stunned. "Well, I wonder if all of them have changed. I mean... all across the galaxy, throughout the entire Expanse."

He had brought up an interesting point. Would all Kroma M8 turn against the MST now that their minds had been opened and their wills made free? I still sensed an overwhelming desire for peace and an urge to protect life coming from each one. I could only hope they would all stand up for those in need and rush in to help no matter what.

I patted Doug's shoulder and then rose a hundred or more feet above the street. Several Kroma M8 had reached the edge of the island where the rogue ships had docked. Fights had broken out, and troops were shouting all around in confusion as to why their genetic weapons had turned against them. The Kroma M8s' smashing fists made a mess of each ship. Gunshots did nothing to them, as their durability was of the highest magnitude.

"Look!" I pointed far off into the distance. "There's a lot more than we saw."

Doug probably couldn't see what I could, but dozens of the Kroma M8 were racing throughout the city, moving from tier to tier, from the old cottage sections to the more refined and grandiose buildings much higher up. They stopped and stood guard in front of stores. They watched over innocent bystanders and knocked rogue troops unconscious before picking up their rifles and shattering them against the streets or edges of the sidewalks.

I took a reassuring deep breath knowing Anourish would no longer be subjected to random acts of violence. The Kroma M8 would stand guard over all levels of the entire island. I could sense devotion in them as easily as I could sense it in my summoned spirits. Speaking of, I dismissed my oversize bear pets and floated down to hover beside Doug.

"I think it's safe to say our new allies have the rogue agents under control," I said happily to Doug. "Wouldn't you agree?"

He laughed mildly as a smile stretched across his face. "Maybe we should swing back by Nheyja's place and tell her and Ellet the good news."

No need to convince me.

In a snap, I shifted us back to the main chamber room of Nheyja's house, with its broken statues and shattered marble floor.

"How bad is it?" Nheyja asked. She was helping Ellet move several large chunks of stone away from the pool at the center of the room.

"A large piece of the island broke away from some kind of attack," Doug explained. "Then the MST's genetic freaks showed up. But David here took care of them like a pro." He leaned close and wrapped one arm around me and then patted my chest with his free hand.

Both Nheyja and Ellet stared into my eyes with confused yet terrified looks from our news.

"I changed them," I stated matter-of-factly. I raised my hands for a moment, emphasizing my point. "I freed their minds, opened up their eyes to see new possibilities, new directions. They're no longer slaves, and they'll fight to protect the city. They'll keep you safe. I promise."

Doug took a few minutes to describe some more details about the fight to them. Until now, I had never seen Nheyja cry so noticeably. But as she walked over to me, keeping mindful of the debris littered across the floor since she was barefoot, several tears ran down her silvery cheeks. She embraced me within a warm and caring hug, and we held each other close and tight for a long moment, no less than best friends who hadn't seen each other in many years would do.

"Thank you," she whispered sweetly. She then leaned back a bit to kiss my cheek. She smelled like the sweetest of flowers. After she stepped away, she gazed at me with abundant care and gratitude. "Again... I apologize for having doubted you, David. Shaye chose wisely. You are the greatest blessing the Expanse has ever received."

Ellet even shot me a smile in addition to Nheyja's.

Doug stepped forward and tenderly rested his hand on her bare shoulder. "We've been friends for many years," he reminded her with a hint of tearful joy in his voice. "I can't imagine not having you or Ellet in my life."

After the three of them exchanged a few rounds of hugs, Doug came back over and stood beside me. He told Nheyja, "I'll get my brother, Bryan, to come over, and we'll help you straighten up your house."

I didn't need my powers to see the abundant joy radiating from Nheyja after Doug's promise to help her. She admired him more than words could say, and she held him very close to her heart, more than the best of friends, to say the least.

Doug texted Bryan, who answered right away. He and Seth were somewhere near the town of K Field in the Shards of Exeter, and apparently they'd recently dealt with some rogue issues of their own. So Doug insisted we shift to his brother to see what had happened.

"We'll be back," Doug promised to both Nheyja and Ellet.

Smiles and grateful nods had become plentiful.

I focused on Bryan's signature, and Doug and I appeared beside him in a flash.

5

Both Bryan and Seth stood shirtless and barefoot, their hairy chests and muscular arms on display to my left and right. The only clothing each was wearing was a stylish pair of shorts that Seth had made. Both pairs of fancy shorts were white with decorative black stitching and details around the edges and around the waists. The shorts ended just above the knee with a snug fit. Seth had once given Doug and me similar pairs as gifts. He enjoyed sewing and fabricating clothing.

Doug and I wasted no time exchanging hugs with them along with pats on the back and brotherly tickles that added some fun to the moment, sparking a lot of giggles and smiles.

"So what the heck is going on?" Doug asked. He stood beside Bryan with his muscular arm slung over his brother's shoulders.

Bryan laughed some as he and Seth both tilted their heads back and stared up into the starry night sky. Far above us, just beyond the breathtaking view of the floating islands and rocks, lay a scattered debris field of shredded spaceships. Against the backdrop of space, the pieces sparkled like a stream of glitter, reflecting light from the suns that were shining around the main landmass we stood upon.

"Bunch of rogue bitches started some shit in K Field." Bryan sounded incredibly pleased with himself as he rubbed his hand against Seth's back and said, "But we taught them a lesson. None of them better come here again and fuck with our home or any citizens over in the town."

Despite the wreckage drifting through space, I felt so happy that Bryan considered the Shards his home and that he was content living here with Seth. They were a perfect fit for one another. Both were lighthearted, with good senses of humor and just a touch of perverted thoughts, which I was sure Bryan absolutely loved about Seth.

"What did you guys do with all the troops?" I had to ask.

Bryan grinned wickedly and then rubbed his hand over my head. "We shifted them to some uninhabited planet Seth and I have been on before. They'll get picked up eventually."

Doug smiled and gave his little brother a supportive pat on the shoulder and then gave Seth one too. "Nice job, guys," Doug told them. "Looks like you both got the art of spirit calling down pretty good."

"We fucked them up," Seth said. His English sounded better all the time.

Despite his improved speech, Doug and I laughed at Seth's outburst. Bryan's raunchy influence on him showed all too well. But it was good to know the Shards of Exeter wouldn't succumb to any random acts of violence by the rogue agents. Bryan and Seth would always see to its protection.

We took a few moments to bring them up to speed concerning the recent attacks on Anourish. Afterward, Bryan rushed in and gave me a superpowered hug, even lifting me into the air for a few seconds before putting me back down.

"Nice job, sweetness!" Bryan told me. He had a much hairier chest than his big brother, although Doug sported much more prominent muscles, looking like a professional wrestler.

"So you think you two could swing by and help Nheyja straighten up her place a bit?" Doug quickly tapped the side of Bryan's face in a teasing, brotherly manner. They couldn't resist harassing each other in some sort of way.

Bryan batted his hand through the air. "No problem," he reassured us. "Seth and I can run home, throw some clothes on, and then shift right over there. You guys go take care of your Bear Paw stuff. We'll go and help her and Ellet."

A satisfied and proud smile grew on Doug's face. Bryan had known Nheyja as well and for as long as Doug had, and I could sense my sweet man's contentment with his brother's support. I took hold of Doug's hand in a show of my love and support for him.

The stars shone brightly. A large nebula in the distance blanketed the Shards with subtle hues of the most beautiful greens, blues, and yellows. It was always such a magical place, like Wyler had told me many times before.

Doug's pdPhone chirped with a text message, and I recognized the tone. It was from James. After Doug read it, he held it up for me to read too. "Shake and Finger Pop have the ship all ready for some lessons in shifting... Can you guys come and help?"

I chuckled while glancing up into Doug's pretty blue eyes. "Guess it's time for a little training exercise."

We told Bryan and Seth about James's upgrades, and they both couldn't have looked more surprised. Bryan gave Seth a firm tap across his shapely rear and shouted, "That is fucking awesome! There'll be no place for those rogue bastards to hide from our little brother."

The four of us worked in some hugs, along with tickles and pinches in all the right spots. While I was in his arms, Bryan actually placed his hand behind my head and rubbed my face against his hairy chest, right between his pecs. He could be such an adorable buffoon. So in turn, I quickly shoved my fingers into his armpits and tickled him. He laughed, and from his raised brows and pursed lips, I think he actually enjoyed it. None of the Colt brothers were as ticklish as I was, though. Doug had proved that fact about me many times over.

"Behave at Nheyja's place," Doug told his silly brother. He then stepped back and stood beside me.

Bryan acted shocked. He shrugged and lifted his upturned hands into the air. "When do I ever misbehave?" he said.

Doug shook his head and sighed while rubbing his fingers back and forth over his forehead. But then Bryan rushed in and gave Doug another warm hug. I guessed it was his way of reassuring his older brother.

"Oh, I'll behave," Bryan promised us. "I'm just messin' with ya."

I grabbed Doug's arm and pulled him beside me so we could shift away. I was feeling excited to help out James.

"Call us if you need anything?" I told Bryan, though I knew he and Seth were more than capable of moving enormous chunks of marble, with or without the help of spirits. After all, both were as powerful as me.

Bryan nodded, and he and Seth shifted away quickly.

I focused on James's signature. I could sense our captain as he stood on the bridge of his ship, his excitement, his anticipation of shifting his ship from galaxy to galaxy.

With a much more affectionate approach, I slipped my arm around Doug and held him close beside me. "Here we go, handsome."

We shifted away and appeared about four feet from James as he stood in front of a workstation with tall Willie at his side. James jumped a bit at our sudden appearance, but Willie only smiled with a hint of laughter. It would take more than our sudden arrival to shake Willie's nerves.

"You guys all ready?" I knew they were, but it couldn't hurt to ask.

James glanced at me with a single brow raised, and Willie gave me an affirming furry thumbs-up.

The three Devil Bunnies were still here, each clad in a skintight dark bodysuit with the top opened just enough to show off a small amount of cleavage. They were keeping busy working with Bray and Woofa fine-tuning the bridge's gigantic holographic display, from what I could tell. Numerous technical readouts, displays, and charts rapidly scrolled through the air in outlines of green, orange, and blue. None of it made any sense to me, but I was sure they all understood the technical lingo.

Shake and Finger Pop were simply hanging out, casually stepping here and there, taking turns following one another around the bridge, likely waiting for the show to get started. Both of them were so interesting to observe, especially with their extreme difference in height. Shake was so tall in comparison to waist-high Finger Pop. A small demon and a mechanical man—what could be better?

"You guys excited?" I asked them both.

Finger Pop chuckled while flamboyantly batting his demon hands through the air. "Young man, I am *always* excited for James to try new things. There's nothing Shake and I wouldn't do to help out our best friend."

Good to hear. With their vast number of resources and contacts, James had an ample supply of assistance within arm's reach. I could only imagine all the different kinds of items they could get for him.

Bray and Woofa slipped in some subtle friendly waves to me and Doug while they kept busy beside the Devil Bunnies.

"I think we're ready," Willie said nice and loud. He reached up high and tapped some glimmering holographic buttons with his furry fingers.

James nodded in agreement as Doug rubbed his hand over my back.

"So what's the plan?" I asked. "I'm guessing I need to shift to Earth, and then you'll just follow me?"

James took a few steps back from the workstation before turning around to face me and Doug. "You should probably appear somewhere in the upper atmosphere," he suggested. He was dressed in his usual tough-guy apparel, his holstered handgun hanging along his thigh. "The biggest hurdle is getting there. After we arrive, the ship's systems will scan for signatures, and we'll be able to go back and explore whenever we want to."

"How long does the ship need to be there?" Doug sounded sort of apprehensive.

I slipped my arm around his waist and took a few seconds to ease his worries with a tender hug. I imagined he was concerned about alarming any military on the planet or being seen by someone and ending up on the evening news.

"It should go fast," Finger Pop said with confidence as he and Shake walked closer to us. "The upgrades are designed to constantly scan for signatures and store them for future use. It'll download a million or more in less than a minute, including objects *and* people."

Doug rolled his eyes with a disgusted-sounding huff. "No wonder the MST had such a strangle hold on everyone for so long. Glad those bastards got what they deserved."

Shake uttered something in his machine voice that left Finger Pop laughing.

"I totally agree," our tiny gray-skinned demon said, looking me in the eyes. "How is the transition going with your Bear Paw troops?"

"Good," I told him. "In fact, I've got a nice surprise up my sleeve that will make quite a difference throughout the Expanse."

Everyone on the bridge looked intrigued by my comment. They all stopped for a moment and stared at me.

Before a ton of questions rolled out of their mouths, Doug patted my shoulder and stepped forward. "I guess we'd better get the show on the road!"

"Upper atmosphere," I confirmed again with James.

He nodded yet still looked curious about my announcement. So did his boyfriend, Willie.

Doug leaned down and gave me a kiss while tenderly holding my chin in his hand. I loved when he touched my face and guided the moment. Afterward, he wrapped his strong arms around me in a nice tight hug.

"Love you, sweetie," he whispered in my ear. "Be careful."

"Love you too, handsome. And I promise to be careful." I patted his muscular chest a few times.

My sweet man then stepped back a few paces, and after flashing him a silly smile and wink, I left the Expanse and shifted to Earth. It was a sunshiny day, and I appeared high in the sky beside puffy white clouds. I stretched out my arms and savored this soothing moment. I took in a deep breath with my head slightly tilted back. I felt as if I were inside a lullaby. Calming silence surrounded me as the winds carried my body along and I drifted through warm pockets of air mixed with sparse and dense patches of cooler clouds. Miles below lay a sandy-brown continent bordered by a deep blue ocean. It was the western edge of North America.

"Beautiful," I whispered upon my breath.

Patiently I waited. Minutes passed, yet there was still no sign of James's ship. Thankfully no commercial airplanes had flown by either. I wasn't sure what the pilots would have thought of seeing this midwestern young man hovering in the sky.

My pdPhone rang, and I knew it was Wyler from the ringtone. I pulled the phone out from my pants pocket, a bit surprised by the suddenness. He obviously had sensed my presence.

"Hey there," I answered. "Are you spying on me?" I couldn't stop myself from making a joke.

"Oh, Davie," Wyler muttered in a miserable-sounding voice, "I think I may have screwed myself pretty bad."

He totally caught me off guard. "What happened?"

"Can you and Doug come by... please?" He sounded desperate. "I could really use my friends right now."

A million terrible ideas suddenly raced through my head. "Are you okay? Is Josh okay?"

"Yeah, we're both fine." He sighed heavily into his phone. "I just fucked things up. James's ship will appear in a few seconds. Come over after that, and I'll tell you what happened."

My demon buddy must have used his gift of foresight, because right after I slipped my phone back into my pocket, a startling boom of thunder struck right in front of me, scaring the crap out of me. The hull of the James's ship lay easily no more than ten feet away from my face!

I shifted back to the bridge. James's crew were busy at their workstations, tapping glowing buttons or sliding their fingers across floating screens hanging in midair. Shake and Finger Pop stood in front of a workstation with James and Willie flanking them.

"Looks like it worked great!" I shouted out happily.

"Sure did!" Willie sounded so excited and pleased.

Doug hurried over to me and dropped his arm across my shoulders. I pressed the side of my face against his chest. "We need to stop by Wyler's after we're done here," I quietly told him.

"What's going on?" He sounded surprised, a bit confused.

"He didn't say too much. I guess we'll find out when we get there."

Doug conveyed his support to visit our friends with a few tender pats against my back.

Floating between the two decks of the bridge was a holographic likeness of Earth made in glowing outlines of orange and green. After a few seconds the display changed to an enlarged and more detailed view of our location in the sky. Colorful streams of data scrolled along the map's edge, racing through the air.

"Is that all the signatures the system is collecting?" Doug took the words right out of my mouth while both of us stared in wonder.

"We set it up to just scan the planet and all human life," Finger Pop explained as he tapped a few buttons. "You really don't need much more than that with such an impressive ship *and* an equally impressive captain commanding it." Always sucking up, he turned his bald gray head to gaze up into James's eyes with a delighted smile. Personally, I though Finger Pop was attracted to James, but that was just my opinion.

"Unfortunately we can't run the risk of staying too long," James said in a strict tone.

"Another minute and we should be done." Finger Pop tapped some more buttons, and the main holographic display changed to an impressive full view of Earth, with more details of its surface than I had ever seen on any hologram before.

I stood and stared for a long moment at my home world, reflecting on how far I'd come since Wyler had shifted me into the Expanse—my powers, the fantastic places I'd seen, the loyal and kind friends around me, along with the most loving and passionate man I could have ever wished to have in my life.

"Time to go," James said. There was a noticeable touch of sadness in his voice. After all, he and his brothers had been in the Expanse for more than forty years, so I imagined coming back to Earth (even if it was a parallel version) struck him profoundly. All those years of being lost, and then suddenly a touch of home.

"Are you guys heading back to the Expanse?" Doug asked, walking over to his younger brother.

James shook his head as an adventurous grin slowly grew on his face. "Actually, I think we'll grab some more signatures before we head back." He shrugged. "Might as well make the most of it while we're here, right?"

Doug nodded, then gave his brother a pat on the shoulder. "Well, David and I are going to swing by Wyler's place for a bit. So I guess we'll see you guys back home."

"Sounds good," Willie said. He raised his fist to bump it against Doug's.

I laughed at the two of them. Bray and Woofa did too.

"Okay," James announced, "we're going to shift into a high orbit above Saturn and then maybe take a trip across the galaxy."

I liked the sound of that. It would be fun to see more of my universe, but I'd promised Wyler we'd stop by. Exploration would have to wait for another time.

"See you guys later." I wiggled my fingers in the air with a friendly good-bye for everyone. They all reciprocated, including the three Devil Bunnies.

As Doug walked over to stand beside me, I focused on Wyler's signature, getting a feel for his surroundings to make sure Josh wasn't around. I then shifted me and my man near Wyler's kitchen by the patio doors. Bright afternoon sunlight poured in on us. My two large dogs that Wyler took care of hurried over to greet us with their tails wagging and tongues flapping. I petted both their heads as they vied for my attention. Sian was black, and Zoe was a light-brown color. They were sisters from a litter of nine puppies, a mix of Akita and Chow breeds.

Wyler was sitting on his couch, hunched over, holding his head in his hands. I could sense a great deal of anxiety and sadness coming from him.

"Wyler... you okay?" I moved forward with Doug close behind me.

He sat up and stared at us with a tear-soaked face. The front of his light-gray T-shirt had been soaked from his tears. We hurried over and sat on either side of him. Both of us rubbed a hand over Wyler's back in an attempt to comfort him.

"I told Josh everything," Wyler explained as he blubbered and wept. Barefoot, he wore only a pair of black-and-red shorts. "I even showed him the *real* version of me."

As shocked as Doug and I were, in the back of my mind I had earlier assumed whatever problem had come up involved the truth finally coming out. Wyler was a demon in human disguise.

"What made you do that?" Doug moved his hand higher along Wyler's back and massage his shoulder a bit before moving over the back of his neck. It was nice to see my tough guy treating Wyler with ample amounts of care.

"It just felt like it was time," Wyler said. "Josh surprised me the other night and started talking about the two of us getting married someday, so I figured I shouldn't keep lying to him."

I slipped my arm around Wyler and pulled him close beside me. Still weeping, he rubbed his hand along my thigh.

"So where is Josh?" Doug asked.

Wyler leaned the side of his face against my arm and said, "It devastated Josh, and he took off last night. I used my skills to remotely spy on him. He's been sitting at a twenty-four-hour club downtown drinking all night. I couldn't muster up enough courage to go and confront him. Not in public."

It didn't take any special godlike abilities to see how much Wyler cared about Josh, how deeply he loved him, as he cried. In fact, sitting there and comforting him made me sort of teary-eyed too.

The sound of the patio doors sliding open made both of the dogs perk up their ears as they lay on the area rug in front of us. All three of us turned to see Josh coming in from outside.

Doug stood up and nodded to him, saying in a friendly tone, "Hey."

Josh said nothing as he closed the door and then made his way over to us. He had on a white tank top and old dark jeans with tan work boots. He looked absolutely exhausted. He knelt down and placed his hands on Wyler's knees. I could tell he had been crying a lot. Both of his cheeks were slightly red. He took hold of Wyler's hands, and I hoped for only the best to come.

"Please don't cry, sweetie," Josh begged in a soft and comforting tone as Wyler gazed into his eyes. "I'm sorry I busted out of here like a complete jerk last night without letting you explain things. You don't deserve to be treated like that. All the stuff you told me just caught me off guard. But I love you more than I can say, so I'm willing... no... I'm *asking* you to show me more and let me be a part of your life. That is, if you still *want* me to be a part of your life."

Wyler damn near jumped off the couch and happily slung his arms over Josh's strong shoulders. He buried his face against Josh's neck, below his beard, and then both of them squeezed each other in a tight and loving embrace. They whimpered and cried and then passionately kissed a few times. Eventually Wyler leaned back a few inches, and Josh reached up and gently wiped away his boyfriend's tears.

Josh gave Wyler a kiss on his cheek. "I guess you've got some incredible places to take me to, being a shifter and all."

Doug patted Josh on his shoulder, and I chuckled as I scooted forward onto the edge of the couch. I rubbed my hand over Josh's head in a loving manner. "And I know *exactly* where we should take you first," I told him with ample excitement.

6

We all stood up, and Doug moved in with opened arms so all of us could share a group hug.

"What place did you have in mind, Davie?" Wyler's smile couldn't have been any brighter. It was so nice to see the love he and Josh had for each other, the cute glances they exchanged as they held hands and touched each another in tender, passionate ways.

"I'll handle it," I told him. "Just a quick trip, then we can come back." I glanced into Josh's eyes. "Wyler did explain to you I'm also a shifter, right?"

"Yeah, he told me," Josh answered with a slight nod and an intrigued gaze.

"And the beauty of where we're going," I explained, "is that we don't have to change our clothes. In fact, we won't need our clothes."

All three of them stared at me with raised brows and questions plastered all over their faces.

"I need to let the dogs out before we take off," Wyler said. He hurried over to the patio door, slid it open, and both dogs took off like rockets to go out and pee in the yard.

Doug stood close beside me and playfully bumped me with the side of his arm before wrapping it around me and giving me a kiss. "I have an idea of where you're taking us."

My sweet man couldn't have been more adorable.

Wyler whistled out the patio door, and the dogs raced back inside and headed into the kitchen, where they lapped up some water from their dishes. Wyler then returned to us and slid his arms around Josh, locking his hands around his tall lumberjack man.

I reached over and tickled my fingers along Josh's tummy. I could sense his nervousness, his fear of not knowing what to expect with shifting. "It'll be fine," I reassured him. "Are you ready?"

He slipped his arm around Wyler and nodded. His eyes showed growing tears of happiness.

After I gave an "okay" wink to Doug, I shifted the four of us into the Expanse, to some pools in the Shards of Exeter that weren't too far from the village where Seth and Bryan lived.

We appeared beneath a star-covered sky filled with mountains of floating rock plastered in front of a green-and-blue nebula in the distant background. Josh stared skyward in silent wonder. I could sense his awe, his growing peace and contentment.

"C'mon, sexy butt." I smiled and took hold of Doug's hand so we could lead the way through the trees and bushes lining the stone path that led to the pools that we so enjoyed.

I heard Josh's work boots and Wyler's bare feet tapping upon every ancient stone as they followed us. The giant floating flowers high above us glimmered ever so softly with a subtle and ghostly light as we emerged and stood before the waters. Josh stopped and marveled at the sight of such things. I recalled how amazed I had been the first time I had come here.

"How can they just float there?" Josh asked. "And why do they look like some kind of ghosts?"

The three of us laughed mildly at his question. Then Wyler leaned his face against Josh's arm and whispered, "I think it's best to just accept such marvelous facts, without trying to understand them, sweetie."

Doug wasted no time pulling off his boots, socks, shirt, and pants. And since he preferred to go commando, he stood naked before us as he leaned over and piled his clothes near the edge of the pool. He stood and turned around, then reached out and tickled his fingers along my thin beard. "C'mon, Little Bear... time to jump in the water."

Oh, the sight of Doug's naked and hairy body left my heart racing. As I watched my sexy man step down onto the small ledge beneath the pool's surface, I hurried to get naked and joined him. Wyler and Josh wasted no time either in stripping down to their bare skin.

"Here," Wyler said as he held Josh's hand and led him into the water. "There's a narrow ledge around the rim, so be careful."

One after the other, they stepped into the pool and then made their way down into the chest-high water. Josh faced Wyler, both of them smiling and holding hands. Then Wyler led him farther along through the water, heading away from me and Doug until they were out of sight.

High above us, silhouettes of the glowing lotus flowers reflected upon the water's rippling surface, all backed by a beautiful black sky filled with tons of stars.

Doug and I stepped off the ledge. The water lapped against my shoulders and chin. He took hold of my hands and swirled his way around, moving back and forth, dipping his body farther beneath the surface while making his way into a comfortable position along the ledge.

I floated closer to Doug until I lay upon him. We pressed our chests together and couldn't stop grinning into each other's eyes. Safe to say, I think both of us desired some fun time while lying here beneath the stars. Plus, I could feel Doug's rock-hard piece of meat poking firmly against mine.

We shared several tender kisses, taking turns slipping our tongues into each other's mouths. I leaned a bit to the side so I could pinch and play with one of Doug's nipples. It definitely turned him on even more.

"Here," he said as he backed away from me and carefully stood up on the ledge, with no more than several inches of water covering his sexy feet and calves.

I knelt before my tough guy. I wrapped one hand around his manhood, then slid my other between his legs, moving my fingers deep between his cheeks so I could tease his tender spot. I placed a few kisses along the tip and shaft of his impressive erection before swallowing all of it over and over again. I could tell he enjoyed my work from his pleasurable sighs.

"Oh, Little Bear," Doug whispered. "You really got a knack for makin' me feel good, sweetie."

I gazed up at my sexy man and smiled as much as I could with my mouth full. He was such an impressive sight from this angle. I loved admiring his hairy stomach and chest. His muscular silhouette was especially enticing beneath the backdrop of the glowing flowers so far above his head.

Ample amounts of precum oozed from him, which meant he was probably getting close. So I pulled back a bit and buried my face along the side of his thick patch of hairs. I took a deep whiff of his intoxicating scent before running my tongue deep between his boys and along his thigh. Doug always tasted so good.

"I can't hold out any longer." He cradled the back of my head and stroked himself with quick, lengthy twists of his hand.

I leaned back and opened my mouth, then added a few swipes of my tongue along the tip of his wiener just to tease him, to show him how much I wanted it.

"Oh, yeah," he said. "Here it comes."

Instead of letting him merely feed it to me, I pushed Doug's hand away and swallowed all of him in my mouth. I buried my nose deep against his hairs and kept a tight seal around him with my lips as I reached up and held on to his waist. Doug shook and trembled with ecstasy as he got off, completely filling my mouth with a few huge loads of his deliciousness.

"Holy shit!" He took several deep breaths. "That was incredible, David." He paused for a moment, shook his head, and then looked down into my eyes. "Your turn," he said with a wink.

My eyes locked on Doug's. I swam backward a few feet along the side of the pool and then lifted myself onto the outside edge, letting my feet dangle in the water. Doug happily moved through the water, reached down to grab hold of my calves, and then lifted my legs up high. I gently slid back onto the ancient stones as my well-known ass man did what he loved so much. He placed tender kisses deep between my cheeks, sensuously twirling the tip of his tongue. Then came the ultimate joy as he pushed his tongue inside me as far as he could, slurping, licking, and swirling it around for the longest time.

Slowly he pulled back and lowered my legs. My feet and calves dangled in the water along both sides of him. He then reached up and stroked my hard wiener several times before taking it into his mouth.

An overly delighted sigh rolled out of my mouth. "You're pretty good at that too," I told him.

He chuckled mildly while tapping the side of my thigh. He then softly glided his strong hands over my stomach, moving his fingers through my sea of hair. He reached higher and played with my nipples, pinching and pulling at them both. It felt incredible.

"I'm hungry for it, Little Bear." Up and down, he kept slurping, licking, and sucking nonstop while tweaking my nipples.

I reached down and rubbed my hands along his hairy arms, overjoyed by the sensation, the feel of his muscles. I loved him so much. Life felt so incredible with Doug beside me.

Slowly the feeling grew inside me. The pressure built. I gently moved my hips up and down, feeding him all of me as he buried his face against my pubes and took a deep whiff. That did it!

I grabbed his head and filled his mouth full of my love for him. He moaned with delight as he gulped down every single drop. A great thing about Doug was that after I got off, he liked to continue sucking me until I became soft. Once I was no longer hard, he moved his face a bit to the side where he kissed my boys and gently pulled at the multitude of hairs with his lips. My lovable man could be such a playful tease.

"Wonder where Josh and Wyler took off to?" Doug raised his head and kissed me along the inside of my thigh.

With my remote viewing, I briefly sensed what those two were doing. I turned my attention back to Doug. "They wandered off down through the pools to enjoy themselves." I gently rubbed my hand over his head and took a few seconds to play with his ear and brush the back of my fingers down his sideburns and along his beard. He had such a manly, handsome face.

"Can't imagine what Josh is thinking about all of this," Doug said.

The tiniest of laughs rolled out of my mouth. "Oh, I think the Expanse is the *furthest* thing from Josh's mind right now."

As Doug stood up and took hold of my hands to ease me back against the edge of the pool, my pdPhone chirped with a couple of text messages. I sighed, figuring they were both work related in some way.

Doug grabbed my phone out of my pants pocket and handed it to me. "Fun never ends for the Keeper of the Citadel, huh?" he said playfully.

I reached forward and gently tapped his cheek a few times for being a joker. He let out a silly laugh, then took a step back and sank into the water while blowing me a kiss.

One of the messages came from Jay. "Keeper, I have more than enough Bear Paw troops headed toward the Citadel. We should be ready in a few hours."

The second message came from my journalist friend, Fred. "Lots of reports coming in about those MST genetic weapons you told me about. Seems like they've turned against their masters and are causing a lot of headaches. Wasn't sure if you knew anything. Care to offer any quotes for an article?"

Reading Fred's message left me smiling. His text definitely proved all the Kroma M8 had changed. I could only imagine all the headaches they were causing for the MST.

After I relayed the good news to Doug, he floated toward me through the water with a mischievous grin. He wrapped his hands around my feet, briefly massaging the bottoms of both before gently pulling on them to lure me into the water. He added some goofy flicks of his tongue and equally silly looks to match. How could I refuse to play with him?

I eased myself down into the water, moving along the ledge before I swam forward into the pool. Doug quickly snared me in a warm hug with his powerful arms. He held me close against his body as we shared several passionate kisses.

"I love this place," he whispered while sweetly kissing the side of my face, and then he nibbled on my ear for a few seconds. "But I love you even more, David. You mean the world to me. I feel like I'm the luckiest man alive, having you all to myself."

With both hands clasped on his behind, I firmly squeezed his cheeks and kissed him again. "I love you too, sexy butt." I kissed the tip of his nose, then stared into his blue eyes, which reflected a small amount of the light from the glowing flowers above us. "My life would be miserable without waking up beside you every day," I told him. "I've never been so in love with a man until now, and I'd be happy to spend the rest of my life in your strong arms. I truly would."

Doug loosened his hold around me and placed his hands along the sides of my arms. I took the opportunity to reach down and fondle his privates. I held them in my hand with some tender massaging that left him sighing in delight. With my other hand I squeezed his muscular, hairy pecs. "I just can't get enough of your chest," I said. "It feels so good when I squeeze your muscle boobies."

We both laughed at my silly description, and then in a playful move Doug squatted a few inches so he could raise me up and slowly twirl us around in the water, making mild splashes as he did. With his face pressed against my chest and his hands firmly against my back, I watched the reflections of the flowers as we spun around. There were so many shimmering hints of white light upon the rippling surface. It was as if we stood inside a wonderful dream, an image of bliss and color and magic.

I gave Doug a kiss on his forehead. "You're so adorable," I told him.

He lowered his hands down my back until he cupped both of my cheeks and squeezed them a few times. "You're making me horny again, Little Bear."

I chuckled and playfully reached up to tweak the tip of his nose. "I like the sound of that."

Nothing would have been better than making love to Doug again in this magical place, but an odd tingling started to wash over me. A signature grew inside of me, one I was familiar with. For some unexpected reason, the Silver Tree was calling to me, urging me to shift to it. We had visited the tree before when we were looking for a means to defeat that supernatural freak Ahzoul. But why it was calling to me now, luring me toward it, was a mystery.

Doug could tell something had happened to me. I was sure it was fairly obvious. He rested his hands on my shoulders, then leaned back and curiously stared at my face. "What's wrong, sweetie?" he asked.

I took a deep breath to try to calm myself. "The Silver Tree... it's pulling me to its signature," I told him.

Doug rubbed my shoulders and smiled into my eyes. "Then let's go see what's going on," he said. "It could be important."

His support left me feeling loved and incredibly satisfied.

After he gave me a quick kiss on my cheek, both of us climbed out of the pool and quickly got dressed. Pants up and zipped, shirts on, socks and shoes in place.

"Should you tell Wyler before we head out?" Doug asked.

I shook my head. "He'll figure it out. Plus they're still going at it. No need to interrupt their special moment under the flowers."

My comment left Doug grinning. He was surely picturing some dirty scene with Josh and Wyler, no different than the two of us had done in the same enchanting waters, although Josh and Wyler had explored more of the waters than we had ever done. They were pretty far away.

Doug stepped closer and wrapped his arms around me. He held my face gently against his chest and kissed the top of my head.

"The signature is really getting strong," I mumbled from the side of my mouth. "Are you ready?"

"Take us there, sweetie." He patted my back a couple of times.

Since the potency of the signature was close to overwhelming me, I barely had to focus on the Silver Tree at all to shift us there. However, I made sure I kept Doug's signature in my mind. I wasn't about to leave him behind.

We appeared at the base of the enormous green hill leading up to the tree. We stood in ankle-high grass, still holding each other in a hug beneath a beautiful blue afternoon sky filled with cotton ball clouds. We parted a bit yet still held hands. We turned to face the hill. An abundant number of feathery, winged black-and-white females were hovering and flying around the tree's enormous limbs and canopy. The gentle breeze from their flapping wings dangled the tree's metallic leaves. A sound of chimes filled the air in a subtle melody accompanied by the barely audible sound of voices humming in the background.

Slowly we made our way up the hill, the tree's comforting influence washing over us with every step we took. This was such a magical place, a land of passion, comfort, and care, which were all projected from the huge tree.

Doug leaned down a bit and whispered in my ear, "I wonder why there are so many more of them flying around. You think it's because of what happened to the Ravages?"

The winged females had long, flowing snow-white hair, and thin black lines ran over their vivid white breasts and legs.

"I think you might be right about that." I tenderly squeezed Doug's hand. "And I'm guessing that's why the tree brought us here."

We climbed more of the hill, stepping through the tall green grass until we reached the huge trunk that perfectly resembled any other tree's, complete with grooves and knots. What set the Silver Tree apart from other trees was its metal surface and its massive size. It stood at least a few hundred feet tall.

It couldn't have been a more picture-perfect day. A gentle breeze carried delicate scents of flowers, and green grass covered the wandering hills for miles in all directions. It looked as though an invisible hand had brushed over each strand, moving every blade in a synchronous back-and-forth harmony.

"Think they'll come down and visit with us?" Doug asked, staring up at the flying females who tended to the tree, caring for it, all the leaves and limbs, its full and tremendously wide canopy.

"I hope they do." I couldn't resist staring at all of them either. They were all so captivating, so wonderfully different and unique.

A large group of the females had gathered around a particular section of the canopy, busily fussing with it. Watching them reminded me of the last time we had been here, when they had brought down the vessel from one of the tree's branches.

Doug brushed his hand along the side of my arm. "It looks like they might have another gift for you, David."

Sure enough, high above us, several of them opened a dense pocket of the canopy so that a single female with bold black lines wrapped around her thighs, ankles, and breasts could stick her snow-white arms deep inside and remove something. Slow-flapping feathery wings and long, flowing white hair dominated the scene. From the canopy the single female descended toward us, a graceful beauty not so dependent upon flight, as she obviously defied gravity. They all did, just like I could. With her elbows bent, her hands turned upright and cupped together, she carefully and respectfully held the object she had removed from the dense tree branches. The gentle breeze from her wings moved over us, ruffling the ends of our shirts. She stopped and hovered no more than a few feet away from me. Her white feet dangled inches above the grass as her wings gently folded and unfolded.

I had never been this close to one of the females before. The vivid sharp edges of the two black lines that ran over her eyes and down her cheeks stood out with striking vividness. Her lips were also black.

She stretched out her arms and offered me the item in her hands.

The perplexed look on Doug's face probably matched mine.

The object was a large chunk of blue stone with a sort of ethereal glow to it. As I slowly reached out and took it from her with both hands, the signature of the Ravages rushed into me, which totally caught me off guard. However, the signature presented more than just the Ravages's identity. Each of the four pillars was also embedded within the signature. I could feel them all as I held the stone, an incredible blend of each that left me feeling fascinated.

"You okay, David?" Doug could tell I was lost in the moment. He rested his hand on my shoulder and curiously gazed into my eyes. "What's with the stone?"

"I'm not sure." I shook my head a bit. "It's sort of like a collection of family signatures... the Ravages and her four children."

I turned the stone over a few times and inspected it with each move. Could it have come from the Ravages? Had the pillars somehow obtained a fragment of their beloved mother after the MST destroyed her? But how could they have done that?

The winged female moved back several feet and then rose slowly into the air, making her way toward the vast canopy to join her sisters. She glanced back down at us with her solid black eyes.

"I think I'll take the stone to the Citadel," I told Doug as I gazed into his pretty eyes. "It seems like the respectful thing to do."

He leaned in and gave me a sweet kiss. "Well, Jay and his bear buddies are probably waiting for you." Doug then squeezed my hand a few times. "But before you shift on over to the Citadel, could you drop me off in downtown Kakadu, near the Arkenstone Bar? I've got some property stuff to deal with."

I reached up and cradled his beard, rubbing my fingers through its impressive thickness. "Is everything okay? Please tell me nothing happened to your rental properties."

A wide smile stretched across Doug's face. "No, it's all good. I just need to take care of some business stuff."

I nodded happily while rubbing my hand over his enticing chest.

Both of us took one more look at the canopy and winged females above us. The Silver Tree projected such noticeably intense feelings of love and comfort, of invitation and friendship. I could have stood here all day with Doug and enjoyed holding his hand or lying beside him at the base of the tree, my arms wrapped around him with the side of his face resting upon my chest. A wonderful image of us both.

"Ready?" I asked.

Doug nodded and flashed me one of his adorable crooked smiles. He could be so damn cute.

I focused on our beloved town of Kakadu, on the bar and grill our friends owned. It was early in the day, well before noon, but the downstairs to the bar, a private space for men only, would be open, as it never closed. I shifted the two of us outside of the bar's front doors beneath a gorgeous blue sky.

7

"You sure you don't need me to take you around to your properties?" I gave Doug's hand a gentle squeeze while holding the blue stone with my other. I didn't want him to get stuck depending on public transportation all day.

He let out a mild chuckle, then leaned down and gave me a kiss, along with a reassuring squeeze of my hand. "I'll be fine," he promised with a delighted smile. "Bryan is supposed to show up here soon, so we'll wait around for you to get done with the bears, and then we can all grab some food or something. How's that sound?"

A good dinner with Doug and Bryan sounded fantastic, especially knowing it would probably take a few hours to alter the bear candidates Jay had chosen for me.

After Doug and I kissed one more time, he gave me a playful wink and made his way down the sidewalk to catch one of the hovering cabs waiting along the street. He hopped inside, wiggling his fingers to me in a playful good-bye wave. The cab rose into the sky and soon blended in with the airborne lanes of traffic moving above the city and its skyscrapers.

As I stared at the sky, the Citadel's signature coursed throughout my body. Jay's did too. Within seconds I shifted away and stood beside my immense bear friend outside in the surrounding gardens. I watched intently as several bears frantically raced around the grounds. Something serious must have happened.

"What the hell is going on?" I looked up at Jay's furry face, at his thick brown snout, as he grimaced and stared toward the edge of the

Citadel's island. A few plumes of smoke were rising in the distance, and about a dozen Bear Paw ships had amassed around the site.

"A ship full of rogue trash decided to attack a few of our smaller vessels in orbit," Jay explained with a detested growl. "After several well-placed shots, the rogue ship plummeted toward the gardens and ended up crashing into the edge of the island."

"Were they all killed?"

Jay laughed. His huge hands were locked on his waist. The gentle afternoon breeze played with the sea of thick fur covering his shirtless torso. "A few managed to crawl out and fire their weapons at us," he said. "They shouted hatefully before we put them down."

"You killed them all?" I was sure I sounded shocked.

Jay looked down at me with a confused look. "Of course we did, Keeper. I promised to protect your Citadel, and that's *exactly* what I mean to do."

"What were they shouting?"

My furry friend shook his head with a smirk and mild laugh to match. "The usual bullshit... how the MST will not give in to any demands, that they will *always* be the dominant force throughout the Expanse."

I nodded, then reached up and patted the side of his furry arm. "I imagine hearing all their spewing crap probably pissed you off like crazy."

Jay nodded, confirming my thoughts. "What's that you're holding?" he asked.

"Oh," I answered with a surprised tone. "Doug and I just visited the Silver Tree, and it gave me this as a gift. Not quite sure why, but it's got a blend of all of the Ravages children, including hers."

Jay nodded and gently tapped my back with his massive, furry hand. After so many months, he had finally become comfortable touching me in a friendly, supportive way.

"There's an old marble pedestal near the main chamber room in the Citadel," I said to Jay. "I think I'll sit the stone on top of it."

"I know which one you're talking about," he said. "And we can move it anywhere you'd like. Maybe near the windows in your throne room?"

I liked his suggestion.

"Are your bear candidates ready for me to enhance them?"

Jay softly patted my back again. "The final group arrived less than five minutes ago. There should be exactly four hundred of them for you to alter."

"That was fast," I said. "Are they all excited?"

He let out a delighted sigh. "All of us are excited to see the Bear Paw finally take charge of the Expanse. We've waited far too long... suffered through too much humiliation and abuse over the centuries."

I brushed my hand down his arm in an appreciative gesture. I couldn't have asked for a more devoted friend.

"Just promise me one thing," I said. His humble stare down into my eyes was all the confirmation I needed. "If *any* rogue ships show up here again... please call me so I can shift here and help out. Okay?"

Jay smiled proudly, then patted my back for a third time. "You have my word, Keeper."

Bear Paw ships of all sizes blanketed the sky high above the Citadel. Some were shaped like bullets, while others were long and bulky, resembling futuristic rifles. Two of the Makers' ring ships also lay positioned far in the distance, looking almost like distant moons.

Together, Jay and I walked through the gardens, Jay leading the way toward a huge gathering of bears at the far side of the grounds. It was a sea of fur, muscles, and claws.

It couldn't have been a more beautiful day here at the Citadel. Flowers throughout the gardens were in full bloom. Some had vibrant colors of blue and shimmering silver or gold, and many were larger than a dinner plate. Bright green-and-yellow birds with long tails darted between each of the plants. They moved like hummingbirds from flower to flower, drawn to the sweet aroma of each. Green grass edged the wide and winding path we followed, with small patches of blue around the ponds and along the flowing streams. A gentle breeze brushed over each strand so softly.

Several bears passed us, and each nodded to me courteously. Some even said "Keeper" as a greeting.

There were a variety of candidates, both males and females. Some were brown bears, gray bears, or a mix of the two. Some were solid black, and some had silvery chest hair. All were muscular and wore cargo shorts or slightly loosened pants, similar to blue jeans. Wearing tops was optional for both males and females.

"Wow," I said to Jay. "You really got a formidable-looking group gathered together."

"I aim to please." Again, he gave me a gentle pat on my back. "My race is so thankful, Keeper, for the gifts you are about to bestow upon them."

Jay's words delighted me. I was more than happy to help his race. But as we got closer to the group of bears, I started to feel somewhat overwhelmed by the task at hand.

Upon a very flat section of the gardens, all of them stood quietly in the sunshine, each a motionless tower of fur as Jay and I came to a complete stop and stared for a moment. Talk about feeling like a munchkin. Some of these bears stood at least twelve feet tall, more than twice my height.

Jay unleashed a few growls in his language, and all the bears grunted happily in agreement with whatever he had said.

"They're ready, Keeper," he told me in a humble voice.

I took a deep breath, then let it out slowly as I raced through several ideas tumbling around in my head. I gave ample thought about how to change them, how to do it efficiently.

"Tell them to raise a hand into the air," I told Jay. "They'll need to make direct skin-to-skin contact with me."

After Jay growled his order, I handed him the blue stone and then took off my shirt and handed it to him too. I needed to provide as much hand-to-body contact as possible. I could have taken my pants off also, but I didn't want to freak them out with a view of the Keeper's rear.

With a gentle push of my foot, I rose and hovered at eye level with the bears. Before I even started to move through the group, I could feel my imbuing ability surging and coursing throughout my body, as if an inner flame had ignited and set my body ablaze. An overwhelming experience for sure, but it also felt amazing.

Slowly I floated forward, and bear after bear stepped close to lay a huge, furry paw upon me. Several bears at a time covered my shoulders, my back, my stomach and chest, and both arms, and some even grabbed hold of my hands. As I floated along in my hypnotic frame of mind, their emotional states came across to me vividly. Each one stood dazed and amazed, staring ahead with new and wondrous sensations, a fresh view of life, all of which I was more than familiar with.

As I moved through the crowd and changed them, I thought about Shaye and Wyler. Perhaps this had been Shaye's ultimate goal in bringing me into the Expanse. Without even realizing it, she had expertly guided me and shaped me into a god hunter, the one who sought out suitable candidates and imbued them with supernatural abilities in order to make their lives better and to help those in need. However, I wasn't about to complain. I didn't feel duped in any way from having been maneuvered into my position. I liked my role as Keeper of the Citadel. I loved the Expanse and its diversity of races. So I would honor Shaye's intentions to the fullest degree.

In small groups I changed each bear. A few times I looked back at Jay, who had such a proud smile stretched around his snout. It warmed my heart to see him so pleased, but then I laughed a bit as I thought, *Just wait until Jay sees all his bear friends learn to shift and call spirits!* That should be entertaining for him.

In less than an hour I had gifted the powers of flight, shifting, and spirit calling unto all four hundred of them. Surprisingly, a few adventurous bears had started to hover several inches above the ground, anxious to get started, no doubt.

Doug texted me near the end of the process. "Got a big surprise for you, Little Bear."

I replied with three questions marks, and my handsome man answered, "You'll see when you get here. Love you, sweetie."

I could have done some spying and used my remote-viewing ability to get a feel of where and what Doug was doing, but I didn't want to spoil his surprise. I wouldn't do that to him.

Back on the ground beside Jay, I put my shirt back on. He still held the blue stone.

"Now the fun begins," Jay happily exclaimed.

I rolled my eyes and jokingly sighed as I leaned in close to nudge his thick, furry arm with my tiny shoulder. Just to be an ass, I added some extra oomph, which caught Jay off balance for a moment. Afterward, we both shared a brief giggle together.

"I think the best way to do this," I told Jay, "is to train a small group, and then they can teach all the others." I looked up into his dark eyes. "You think they could do that?"

Another proud smile grew along his snout. "I will make sure they do."

"Once they learn the basic techniques, they'll be able to fine-tune their skills on their own." I patted my hand along Jay's arm in a reassuring and grateful manner.

So I took twenty-five bears to the opposite side of the Citadel's island to train for an hour while Jay kept all the others occupied with plans of where each would be stationed and what their responsibilities would entail.

Before long my trainees all had flying down fairly well. Spirit calling came easy for them too. And the creatures they could summon completely blew my mind. They called huge, furry beasts (both four legged and two legged) with armored plates running along their spines. Some spirits resembled enormous winged insects but with long necks, beaks, and grasping talons. A few bears even summoned these amazing cloud-like beings. Comprised of a million tiny specks of light, these cloud-like beings could morph into various forms, like different animals or unique shapes like gigantic weapons or blades. I could only imagine how useful this type of spirit would be for the Bear Paw, knowing how much they enjoyed wielding armaments.

Shifting took the bears some time to get a grasp on. I taught them the basics of sensing signatures and using their remote viewing.

Once I shifted them to an uninhabited world, then they truly picked up on the ability. Their eyes opened to a whole new way of seeing life throughout the Expanse. I could sense the awe and amazement flowing throughout each of their powerful bodies.

After we returned to Jay in the gardens, the bears dispersed throughout the crowd to train all the others. I imagined it would be a long day for them, but I could tell the handful I'd trained had a good grasp on their newly acquired skills.

"Where are you off to, Keeper?" Jay couldn't have acted or looked happier with the results so far.

"I'm going to meet Doug," I told him. "Apparently he has a surprise waiting for me in Kakadu."

I noticed the blue stone was gone, and Jay must have been able to tell I was wondering where he had put it, as he said, "I had the pedestal you mentioned placed in your throne room. The stone is sitting on top of it, just as we talked about."

I brushed my hand along his arm as we stood and stared at the revamped bears. "Thanks for doing that," I said.

Jay gave me a respectful nod. "I'll make sure each one of them is capable of using their skills before I send them out. The shifting alone will be a huge benefit for us."

I gave another playful nudge against his arm as I focused on Doug's signature. "Call me if there are any more problems."

Jay agreed by giving me another friendly pat on the back just seconds before I shifted to Doug.

My sexy man glanced at me as he kept busy fine-tuning what looked like a nice meal set upon a huge mahogany dining room table.

"Where are we?" I gazed around at the beautiful Victorian-style house, with its dark wood accents and hardwood floors. Comfortable-looking furniture lay atop large, colorful area rugs. To my left, beyond a wide and tall arched entryway, was a spacious living room.

Doug stopped fiddling with the plates and dishes of food on the table. A mouthwatering aroma of slow-baked chicken and pasta filled the air. He stood with both hands firmly on his waist and one of his adorable crooked smiles on his bearded face. "Welcome to our new home, Little Bear."

I laughed while shaking my head *and* my finger at my sexy man. "I had a feeling something was going on. Lately you and Bryan have been visiting Kakadu *way* too much for merely hanging out and stuff."

Doug giggled and made his way past four fancy high-back chairs pushed under the table. He stopped right in front of me, placed his hands on my shoulders, and gave me a passionate kiss, playful poking his tongue inside my mouth. He then leaned back and stared into my eyes. I could see the beginning of heartfelt tears building in his eyes.

"You mean the world to me, David," he whispered tenderly. "There's nothing I wouldn't do for you, sweetie. And that includes buying this huge freakin' house for us."

I slid my arms around his strong body and hugged him for the longest time, resting the side of my face upon his powerful chest so that my ear covered his beating heart. A whiff of his cologne delighted me.

"You're the best man ever," I mumbled from the side of my mouth. "I'm so thankful I have you."

I raised my head so we could kiss again. Doug had such soft and inviting lips. I could have stood there all day enjoying his handsome face and the feel of his touch and his arms around me as he rubbed my back.

"So are you ready for a tour, Little Bear? Or would you like a bite to eat?... Or we could get naked, and I'll introduce you to our bed."

Delighted by his offers, I sighed and let myself sink against him again. "I love you," I whispered happily.

He laughed and kissed the top of my head. "I love you too, David. So maybe let's begin with a tour. Does that sound good?"

I wasn't about to argue. All three suggestions were already on my list, especially the third one.

Doug and I held hands as he led me through the house... through *our* house.

We started in the living room. Filtered sunlight poured in through several tall windows, each covered in sheer lace drapery with heavier dark-red drapes tied back to the side. There were decorative cushioned couches with polished hardwood legs shaped like flattened balls and several tables, all fancy, with marble tops and polished dark wood bases. I brushed my hand along the marble top of a tall, ornate wooden table. In the center of the table sat what resembled an orchid in a large, decorative ceramic pot with vertical grooves along its sides.

"Did all this stuff come with the house?" I asked.

"I managed to work some deals," he admitted while tenderly squeezing my hand a few times. "Everything actually cost way less than I would have imagined. Of course being the Keeper of the Citadel's boyfriend managed to get me quite a few discounts. People love you, David."

I laughed in amusement. "Well... I'm glad I could help us out," I said happily.

The ceilings were incredibly high. So much, in fact, that even super-tall Willie wouldn't have a problem hanging out in our house. In fact, any bears would be able to stand straight and not bump their heads against the roof.

Doug led me over to two wide patio doors, and I gawked at the resort-like area outside in our backyard. Gorgeous white tiles surrounded an enormous pool with a raised hot tub off to the side. Several lounge chairs were positioned around the pool, along with two tables and umbrellas. There was a bar out there also, along with several humongous ceramic pots with bountiful ferns, flowers, and tall tropical plants mixed in each.

Doug pointed. "Out there is were we're going to have a lot of sex."

I laughed and spun around to give my handsome man an enormous hug. "Greatest boyfriend ever," I proclaimed as he wrapped me up in his arms.

At the side of the living room, a massive, slightly curved staircase led upstairs. A band of carpeting covered each mahogany step, and two beautiful silvery wrought iron banisters lined the staircase's sides.

Upstairs, Doug showed me the three spacious bedrooms and two full bathrooms. He then introduced me to our master bedroom, which completely blew my mind. I started to get a bit emotional and tightened my hold around his strong hand. Happy tears began to fill my eyes. A crystal chandelier hung from a high domed ceiling, and the king-size bed looked so inviting with its glitzy silver comforter covered with subtle spiral designs in a darker hue. Two mahogany dressers bordered the bed's headboard, and a huge cream-colored area rug lay at the center of the room. Ceramic lamps with decorative stained glass shades sat on the room's four matching tables, one of which was a desk. There were two walk-in closets (one for each of us) and a very roomy bathroom with a shower and a bathtub that could easily accommodate more than four grown men, I imagined.

I let go of Doug's hand and headed over to the edge of the bed, where I sat down and took off my shoes. "Come here, handsome." I patted the comforter beside me, inviting him over. He flashed me an excited smile, clearly aware of what I had in mind.

As soon as he sat down, I stood up and undressed and then helped him do the same. I pulled off his boots and unfastened his belt before pulling off his jeans. I added a few kisses to the tops of his feet, which were still covered in his blue-and-black socks. The socks were going to stay on, and since Doug wore no underwear, that left only his shirt, which he quickly pulled off and tossed to the side of the bed, where it landed on the rug.

I quickly straddled my strong man, and he fell backward onto the bed. We laughed, kissed, and rubbed our hairy chests together. I planted kisses along his neck and beard, moving up his jawline to suckle on his ear while I rubbed a hand over his amazing stomach and then toward his hard wiener, which was more than ready to go.

We made love for over an hour. We took turns savoring each other's tender spots, getting each other moist and wet from sloppy kisses and plenty of licks and pokes from our tongues. Doug always treated me so fine. He savored me either on my back with my legs spread wide apart or lying facedown with him going to town behind me. And since both of us were versatile, we filled each other with ample amounts of warm and flowing love.

"Thank you so much," I said. "I love this house and that incredible patio. I can't wait to swim in the pool." I was curled up beside him, his arms around me. I rubbed my hand over his chest and gave him a few kisses right in the center of it, where it was the hairiest.

As Doug massaged my shoulder, he occasionally leaned down and gave me a few sweet and slow kisses atop my head. Before long he tightened his hold around me and said, "I'd do anything for you, David. I just want you to be happy."

I let out a delighted sigh. "Oh, I am *very* happy... both with this place *and* with you."

I reached around him as much as I could and massaged the side of his butt. We both got a kick out of that. But before I could utter another word, my pdPhone rang. A digital image of Bryan's face floated above its screen in midair.

I grabbed the phone off the nightstand and answered playfully, "What's going on, Mr. Filthy?"

"Hey, sweetness," Bryan said quickly. He sounded nervous. "I know my big brother has probably fucked your brains out in your new house, but you'd better turn on the TV to channel 745. There's a fleet of rogue ships attacking the paper where your reporter friend works!"

Doug had been playfully nudging me with his hand but turned serious as soon as I sat up and told him to turn on the television. Using his phone, he projected a fifteen-foot-wide holographic television screen about four inches in front of the wall facing our bed.

Before Bryan hung up, he yelled, "Shift there, sweetness! Seth and I will follow your signature."

I jumped out of bed and started to get dressed as fast as I could. Doug stood buck naked watching the TV, with his thick and meaty erection pointed directly at it.

Several distant camera shots showed a dozen or more spaceships firing upon the downtown area of Chorgal city where the *Transgalactic Press* was located on the planet Ves Soule. The news anchor described the scene between her horrified gasps.

"Are you fucking kidding me!" Doug hurried over to his closet, opened the door, and stepped inside.

By the time I sat down along the edge of the bed and quickly put on my shoes, my tough guy had stepped out of the closet dressed in his shit-kicking attire, his beloved Kimoon TC rifle in hand. He had put on a padded, heavy black vest with its buckles left open, along with a form-fitting pair of dark blue jeans and his steel-toe black leather boots.

"Looks like you're ready to kick some ass." I stood up and smiled at him.

With a determined look on his face, Doug said, "Let's do it, Little Bear."

8

Right after I texted Bryan, I shifted Doug and myself to Chorgal, focusing on my journalist friend's signature.

"Hey, you two!" Fred hurried over to us. He had on business attire—a dark-blue polo shirt with dress pants and black leather shoes. His mostly bald head was soaked with sweat.

We were in some sort of library storage area, though it looked more like an underground bunker than a storage facility. But I guessed being a newspaper they needed to protect their archival materials as best as they could.

"What the hell is going on?" I asked. I could tell Fred was fed up with bullshit like this. "Why didn't you call me?"

Of all things Fred laughed. With a tilt of his head, he gave me a twisted, goofy look. "I left my phone upstairs. And whatever you did to the Kroma M8, you must have *seriously* pissed off the rogue agents. We've been receiving reports about upheaval from all across the Expanse."

I shot a similar look right back at him. "Well, duh," I said. "And I suppose the scandalous articles you wrote about the MST didn't upset them either."

Fred gasped and acted completely shocked at my comment. "*Me...* do something wrong?" Fred laughed, then placed his hand on his chest. "All I do is report the facts. If people don't like it, then that's their problem, not mine."

A huge blast came from above and shook the entire room. A couple of Fred's associates almost toppled over.

"Well, it sure feels like it's your problem," Doug pointed out.

"Will you all be safe down here if Doug and I go above and check things out?" I asked. There were over a dozen employees in here with us.

Fred batted his hand through the air in a dismissive gesture. "Yeah, we're fine in this bunker slash library. Several crazy-ass people have attacked us before, and we survived." He shook his finger at me and smiled. "But if I were a shifter, we wouldn't be in this predicament. Plus, I'd be able to get around from one guy's bed to another a hell of a lot faster than I can now."

I rolled my eyes at him with a mildly entertained sigh. He just couldn't resist slipping in some sexually slanted joke. But that was how he rolled.

I could sense Bryan's and Seth's signatures nearby. They were already aboveground kicking some ass, so I shifted Doug and myself up into the city a few blocks away from where the newspaper building stood.

We gazed around in shock at all the damage. A beautiful futuristic-looking city of shapely skyscrapers lined with glass, all positioned along the edge of a blue ocean, and so many of them had been shot to shit.

"Motherfuckers," Doug spewed hatefully.

Huge black columns of smoke rose from the all over the city. Tops of buildings had been shattered, and parts of some had fallen down to the streets below. The building for the newspaper was in shambles too. Half of it lay flattened to the ground. Good thing Chorgal had flying vehicles, because the entire street was blocked with debris on both ends.

Above us, though, it pleased me to see Bryan and Seth were keeping on top of things. Both were flying through the air calling dozens of spirits, commanding their ethereal army to shred the dozen or so rogue spacecrafts maneuvering through the dense clouds.

I could only imagine how the Bear Paw would perform with spirit calling. They didn't hold back when the shit hit the fan.

"I guess I'd better get up there and help." I glanced into Doug's eyes. "You gonna be okay down here?" I felt bad leaving him alone on the street. Groups of people were running around in a panic, but I could sense most had taken shelter or fled.

Doug smiled at me before raising his rifle and holding it in front of his chest. "I'll be fine," he reassured me with a shake of his powerful gun. "Any rogue trash show up down here, and I'll blow their freakin' heads off."

He gave me a kiss, and then I squatted a bit and rocketed off into the sky. Unfortunately, I got nowhere near as far as I had planned. A gigantic spaceship full of holes from Bryan's and Seth's spirits came plummeting out of the clouds, headed directly toward the city. On fire and burning out of control, it made a deafening sound as it fell through the sky. Shocked, I stopped, hovered in the air, and watched as tons of sparks and smoke poured out from its shattered hull.

"Thanks, guys!" I shouted out as a joke, knowing Bryan and Seth probably couldn't hear me.

I wasn't about to let this ship crash into the city, especially considering I knew from experience how explosive a ship's power core could be. Even one this size, maybe ninety feet long, would take out an entire city block, or more!

What about the ocean? I could push it toward the sea and drop it there. What was the worst that might happen? A gigantic wave of water would rush against the shoreline? That wouldn't be so bad. Would it?

I flew toward the ship's nose. Overall it was shaped like a bullet, but it had huge, bulky wings angled downward and a similar-shaped fin along its back. Through the clouds it came closer toward me. I slowly backed away so I could catch it without causing any more damage to its hull. But my good intentions failed miserably. The ship had become incredibly fragile, and as soon as I made contact with it, my enhanced strength shattered even more of its weakened frame.

"Great! Fucking great!" With my remote viewing I could sense Doug thought the exact same thing as he watched me from the city streets below.

I wasn't about to let my lovable man get singed by some enormous blast, and of all things, a brilliant idea suddenly raced through my mind. Could I do it? Could I shift a large spacecraft over to the ocean and then drop it in? It was definitely worth a try.

After taking a deep breath, I pressed my hands firmly against the ship's hull, focused on moving myself just above the sea, and then bam! The ship and I appeared far from the shore, probably two hundred feet above the surface of the ocean. Immediately I shifted just myself back above the city and watched as the rogue vessel crashed into the ocean with a huge splash and a harsh noise to match. Its hull shattered and tore apart from the impact.

Luckily there was no explosion, so I smiled, knowing I'd done a good job. But Bryan and Seth were sending down even more heavily damaged ships. Huge ones, in fact! Some were half the size of the skyscrapers below me. Geez!

There was a variety of spirits above me in the sky, a mix of flying, furry, four-legged creatures; enormous whales; and a swarm of tire-size, ravenous insects. I couldn't have been more proud of Bryan and Seth. They had mastered shifting and spirit calling spectacularly.

I then thought about the planet, about the city and all the destruction it had suffered, and about why I shouldn't be littering the ocean with ships. Probably wasn't the best idea. So I shifted over to a bulky ship plummeting through the clouds, pressed my hands against its hull, and shifted it into outer space, directly above the planet's atmosphere. I gave it a seriously strong push, sending it spiraling away from the planet and deeper out into space.

I then shifted back, startling Bryan when I suddenly appeared beside him. He actually raised his fist and came close to knocking the shit out of me.

"Sweetness!" he shouted with a startled laugh. He was shirtless, sporting his hairy chest, with jeans and a pair of skull-cracking steel-toe brown boots. "Did you bring Doug with you?"

I nodded as we floated beside each other in the clouds. "Yeah, Doug's down there," I said. "Keep disabling their ships, and I'll dump 'em off in space!"

To confirm my suggestion, Bryan reached behind me and gave me a firm smack across my rear. "You got it!"

I imagined the media had probably captured Bryan's playfulness on film. Oh well. The citizens of Chorgal would at least see how entertaining he could be.

I shifted all the spaceships Seth and Bryan disabled into space and sent them tumbling away with powerful pushes. A few broke apart from my forceful moves, but I made sure every chunk drifted away from the planet. No stragglers or chunks would fall down upon the city.

Right before I pushed away the last ship, I sensed hundreds of signatures coming from somewhere deeper out in space. I hovered high above the planet for a moment and made use of my remote-viewing ability to get a sense of what and *who* they were. From what I could tell, a fleet of ships had parked far in the distance, a million or more miles away. Rogue vessels, I assumed, after vaguely sensing their intentions and emotional states.

As I panned through their crew, something caught my attention, something that bothered me a great deal. I detected Admiral Rohn's signature on board one of the ships, and I couldn't get a clear sense of why he would be there. Was the admiral playing both sides? Telling me one thing and then doing another? Everything my friends had told me about the MST and their lies suddenly sounded very true. Dozens of suspicious ideas rushed around inside my mind.

I turned back toward the planet, intending to shift down to Doug and tell him what I had sensed, but from the corner of my eye I saw movement to my left. Something inspiring and refreshing to my soul had appeared, a reminder as to why I fought to keep the Expanse safe. A dozen giant sea turtle–type creatures were slowly swimming through space, making their way high above the planet on a course to some unknown destination. Each one had to be the size of a suburban house. Their long limbs gracefully and fluidly moved up and down, pushing and guiding them forward. Their rounded bodies were covered in layered patches of what resembled thick, rough tree bark. Some had curved spikes along their spines, and each lengthy neck gave rise to an armored-plated head.

Slowly I drifted closer toward them, keeping enough distance so I wouldn't startle them. They glanced at me with large, sunken, shiny eyes.

Such an amazing moment. Another reminder of how incredible and unpredictable the Expanse could be. Moments like this really warmed my heart.

I wanted Doug to experience such an incredible sight, so I shifted down to him, totally catching him off guard.

"How's it going, sweetie?" he asked, patting my shoulder.

I immediately slipped my arm around his waist and pulled him close. "Got a surprise for you," I told him real fast. "Hold on!"

I shifted both of us high above the planet, taking us into the cool evening atmosphere of Expanse outer space. Staring at the creatures before us, Doug gasped and released his rifle, which floated beside him.

"Wow!" He slipped his arms around me and held me against the side of his chest. "I've never been this close to a group of porpahlis before. They're really amazing."

"So you know about these turtle things?" I asked. "What do they eat? Can they go down to the planet?"

Doug let out a tiny laugh and kissed my forehead, keeping his eyes on the porpahlis as they continued to maneuver through space. "They defy gravity just like you, Little Bear. I'm pretty sure they can hover and float down to the oceans on the planet. Not sure what they eat, though."

My sweet man snuggled beside me as we enjoyed the awe-inspiring moment. He rubbed his hand over my chest, over my nipple, and then used his finger and thumb to tweak my slightly bearded chin a few times before leaning in to give me a passionate kiss.

"David," Doug whispered affectionately, "you make me so happy. I can't even begin to tell you how grateful I am for having you in my life. I love you so much, baby."

I buried my face alongside his chin and kissed his neck, savoring the feel of his thick beard against my lips. I caught the faintest hint of his enticing cologne and of his beard oil and the balm he enjoyed using.

"I love you too, handsome." I gave him a firm squeeze, then reached lower so I could fondle his behind for a brief moment. Doug had such a shapely ass. It was wonderfully toned and firm from all his years of working out and from all the MMA fighting he had done.

Both of us nervously jumped as we simultaneously noticed two huge porpahlis gliding several feet above us against a star-filled background. We both let out captivated gasps while marveling at the details of the creatures' scales and fins, armored heads, and enormous parrot-like beaks. Those beaks could easily snap a person in two, I imagined.

"Amazing," Doug said.

I nodded, feeling just as captivated, then paused for a moment before telling Doug about sensing the admiral's signature.

"Seriously?" My tough guy sounded pissed. "Are their ships still out there?"

"No," I answered. "All their signatures are gone. They were probably monitoring us, watching Bryan, Seth, and me."

Doug reached out and grabbed hold of his high-powered rifle. "Well, maybe we should go pay the admiral a visit and see what the fuck he's up to. He's probably a lying, two-faced sack of shit like all the others."

As good as his suggestion sounded, I knew we needed to tend to the city below and check in on our journalist friends. Plus I needed to return to Jay and see about dispersing the bears I had empowered.

"First things first." I wiggled my fingers over Doug's stomach, then wrapped my arm around his waist nice and tight.

I shifted us down to the sky above the city, near Bryan and Seth, who were hovering with watchful gazes for any more invading spaceships. I held Doug close to me so he wouldn't fall.

"Looks like we got them all," Bryan happily declared. He gave me a playful wink. An army of spirits swam throughout the clouded sky, all of them ready to shred any ship to pieces.

"Great job, guys!" I couldn't have been more pleased with the way Bryan and Seth had handled the rogue vessels.

"Did everything go okay at Nheyja's?" Doug asked. He had slung his left arm over my shoulders for some added support while we floated miles above the city. He didn't seem super nervous about being up so high, just somewhat cautious.

"Yeah, it went good," Bryan answered. He and Seth had drifted beside each other to hold hands and playfully nudge their shoulders and arms together. "There's some more to do, but Ellet invited a bunch of friends over to help straighten up the minor stuff after we moved all the heavy chunks out of the way for them."

Seth smiled and leaned over to give Bryan a tender kiss on his shoulder. He then reached behind Bryan and squeezed his tough guy's shapely rear a few times. Hopefully no cameras were rolling from down below.

"Well," I said to them, "could you two hang out up here for a while to make sure no more ships attack?" I took a moment and explained about the signatures I had detected far out in space.

Bryan rolled his eyes with a sigh and then nodded several times. "Hell yeah, we'll hang around," he said before slipping his arm around Seth and pulling him closer. Bryan gave him a few quick smooches on his happy cheeks. It was such a sweet display of affection. "Me and my wild man here will keep an eye out for those fuckers and kick their asses if they show up again."

I drifted toward them with Doug in my arms so the four of us could share a mutual bump-and-nudge moment, a loving gesture of how much I appreciated their help and determination. We all shared some laughs and silly looks while floating high in the sky, miles above the city.

"Okay," I announced, "me and sexy butt here are going to head back down to the newspaper."

Bryan gave me a playful shove with his hand, and I shifted Doug and myself down to the newspaper storage room.

"Well, did you beat the shit out of them?" Fred casually walked over to us with a concerned look. He seemed somewhat flustered and exhausted from the attack. "The room down here stopped shaking, so I guess it's safe to assume you sent them running off like cowardly little bitches."

I tilted my head and nodded with my brows raised for a second. "Pretty much," I told them all. "But before we leave, I need to pump you full of a special treat."

Fred's face lit up, and I could sense his thoughts dipped straight down into the gutter. For the life of me, I had no idea why everyone always had dirty thoughts when I mentioned giving them something.

I let out a small chuckle, then took a few steps toward Fred and cradled his bearded, rosy, and round face in my palms. It was time to give him what he wanted.

Fred gasped from the heat pouring off my hands, and after a short moment, his expression went completely blank. As I stared into his eyes, I could tell he now gazed outward with a new understanding, a new vision of all life. He would view his world as he had never done before, sensing all things, all individuals in a much more intimate and personal manner.

"All done," I whispered with a hint of excitement.

I shifted Doug, Fred, and myself to the new house back in Kakadu. Fred needed certain signatures, specific impressions of places, people, and worlds, so what better place to start than Doug's and my new home. Now he'd be able to visit and approach us for help whenever he needed it.

"Are you picking up signatures?" I gently tapped Fred's cheek to snap him out of his daze before dropping my hands.

He giggled, then let out an astounded sort of sigh. "I am," he said. "And it's so freakin' awesome!"

"That's one way to describe it." I glanced at Doug, and we exchanged some warm smiles before I shifted the three of us to the sidewalk in front of the Arkenstone Bar and Grill. I then moved us around the city of Anourish, traveling to each tier, before finally shifting us to where Bryan and Seth were hanging out, a skyscraper rooftop near the newspaper building.

From our bird's-eye view of the city, the damage stood out like a sore thumb. Avenues were littered with huge chunks of broken buildings and shattered glass, plus damaged flying vehicles that had crashed. Plumes of smoke rose up from the tops of skyscrapers, clogging the beautiful sky with what resembled clouds of dirt.

I faced both of my shifter prodigies. "Could you guys do me a huge favor?"

Bryan stared at me with a goofy grin. "Sure we can. Whatever you need, sweetness."

Seth happily nodded also, more than ready to jump on my request.

"Well," I explained, "I gifted Fred with identical powers to yours, so if you have time, would you mind helping him out with some basic spirit-calling skills and then make sure he can fly? I don't want him to turn into a juicy mess all over the streets from this height."

Fred's face went completely blank from surprise. I guessed he hadn't thought I had given him so many abilities. But with all the rogue problems lately, he would need to be able to get around fast, keep himself safe, and probably protect his coworkers too.

With a great big smile, Bryan stepped over and slung his arm across our journalist friend's shoulders. He stood a few inches taller than Fred and gave him a few friendly jiggles. "Buddy," Bryan said with an added tickle along Fred's side, "you are in for *quite* a ride today!"

I had no doubt Fred would pick up flying. That was easy. But for my own peace of mind, Doug and I hung out for a few minutes to make sure Fred could actually summon a spirit. A part of me also wanted to see what sort of creature he could produce.

After Bryan gave Fred some pointers and demonstrated exactly how to do it, Fred summoned his first sprit. The five of us busted up laughing. It was a tiny, fluffy bunny. Its fur glowed in outlines of ethereal blue-and-white light as it hopped around the rooftop.

Blushing, Fred giggled and laughed the loudest, even hunching over a bit from his amusement at the sight of his tiny rabbit.

"Well," he said, "if I can't shred any rogue ships, at least I'll be able to kill them with kindness and some laughs."

I gave Fred a few reassuring pats on his shoulder. "Trust me, you'll get the hang of it. There's no rush."

Overall, he seemed determined to master the art of spirit calling. I could see abundant interest in his eyes and on his face.

"Well," Fred admitted, "I *am* going to rush it. I don't plan on sitting idly by anymore like some terrified kid hiding in the closet. If people want to fuck with *my* newspaper, then they're going to face the consequences. I'll be like your friend Deora... out on a killing spree."

I stopped for a moment and stared with concern. "What do you know about Deora?"

Fred shrugged. "We've heard a shit ton of rumors. Apparently she's been on a rampage since your ordeal at the Ravages. She's assembled a huge army of demons. Her shifter buddy is moving them all around, and they're slaughtering every MST agent they can get their hands on."

I shook my head and sighed before flashing Doug a disgruntled look. "She just isn't going to stop, is she?"

My tough guy wrapped me up in a one-armed hug and kissed the top of my head. "Maybe we should check in on her and make sure she's not fucking up your arrangements with the MST."

Feeling frustrated, I took a deep breath and then let it out slowly in an attempt to calm myself. Of course, Doug holding me against his body helped to ease my tensions more than anything. He would always be my pillar of strength and support.

"Okay," I mumbled before taking a few steps back. I stood and gazed for a moment at four very concerned-looking faces. "We need to get the bears into position around the Expanse, then see what's up with Deora and the admiral."

"The admiral?" Fred sounded intrigued. His ever-curious ears perked up a bit. He raised his eyebrows too. "More MST headaches, I'm guessing?"

I rolled my eyes and nodded. No need to say too much since I wasn't entirely sure why Admiral Rohn was on one of the rogue ships. But I had a hunch Doug's original assessment would turn out to be true, in one way or another.

In a playful style, I shook my finger at Fred, Bryan, and Seth. "You three behave yourselves," I told them.

They each gave me a goofy look, like they had no intentions of listening to me.

Once again, Bryan slung his arm across Fred's shoulders and shot me a silly smile. "We'll treat him real nice, sweetness. Don't worry."

Seth then stepped up on the opposite side of Fred and gently patted our journalist friend's stomach. "Treat him real nice," he reiterated in his heavily accented voice.

Doug and I glanced at each other and shook our heads. Safe to say, neither of us wanted to know the details of their intentions. But Bryan and Seth had definitely put a great big smile on Fred's round face.

"Call us if anything happens," Doug told his younger brother, but the three of them had already stepped aside and were making their way across the roof to work on some training.

I focused on Jay's signature at the Citadel, then shifted Doug and myself to the main chamber room, where our furry friend stood with a large group of his fellow bear captains.

9

Jay turned around to face Doug and me and courteously bowed his head before me. "Keeper... what perfect timing."

In addition to Jay, forty-six others, all growda ha'tars, occupied the main chamber of the Citadel. There was a mix of males and females with black, brown, and some gray fur. They stared at Doug and me with looks varying from delight to curiosity.

Ample amounts of early-morning sunlight poured in through the arched windows lining my throne room. Each bear's fur glimmered with subtle hints of shine, as did the marble floors and walls. The sunlight also illuminated the blue stone Jay had set on the pedestal he'd moved for me.

I glanced at my bear commander with a pleasant but silly grin. "You didn't have to get a welcoming party together just for *me*," I told Jay.

He got my joke and chuckled a bit while walking over to stand beside Doug and me. He laid his huge, hairy paw, which was damn near the size of my chest, on my shoulder.

In a loud and proud voice, Jay said, "Allow me to introduce the Bear Paw's finest and most honored captains."

Every nine-to twelve-foot-tall growda ha'tar bowed his or her head before me. Many touched their snouts to their prominent chests. Some wore either denim or corduroy pants. Others had on cargo shorts. A few had come in gigantic leather boots lined with silver buckles, and more than half were shirtless, showcasing their silky hairiness. A few older bears had touches of silver and gray in their fur. Several of the bears carried rifles that were about half the size of a steel girder.

I turned my head and stared at Jay. He had caught me completely by surprise, but I had to ask. "So you're already prepared to move the altered bears?"

Jay nodded with a satisfied smile growing along his snout. "We will place a gifted bear in each of the numerous galaxies throughout the Expanse, along with a support team," he said. "We will build temples similar to your Citadel where they will stand guard and watch over less developed worlds, answering to *any* people in need of help. The Bear Paw will stand as the new guardians of the Expanse, serving and protecting *all* life."

Jay's words profoundly touched my heart. The sight of the captains did too. I had to wipe away a beginning tear as Doug lovingly rubbed his hand across my back.

"How will you build more citadels?" I asked, curious and confused. "I mean, will they float in the sky like mine does?"

Jay patted my shoulder before he moved forward to stand with his comrades. He turned around to face Doug and me. "We have the means and the resources," Jay explained in a pleasant voice. "As soon as our ships are in position, construction will begin. Within a few months, four hundred similar citadels will stand erected, and the Bear Paw will take their rightful place under your guidance. Each structure will likely be grounded, as opposed to floating, and they will be somewhat smaller. But, nonetheless, they will stand as a symbol of what we intend to accomplish throughout the Expanse."

Doug hadn't stopped rubbing my back, and I brushed my hand along his thigh, my tower of strength, my love and support.

"Sounds like you've got everything covered." I smiled, and Jay did the same. His loyalty and devotion almost moved me to tears again. A sudden sense of relief filled my soul.

"We will strive to support your wishes, Keeper." Jay slightly bowed once again. "My race is determined to please you, in all ways possible."

Doug lowered his arm to his side. "Just be careful of the Kroma M8. David altered them, and they're on our side now, from what we can tell."

Jay's expression conveyed a touch of surprise and concern. His furry brows lowered, and his thick lips pursed. He quickly nodded a few times. "I will inform our troops," he said. "The Kroma M8 will not be harmed or engaged."

Intrigued feelings spread throughout the room. I had never met any of these bear captains before, but I could sense their desire to shake my hand and to express their gratitude and thanks to the Keeper of the Citadel. *Why not?* I thought. They deserved some up-close interaction.

I smiled and made my way through the crowd, shaking their enormous paws, enjoying the feel of their soft fur, their laughs, and their gracious nods while meeting me. Many of them patted my shoulders or lightly brushed their hands over my back. Gratefulness rolled off of them like sugar from a powdered doughnut. It felt amazing.

As the bear captains mingled with each other, I headed back over to Doug and Jay, who stood together, waiting patiently for me to finish.

I shook Jay's hand again, his palm and fingers wrapping around my entire forearm. "I really appreciate all your help." I raised my other arm and patted Jay's broad and furry tummy. He seldom wore a shirt, and if he did, it was usually a vest left unbuttoned.

"It is my pleasure to serve you, Keeper."

Doug playfully poked my arm a few times. "We probably need to go check in on Deora."

"Do you need my help?" Jay sounded concerned, and his expression had changed.

I shook my head. "Routine stuff," I assured my bear commander.

Jay slightly bowed his head before moving away to stand with his comrades.

Although there really was no need for subtleties, since the bears were getting loud, Doug leaned down and whispered, "Can we swing by the house so I can grab my rifle again?" My lovable man also managed to work in a quick grope of my behind.

"I didn't even notice that you left it back at the house."

Doug let out a mild chuckle. "Yeah, I leaned it up next to the sofa."

"Sure, we can do that." I tickled my fingers over his stomach and then shifted us to our living room.

Doug took a moment to give me some sweet kisses. He firmly gripped my arms with his strong hands and pulled me close, loving me, both of us savoring the feel of our lips pressed together. After a final kiss on my cheek, he picked up his beloved Kimoon TC.

Call me crazy, but he looked mighty sexy carrying his futuristic rifle. I smiled while watching him inspect his weapon. He checked it for scratches and dings and made sure it appeared perfect and functional in every way. Watching him touched my heart.

"You and your big gun really turn me on," I told him.

With rifle in tow, Doug stopped in front of me and tenderly cradled the side of my face with his left hand. "Well," he whispered in a flirtatious tone, staring directly into my eyes, "my *big gun* loves you too, Little Bear. Especially when it gets to fire off a few shots and hear you moan."

I grinned. I adored Doug's filthy humor. Bryan's and Willie's too.

I took a moment to massage Doug's crotch. Beneath his jeans, I could feel him growing harder with every push and pull of my hand.

A silly grin popped up on his face, and he shook his head. "You're going to give me a wet spot if you keep that up, sweetie."

How could I not laugh? But, to be nice, I stopped and pulled my hand away. The fact Doug wasn't wearing any underwear, mixed with how easily he tended to ooze from being fondled, meant that me continuing would indeed have left a noticeable spot on his pants.

"Ready to pop in on Deora?" I leaned forward and planted a kiss on the center of his muscular chest, over his shirt.

Doug affectionately brushed his hand down the side of my face. "You don't think you should call Ruby first?"

"Nope," I answered with gusto. "If Deora can surprise us with unexpected visits, then we can do the same to her!"

Doug smiled and nodded with his brows raised in a supportive look. He leaned down and kissed the top of my head. "Take us there, Little Bear."

I didn't even bother to use my remote-viewing skill before shifting to Deora's signature. Whatever horrible acts she was up to would be a surprise for both Doug and me, I figured.

I patted Doug's side. "Here we go!"

We appeared on a spacious bridge on a spacecraft and gasped at the bloody scene lying all around. Dozens of rogue agents had been slaughtered to pieces. Severed limbs and heads, along with various bits and pieces of shredded bodies, lay mixed among wide pools of blood and entrails. Many workstations were covered in splattered bits too.

"Keeper of the Citadel," Deora said. "You missed all the fun."

Our troll goddess, who was at least twice my height, stood before the captain's chair, which sat atop a three-tiered platform. Her gigantic cleaver-shaped sword was in its leather sheath on her back, and globs of blood covered her chest, arms, stomach, and especially her long, jagged tusks, which she clearly had stabbed through many agents. Impaling individuals with her tusks, after all, was her favorite way to kill a person.

About thirty red hellions manned the workstations around the bridge, and her demon horde was keeping busy maintaining the ship's systems. A theater-size view screen covered one entire wall of the bridge, and above one workstation floated a rotating holographic representation of the ship we were on. It looked about the size of the Empire State Building lying on its side.

Jakloz, Deora's small shifter buddy who resembled a demonic turkey, clung close to her legs, as always. Deora had even brought two bromahst along for their enjoyment. The oversize, muscular freaks stood even taller than Deora, with long, greasy black hair covering their heads. Torn and tattered pants fit snuggly over their prominent thighs, and their pale skin reflected the bridge light more than any of the red-skinned demons' did.

In a loud voice, I asked, "What the *hell* are you doing?"

All her minions ignored Doug and me. They clearly knew who we were.

Deora chuckled as she stepped around the bridge, not at all mindful of stepping on body parts or in pools of blood with her massive bare feet. She stopped and stared at me, then ran her hand along one of her bony tusks. "You have your way of dealing with the MST, and I have mine."

I took a few steps closer. "Yeah, but I'm not trying to start another war."

Deora laughed. "The war has been going on long before *you* came into the Expanse," she said. "I'm just taking out the trash, as you humans like to say."

"Arrival in fifteen minutes," one of her red-skinned minions announced. He was a male red hellion with black horns above his temples, and he stood shirtless before two others who were seated at what I assumed were the navigation workstations.

"The MST agreed to cooperate with me," I told Deora. "And so far they've complied with my demands."

Deora tilted her head and shot me a scrutinizing stare from her scrunched-up face. "You're crazy if you think they won't lie to you." In a haughty manner, she waved her hand through the air before pointing at some of the dead bodies. "Death is all the MST understands. And that's *exactly* what I intend on giving to them!"

Doug shook his head and followed me as I moved closer to Deora. "You're just going to stir up a bunch of shit," my tough guy bluntly informed her. "David's trying to save lives throughout the Expanse, and you're just going to fuck it all up."

Deora shot Doug a hateful glare. Next to the bromahst, she was the tallest person in the room and without doubt the strongest too. I seriously didn't want to get into a fistfight with her.

Spit flew from Deora's mouth as she snapped back at Doug, "*You* don't know nothing about it! I've watched them slaughter my kind for dozens of lifetimes. Neither of you are going to tell *me* what to do!"

Doug and I stopped no more than a few feet away from her. Maybe I could pacify her with kindness. It was worth a try.

"We've been friends for a while now," I kindly reminded her. "Why don't we come up with a better plan? Trust me, I don't care if you kill a lot of the rogue agents, but the MST agreed to work with us. They've stepped down, and a shitload of Bear Paw troops are taking over. This is a done deal, Deora. Believe me, it is."

She shook her head, then pushed her way right past Doug and me in a rage, mashing her bare feet through pools of blood and stepping on bodies and limbs. She stopped in front of the red hellion standing near the navigation workstations, and as Jakloz shifted to right beside her feet again, she asked the hellion, "Have they spotted us yet?"

"No," the demon answered.

"Where are we?" I asked. "And what are you planning to do with this ship?"

She completely ignored my questions, taking long moments to either stare at the view screen or flash hateful scowls at her troops.

In a bold move, I shifted beside our troll goddess and gave her a friendly nudge against the dinged and dented golden armor she wore around her waist. I shouted, "Would you tell me what is going on, please!"

In a somewhat-controlled rage, Deora backhanded me across my chest. The blow sent me tumbling backward. I fell against the corner of an unmanned workstation and broke half of it to pieces with my durability. My hands, butt, and thighs landed right in a puddle of blood that soaked into my jeans.

Doug raced over to me, ignoring any body parts lying in his path. He inadvertently kicked a severed hand and sent it sliding across the steel floor. I could sense his urge to make sure I was all right and his growing anger toward Deora.

"What the fuck is wrong with you!" Doug shot Deora a detested glare, then quickly knelt down and offered his hand to help me stand.

As I got up, parts of the workstation popped and sizzled from the damage. Several red hellions, as well as the two muscle-clad bromahst, glared at me from the corners of their eyes.

Deora didn't give a shit either way about treating me like one of her subordinates. I could read her feelings as if they were written on a billboard.

A red-and-brown planet appeared on the view screen, and our troll goddess exchanged a nod and look with the demon overseeing the navigation area.

"I think the Keeper of the Citadel needs to leave now," Deora stated in a cold tone. She kept staring at the planet on the screen. Feelings of hatred mixed with satisfaction rolled off of her.

Huddled together, Doug and I both stared at her. Doug had his arm around me, mindless of the stains on my clothes as he held me close in a caring, protective way.

Stillness blanketed the bridge. No one made a sound.

In a flash, Deora reached over her shoulder and pulled her sword from its sheath. She turned to the side and pointed the tip of her chopping cleaver directly at me with her brows scrunched together and her head lowered in a formidable pose. "Or would you like to stay and see how easily I can cut through *you* too?" she said.

I shook my head, knowing I had to submit to her demands. She had proved many moons ago that she was stronger and more durable than I was.

"So we're not friends anymore?" I stared at the tip of her huge cleaver, which was thick and long enough to slice through several people at once.

Deora lowered her blade but kept a tight grip around its handle. "Still friends," she said with a twisted smile. "But like I've told you… *don't* get in my way. Keeper of the Citadel or not. I don't care what your title is. You fuck with my plans, then I cut you in two."

Fair enough. I'd ask to stay just to see what she had planned, but I had a better idea of how to watch.

"I'll leave you to your business then," I told her.

She slid her cleaver back into its sheath.

I wrapped my arm around Doug's waist, focused on our destination, and shifted the two of us away. We didn't go very far, appearing high above the red-and-brown planet's atmosphere in a position close enough to watch the commandeered spaceship flying toward it. I could sense Jakloz, Deora, and all her minions still on board. As Doug and I watched, I had a good sense of what Deora had planned.

Doug pointed at the land far below us. "There's a huge MST command base down there, a city of some kind. Do you see it?"

I nodded. "Looks like she's going to crash the ship into it."

Doug shook his head and sighed. He gave me a heartfelt squeeze. "You could intervene, sweetie... use some spirits to stop her."

I took a moment to considerer his suggestion. The thought of what was about to happen made me ill, but I knew I couldn't risk angering Deora. I sighed and pulled Doug closer. "Oh, trust me, I'd love to. But I don't think we need Deora racing around the Citadel slaughtering a bunch of bears."

Doug gripped me tightly and kissed the side of my head, and I found myself once again grateful for his support. I definitely needed it right now.

As we watched, the vessel accelerated. Its rear engines roared and grew brighter, shooting out beams of blue-and-white light. Doug and I stared with blank expressions as it plummeted toward the planet, on a straight path for the base. It entered the atmosphere, parting clouds and swirling them as it moved deeper.

"They still on board?" Doug asked.

"Yep, every one of them." I hadn't stopped using my remote-viewing skills to spy on Deora and her crew. The desire to stop her made my stomach churn. But as I had told Doug, the payback would be bitter and extreme. All we could do was watch.

Small assault crafts zoomed out of the MST base and traveled high into the sky. Their flashing weapons fired at Deora's spaceship, but to no avail. It was far too big. They were unable to stop it. As the ship continued along its path, it turned into a faint blur of movement and glares beneath the clouds.

We waited for several seconds, no longer able to see the ship. But then we heard the crash, an explosion of monumental proportions. There was a blinding flash, the force of which parted the heavens and gave us a clear view of a dark mushroom-shaped cloud rising up from the base's location.

"Holy shit," Doug mumbled, clearly shocked by the magnitude of the blast. He continued to stare. "Deora must have stuffed that ship with a ton of explosives!"

Before the crash, I had sensed thousands of signatures inside the MST base, both humans and aliens. But now there were none. All of them had died.

Doug gave me a tender squeeze with his left arm while holding his rifle with his right. He could tell I wasn't too thrilled right now. "Did Jakloz take them all back to Deora's mountain?"

I nodded without interest. "Yep, and I'm guessing she's got a lot more bloodshed planned."

My handsome man leaned in and kissed my cheek. "Well, look on the bright side, sweetie," he said. "Maybe the rogue agents will see how much of a threat Deora and her army are, and they'll knock off all their bullshit."

Oh, Doug could really make me laugh at times. I reached up and patted his cheek. "You're so cute," I told him sweetly, with a hint of sarcasm. "But you know damn good and well Deora won't stop until she's up to her chin in blood, guts, and body parts."

A faint giggle erupted out of Doug as he gently hugged me. "So what's the plan?"

I gave that some thought, though I already knew exactly what needed to be done. "I think we need to find out what's up with the admiral and why he was on that rogue ship. That should be our priority right now."

Doug nodded slightly. He looked as determined as I felt.

Despite Deora's handiwork with the MST base, I took some time to marvel at the view. How many people could say they had hovered in space above a planet?

I kissed Doug. From his overly receptive response, I could tell he was eager for more affection. His beard always felt incredible.

"Want to go back to the house and make a game plan?" I suggested.

A wide smile grew across Doug's face, and he tapped my upper back a few times in confirmation. "Yeah, take us home, Little Bear."

Of course, the second I started to focus on our place, my phone rang. No biggie, though.

"It could be important," I told Doug as I pulled my phone out of my pants pocket.

I saw Wyler's name and picture on the screen and answered. "Hey, what's up?" I tried to sound relatively happy, considering the destruction and deaths we'd just witnessed.

"Oh my gosh, Davie," Wyler said with ample amounts of excitement, "you're never going to believe what just happened. Josh proposed! He wants to get married."

10

While still talking to Wyler on my phone, I shifted Doug and myself back to our new house, inside the master bedroom. Doug gave me a quick kiss on my cheek before leaning his rifle against the wall with its heel on the floor and then heading into the bathroom.

"You don't think getting married is too soon?"

My question left Wyler chuckling. "Not at all, Davie," he answered. "Josh and I are meant to be together. The love we share is absolutely incredible. Everything about this feels right. It feels good." He took a moment to clear his throat. "Plus... I peeked into the future and saw nothing bad."

Well, I wasn't going to argue against love. I felt the same way about Doug.

"So when is the wedding?"

"I've contacted Rommie and Max at the Arkenstone," Wyler said. "They invited us to have the ceremony there, and then I plan on taking Josh on an exclusive tour throughout the Expanse."

"Sounds like it's going to be an incredible adventure," I said cheerfully. "Let me know if you need anything."

Doug came out of the bathroom and stopped behind me. He slipped his muscular arms around me and patted my stomach. He added some kisses along my neck.

"Speaking of needing anything," Wyler said, "how are things going with the MST and those rogue agents?"

While Doug wiggled in place against my back, I quickly filled Wyler in on recent events.

"Show them you mean business, Davie," Wyler suggested. "Don't hold back. They only understand a firm hand and maybe a fist across the face once in a while. Never trust the MST. I've learned that the hard way."

I recalled sensing the admiral's signature on the rogue ship and nodded in complete agreement with Wyler's assessment.

"Let me know when to be at the Arkenstone," I told Wyler.

We then said our good-byes.

After I slipped my phone back into my pants pocket, I turned around to face Doug. He and I needed some kisses.

Doug playfully brushed the tip of his nose over mine. "Ever think of getting married, Little Bear?"

I chuckled and raised my brows as I pretended to give his question some thought. "I *have* considered getting married." I let out a hopeless sigh and joked, "I just need to find a super-sexy bear who wants me."

Doug laughed and gave me a strong smack across my butt. "Well, the man of your dreams is standing right in front of you, goofball!"

I rose several inches into the air and drifted toward Doug until our bodies softly collided. I gave him several kisses all over his face, savoring the feel of his beard against my lips.

"You *are* the man of my dreams," I whispered with a warm smile. "And having you as my husband would make me the happiest man in any universe." I kissed the tip of his nose. "For years I always wondered if I'd find someone to seriously fall in love with. And now that I have, it's the greatest feeling I've ever known. I never want to be without you, Doug. I mean that."

He tightened his strong arms around me, holding me close while affectionately massaging my back. I rested my chin over his shoulder and leaned the side of my head against his. My heart smiled, knowing we were connected in every way possible.

"First things first, though, sweetie," my tough guy said.

I leaned back and stared curiously into his beautiful blue eyes.

"The admiral," Doug reminded me in a firm tone. He even raised his brows. "You need to know what the hell he's up to—why he was on that rogue ship and whether he's in danger."

I paused for a moment, slipped in one more kiss, and said, "Maybe the Keeper of the Citadel and his gun-toting boyfriend need to drop in on him and demand some answers."

Doug's face lit up with eagerness. "My thoughts exactly."

He lowered his arms and stepped away from me, leaving me hovering a few inches in the air as he went to grab his rifle. Doug stood rigid and ready, holding his gun in front of him with both hands wrapped firmly around it. "All set!" he said. He looked sexy, tough, and more than determined to find out what was going on.

I focused on Admiral Rohn's signature. With my remote-viewing skill, I was able to sense twenty or more signatures around him, all on board the bridge of a spacecraft, each busy with work or piloting the vessel.

After a short moment, we appeared about twenty feet from the admiral. Doug stood like a formidable warrior, and I floated in the air beside my handsome man. The bridge was the largest I had ever seen, with dozens of workstations surrounded by three large view screens. Raised platforms were positioned around the perimeter, with the captain's chair sitting on a three-tiered platform at the center of the room.

"Keeper of the Citadel," the admiral said. He stood and took a second to clear his raspy throat. He didn't seem surprised at all by our sudden appearance. "I suspected you'd eventually pay me an unsolicited visit."

Rohn was a tall and overweight human male with gray hair. He was dressed in his usual garb of stylish dark slacks with a matching shirt and opened jacket. Around the bridge were his subordinates, bunches of humans and several aliens whose race I was unfamiliar with. Not surprisingly, the crew wore casual attire. No MST-style bodysuits, which could only mean one thing.

"Hanging out with rogue agents today, Admiral?" I gave him a questioning gaze, one to match my tone.

His face blank, he clasped his hands behind his back and paced around the bridge, moving up and down a few steps, around workstations, and stopping briefly to glance at the two of us.

"You seem to have successfully altered the Kroma M8," Rohn said. "Truly your powers are worthy of your predecessor, Shaye. Perhaps they are even greater."

"She taught me a thing or two," I answered in a somewhat-bitter tone.

He laughed ever so slightly as he made his way back over toward us, stopping by a large workstation with an orange-and-green holographic representation of a world floating above it.

"In our many years of researching supernatural abilities," the admiral said, "we were unable to recreate any powers in the laboratory exactly as they exist throughout the Expanse. However, we did come across something that you might find interesting, something I had completely forgotten about, until recently."

Doug and I exchanged a quick sidelong glance.

Maintaining eye contact with us, Rohn pulled a small handgun from a holster strapped around his right thigh. He took a few seconds to turn and admire its craftsmanship. It resembled a plastic children's toy, in my opinion.

"A prototype," the admiral said. He suddenly seemed more animated, somewhat delighted. "It takes a while to recharge, but it's capable of firing off several shots before that."

Rohn rapidly stretched out his arm, aimed the tiny gun at Doug, and fired. A puffy silver cloud shout out quickly, hit Doug directly on his chest, and then dispersed like falling water over a rock. What the point was, I didn't know. The admiral then shot me too. To my surprise, I slowly descended to the ground. My ability to hover now felt slightly inhibited.

"As I said," Rohn explained, "in our years of laboratory experiments, we stumbled upon a great discovery. We learned how to temporarily suppress supernatural abilities." He cleared his raspy throat. "There's a whole complex science behind it, all of which I don't understand," he admitted. "But it does work well."

He shot both of us again, and the blast left me feeling dizzy.

"Fuck you!" Doug pointed his gun at the admiral, but before he could fire, a crewman shot him in the shoulder with an energy weapon. Instead of the bolt bouncing off of Doug's enhanced durability like normal, a fair amount of blood spurted into the air. Writhing in a considerable amount of pain, my tough guy dropped his rifle and fell back against a workstation.

I rushed toward Doug to help him, but the admiral shot me again. It left me seriously disoriented. The room started to spin.

"Keeper of the Citadel," Rohn said in a haughty tone, "this is where your reign will end. You and your man will die here today. And soon your Bear Paw minions will follow. Then the MST will take back what is rightfully ours."

What the hell had happened to me? It took all my strength to remain on my feet. Hunched over, I stared at Doug, who squirmed in place on the floor. Blood coated his left shoulder and upper chest and ran down his arm. All I could think of was getting to him, helping him. Another shot hit me in the back, and this one came close to making me pass out.

"Get us... out of here, David," Doug mumbled in excruciating pain.

I could barely focus on the moment, let alone shifting. But from the corner of my eye, I saw the admiral moving closer with several troops behind him, so I needed to try to get the hell out of here. After taking a deep breath, I concentrated on Doug's signature with the intent of moving us back to our new house. However, I only shifted myself. And it wasn't home either. I only moved a few decks through the ship, appearing beside six angry rogue agents who obviously knew who I was.

"You piece of shit!" a large, muscular alien male said to me. He had dark-green skin, was bald, and wore a tank top, jeans, and brown leather boots. He hit me right in the jaw, and I actually felt a significant amount of pain.

I was still stronger than all of them combined, though. I slammed my palms against his chest, launching him several feet backward through the air. As the other five rushed toward me, I stretched out my arms and, despite my induced dizziness, spun around. They all went flying toward the steel walls, hitting with loud thumps.

My victory abruptly came to an end. As soon as the rogue agents landed on their butts, each one scurried to stand back up, including the first alien I had shoved.

I focused as clearly as I could, but my head was a jumbled mess filled with dozens of signatures. I spun around to run and was caught off guard as a vision of Sanvean appeared directly in front of me.

Time seemed to stand still. She raised her hands and cradled my face, her touch warm. I could smell her floral perfume. She looked as beautiful as ever with her striking cobalt-blue hair rolling over her delicate, pale shoulders.

"Awaken, David," Sanvean whispered to me with a loving smile. "You are stronger than you realize." She stared deeply into my eyes. "Recall your past, and live again. Remember *who* you were, and you will triumph over all."

I knew she was referencing the idea that, in a past life, I was the first shifter who had left the Expanse and created all life outside of it. Could it be true?

Before I could give it any more thought, Sanvean disappeared, and a striking clarity filled my head. I could suddenly focus again. In the blink of an eye, I shifted myself to Deora's dark mountain, of all places. I appeared in her huge black hall beside her enormous fire pit and the cauldron she liked to cook people in. She loved referring to anyone she cooked as "smart meat," which seemed wrong and appropriate at the same time.

In less than a second I dropped to my knees, panting and out of breath. Two huge rust-colored bare feet lay before me on the dark stone floor. I lifted my gaze, following the legs up to the familiar-looking body.

Deora of the Shadows leaned down and offered me her hand. "What the fuck you been doing?" She laughed a little while helping me to stand.

I stumbled and braced myself against her powerful thigh as I slowly regained my stability.

Jakloz shifted in and stood around Deora's feet, his favorite spot. Red hellions kept busy around the dark and smoke-filled room, lurking in the distant shadows, doing whatever tasks their troll goddess had demanded of them.

"Admiral Rohn..." The words stumbled out of my mouth. "He used some kind of suppression gun to... interrupt my abilities. He's on a spaceship. Doug is still there. They shot him in the shoulder. He's bleeding like mad. I need your help."

Jakloz lifted my pant leg and pulled down my sock. He wrapped his three-fingered, bony, clawed hand around my ankle and probed my mind, acquiring all the details about the admiral's ship and the signatures I had sensed. He lifted his head and long beak and stared up at Deora with his beady, dark eyes before letting out several high-pitched screeches. From the look on her face, I could tell she understood the gist of the situation.

She spun around and yelled in some alien language. Whatever she had said, everyone in the room reacted without hesitation. Red hellions ran around grabbing weapons as more of the demons poured into the hall from several huge arched doorways. More than a hundred had filled the chamber within a few seconds. Two of Deora's demons fetched her enormous cleaver sword. They bowed respectfully while handing it to her and then quickly backed away as soon as she'd taken hold of its handle.

"Let's go get your man back," she said to me with a hefty amount of determination, blended with an eagerness to kill. She ran her hand along one of her lengthy, bony tusks. I imagined she was anxious to impale a ton of MST troops.

Jakloz let out a shrill cry as he shifted himself, Deora, me, and dozens of her armed demons to the bridge on the admiral's ship. We appeared right beside Doug, who had remained conscious and was still lying on the floor with his head propped up on the workstation he had fallen against.

I dropped to my knees beside my sweet man as the bridge crew shouted out in panic. The red-skinned demons raced around the room, hissing and snarling. Black-horned males and females stabbed troops in the back, chest, and even right in the face. They cut throats and sliced open stomachs, covering the floor in pools of blood and spilled guts.

I checked Doug's wound. Someone had shot him again in his side, and he had lost a lot of blood. A huge pool had formed around him.

"I'll be okay," he whispered. But I could see pain written all over his scrunched-up face. "Deal with these assholes."

I heard some nearby cussing followed by gunfire. As I turned around, Jakloz appeared on the admiral's left shoulder. Rohn had lifted his gun at Deora. Jakloz opened his beak wide and clamped his sharp teeth onto Rohn's neck, which caused the admiral to drop his precious little weapon. The admiral tired to grab at Jakloz and pull him away, but Deora quickly grabbed hold of Rohn beneath his armpits and lifted him high into the air.

"I've been waiting to do this for years!" Deora shouted. She tilted her head a bit to the side and rammed her enormous tusks through the admiral's overweight body.

Jakloz jumped onto Deora's shoulder; wrapped his long, bony arms around her thick neck; and hung on tight.

Admiral Rohn squirmed, twitched, and moaned as Deora slowly pulled him all the way up her tusks, until his body pressed against her lips. She stared heartlessly into his eyes. Both tusks had punctured him thoroughly and jutted far out of his back.

"*You* are the piece of shit now," Deora told him. Slowly, she pushed the admiral back along her blood-soaked tusks. She held him in front of her and gave him a powerful kick with the bottom of her massive bare foot. He flew twenty or more feet across the room and landed on top of a workstation. The impact damaged the console, sending sparks and small puffs of smoke into the air, and ample amounts of blood poured all over the controls from Rohn's gaping wounds.

My dizziness had faded entirely, so I stood and looked around the bridge. Every rogue agent and MST sympathizer had been killed. Our sudden appearance had completely caught them all off guard.

Deora barked some alien orders, and the demon horde ran out of the bridge, probably off to slaughter the rest of the crew, I imagined. I didn't even care. Rohn had proved to be a lying sack of shit, and Deora's wrath was what he and his associates deserved.

With the ship under our control, I pulled my pdPhone out and called Chuppo, my healer friend who was also a troll but much smaller than Deora. Doug needed serious help.

"We're aboard my ship," Chuppo said after I'd explained the situation. "Come now. I'll fix you both up!"

Deora had walked over and stopped in front of me as I hung up my phone.

"Just to let you know," she said, "I plan on crashing this ship into another one of their bases."

I shrugged indifferently. "Fine with me," I told her. "You were right about them. We can't trust the MST, no matter what. Do whatever you feel is necessary. I won't get in your way."

She nodded a few times, smiling with satisfaction. Blood and bits of flesh clung to her huge tusks. I was sure it'd take her minions hours to get every crack and crevice scrubbed clean.

"Get your man out of here," Deora said.

I patted the side of her arm. She towered over me, but we took a moment to gaze into each other's eyes. "Thank you," I said, and then I shifted Doug and myself to Chuppo's ship.

We appeared in the kitchen, which was the heart of their vessel. Doug was lying near a stack of fluffy floor pillows. I knelt down and helped him to sit up more by placing a few behind him. Ni rushed over and patted both our shoulders. She was always so kind. Chuppo and Ra Wee were here too.

"Little one," Ni mumbled softly as she squatted beside me. Her and Chuppo had been dating ever since I'd first come into the Expanse. "You boys always find so much trouble, don't you?"

Ra Wee patted my shoulder and then sat down and propped Doug's booted feet on top of a hefty pillow. "That's because there's a lot of unsavory folks who need their butts kicked," he said. He had small tusks, as did Ni.

"You got that right," I told him. "The MST is full of liars, and I should have listened to all my friends."

Chuppo stopped beside Ni and cast a glittery, bright spell that enveloped all of us. I could feel his magic penetrating me, calming me, healing my wounds, restoring my vigor, and washing away every ounce of stress from my body.

I ripped open Doug's T-shirt and pulled it off of him. Before my eyes, his two bloody wounds slowly closed as he was fully restored to his original condition. Every tiny dark hair reappeared as sparkles of energy drifted over him and disappeared deep inside his flesh.

My handsome man looked into my eyes. "Much better," he said with a smile.

I leaned closer and gave him a kiss.

"You never cease to amaze me," I said to Chuppo.

My healing friend laughed. "Anytime you need me, just come here, and I'll make things right."

Ni nudged me with her green shoulder. She had on a tank top and shorts. In fact, all three of our troll friends were dressed alike, except for Ra Wee, who was shirtless. Some gray hairs showed within the vast amount of black ones covering his chest.

"I've got a few boxes of feel-good cookies for you to take back to James's ship," Ni told me.

"Actually, we got a new place," Doug said. "I bought a house."

Our friends all laughed, and Ni happily nudged my shoulder again. "And you didn't invite us over for a party yet?"

Ra Wee reached over and gave me a shove too. "Does it have a pool, like your friend's place on Earth?" he asked.

"It does," Doug said. "A hot tub too."

Chuppo squatted beside Ni and laid his long green arm across my shoulders. "I think you should shift all of us back to your new pad so we can have some fun!"

I nodded. "That's the least I can do to thank you for helping us."

"It's all good, little one," Ni said. "Friends take care of each other. You know that for a fact."

Chuppo stood up and walked over to a control panel positioned upright on the counter next to the one of the sinks. Dishes and cutlery plus lots of gadgets for cooking meals were laid out.

"Ready to roll," Chuppo announced after pushing a few buttons with his long fingers. "Ship is secured, and we've been docked at a port for over an hour."

I would have asked if they needed to bring any additional clothing, but from my experience I knew they preferred to swim naked.

"Let me grab the cookies." Ni stood up and hurried over to the counter, where she picked up two square white boxes and arranged some dishes inside one of the sinks. I could only imagine how many cookies were inside the large boxes.

I helped Doug stand up, and then Ra Wee picked up his torn shirt and tossed it into a trash can. My sweet man looked like his old self, smiling and playful as always.

I shifted the five of us into the living room of Doug's and my new house in Kakadu. Our guests turned around, admiring all the fancy woodwork and detailed edging along the high ceilings as well as the cushiony couches and chairs and the decorative area rugs. Doug had spared no expense.

"Beautiful home," Ni said. She set the two boxes of cookies on top of the glass table in front of the couches.

Chuppo slipped his arms around his girlfriend in a tender hug from behind and kissed her neck. Both of them sported wide smiles.

The sun was just slightly above the horizon, and the early-evening sunlight poured in through the windows, lighting up the room with a dark-orange hue and reflecting off the polished hardwood and glass tops of the tables.

"Well," Doug said, "I'm going to go upstairs and hose myself off before we get in the pool. I'll grab some towels too."

I tenderly rubbed his shoulder. His chest felt sweaty, and his jeans had dried blood around the waist and also down one leg. There was a little bit of blood on the side of his face as well.

"Hurry up, sexy butt," I told him happily. "You've earned some relaxation time, for sure."

While Doug headed upstairs, I fixed some drinks for our troll guests. Well, actually I just opened the fridge and took out some bottles of beer. They weren't picky at all. Doug had taken some time to buy a bunch of groceries, so we also had chips, cakes, and snacks in abundance.

"Well, let me show you guys to the patio." I walked over and slid open the patio doors. Chuppo, Ni, and Ra Wee followed me out onto the decorative tiled surface. They had already started to take off their clothes.

"It's beautiful, little one." Ni rubbed her hand along my back. She was already topless, and Chuppo and Ra Wee had managed to quickly ditch their shorts. Their big floppy green wieners dangled from side to side as they made their way over to the pool. I noticed some love marks from Ni's tusks along Chuppo's legs and even a few on his butt cheeks—the sign of two trolls truly in love. It made me smile.

All the patio lights—a mix of short solar lanterns throughout the yard and taller torches in large ceramic urns beside the pool and hot tub—had come on. The pool had lights beneath the water as well, so we wouldn't be swimming in total darkness.

My naked troll friends sat down along the edge of the pool, dangling their long green legs in the warm water and sipping their beer, their bulbous noses touching the bottles with every sip. The cream-colored ceramic tiles that lined the pool had slick rounded edges, so we all could slide into the water without any difficulty.

"Come on over here, little one," Ni said. "Don't be shy."

I sat down in a cushioned chair beside the patio table and took off my shoes and socks. I then stood up, pulled off my shirt, and dropped my pants and underwear, piling everything into a stack on the ground.

I sat down between Ra Wee and Ni. The water felt good around my legs. We all decided to finish our beers before jumping in.

Our view across the backyard was absolutely stunning. It was a beautiful mixture of the setting sun behind tall trees, colorful blooms and vines in the huge ceramic urns, and the subtle blue lights shining below the water's surface.

"I'm glad you and Doug got a new place," Chuppo said. He took a swig of his beer.

"Yes," Ni said. She leaned to the side and nudged my arm with hers. "We were worried about you two and all that MST bullshit."

I laughed and gave her a nudge of my own. "Well, I think we're finally getting things under control." I took a moment to explain about the bears I'd gifted powers to, the Kroma M8, and all of Deora's activity. None of my stories seemed to surprise them at all.

Some jamming music started playing, and I knew Doug had finished with his shower. He was a huge fan of classic rock and dance music and had synced his pdPhone to the wireless speakers around the patio to play us some.

I glanced over at the patio doors. My lovable man had come out wearing only a towel around his waist, and he had brought a box of Ni's cookies, two six-packs of bottled beer, and a stack of towels. I laughed while watching him walk over to us. He definitely needed some time to unwind after what he had been through.

Doug placed the cookies and beer close to the edge so none of us would have to leave the comfort of the water in order to refill our stomachs with deliciousness. As he bent over to set our treats down, I got a tantalizing view of his super-hairy crack that totally made me smile. Ra Wee slid into the pool, and Doug sat his nakedness down beside me after tossing his towel to the side. Chuppo and Ni jumped in after finishing another round of beers, and Doug and I joined our friends in the water after sharing a few kisses.

Doug brought out a few inflatable rafts (my thoughtful man). Ra Wee got one to himself, and Chuppo and Ni shared one, as did Doug and I. We all floated around, bumping into each other, laughing and giggling, eating cookies, and drinking beer as the stars came out and spaceships zoomed by overhead.

At one point I mentioned Wyler's wedding at the Arkenstone.

"Well, since you all like music like this," Chuppo said, pointing his finger into the air, "we know a band that would be happy to play at his wedding. I think you saw them at the festival we took you to."

I nodded. "Oh yeah, I remember them. I'm sure Wyler and Josh would enjoy hearing them play. That's a good idea."

Just to be a little shit, I playfully splashed some water at Ni and Chuppo. They laughed and returned an even bigger splash, most of which hit Doug in the face. I leaned in and gave my sexy man a kiss in between our laughter. I moved my hand down his back and fondled his delicious bubble butt. I couldn't resist touching his tantalizing rear while in the pool.

Night descended upon us slowly. Minutes became hours. We took turns floating over to the edge of the pool and grabbing drinks and cookies for one another. I had no idea what secret ingredient Ni mixed into her delicious treats, but whatever it was, it washed away all our worries, leaving us feeling giddy, delighted, and incredibly relaxed.

After we climbed out of the pool, we scurried over to the nearby hot tub and jumped in for a short time. The tub was large enough for all of us to sit comfortably with plenty of leg room, although our feet occasionally brushed together. Our troll friends had seriously large feet, though, probably fourteen or sixteen inches long. The glowing lights below the churning water slowly alternated through a variety of colors.

It had gotten late, and a few of us started to yawn. The beers and cookies were most likely the culprits behind our tiredness.

"Thank you for this great evening." Chuppo raised his bottle to me before taking a drink.

"You guys are welcome to come back anytime," Doug told them. He had his left arm around me, holding me close against his hairy chest. At times he placed a few kisses on the top of my head or played with my nipples beneath the surface.

"Definitely," I added happily. "Those cookies are the best!"

Our troll friends all laughed. Chuppo pulled Ni close to him and kissed her cheek, close to where her tusks grew out from the side of her jaw.

Another thirty or so minutes passed before we climbed out of the hot tub and our guests gathered their clothes. None of us bothered to get dressed. Doug went around naked, shutting off the patio lights and then turning off the tub.

After a round of warm hugs, I shifted our guests back to their ship's kitchen area and said good-bye. I returned home to join my naked man in our bed. We cuddled and kissed a bit before finally falling asleep in each other's arms.

11

Dean left the bridge of the MST spaceship to use the bathroom down the hallway. His intentions were more than taking a simple break, though. Word of Admiral Rohn's death, as well as news of the destruction of one of the MST's largest command centers, had started to fill the communications network. Dean figured it was only a matter of time before there was a strike on the Citadel. He needed to warn someone.

He had been keeping a close watch on his longtime friend Rhynor from across the bridge, watching every move, every button pressed, every holographic image displayed. Occasionally they would exchange a few words or a somewhat-friendly glance but nothing more. They were suspicious of each other and shared an uneasy truce, at best.

Fortunately, no one else was in the restroom. So Dean sat down in one of the stalls and tried to send a message to any Bear Paw ship using his pdPhone, but an error message flashed on his phone's screen. With all the numerous attacks by rogue agents throughout the Expanse, the Bear Paw had closed off their communications to all nonessential personal.

"Dammit," he mumbled hatefully. "I guess *that's* not going to happen."

But Dean possessed some expert hacking skills, so he felt confident he could get some kind of message out to somebody of importance. He just needed a few more minutes. No such luck, though.

"You feeling okay?" Rhynor asked as he came into the bathroom and walked past Dean's stall. "You've been in here for a while."

Dean shook his head, feeling annoyed and frustrated. He couldn't have any private time, even in the bathroom? What the hell?

"Guess that salad I had for lunch didn't agree with me." Dean smiled, so proud of himself for coming up with a quick and plausible response.

Rhynor entered the stall next to his friend's, dropped his pants, and sat down on the toilet. Before any more words were exchanged, Dean flushed, exited his stall, washed his hands at the sink, and left the bathroom.

He seriously wanted to warn someone about the impending attack, and only one solution to his problem came to mind: access the ship's systems, disrupt all internal and external sensors, and then steal a shuttle from one of the bays. Each shuttlecraft was equipped with shifting engines, so getting to the Citadel shouldn't be too difficult. Or so he thought.

Instead of turning left to head back to the bridge, he hung a right and continued down the pristine white corridor until he reached a small elevator. The door split in two, and he stepped inside. "Shuttle bay fourteen," he stated in a rigid tone. He rapidly tapped his dark-blue thumbs all over his phone's glass screen to hack into the ship's computer core. He then initiated a complete system update that would take the primary sensors (both inside and out) offline for about ten minutes.

"Yes!" Dean declared triumphantly. "In your face, Rhynor. That'll teach you not to treat your friends like shit."

As soon as he slipped his phone back into his pant's pocket, the elevator door opened, and he stepped out into the small shuttle bay. Per standard procedure, two shuttlecrafts, each the size of an 18-wheeler, sat ready to launch on a moment's notice.

Dean grabbed one of the few handguns hanging inside a case near the door. Considering how his friend had been acting, it probably wasn't a bad idea to be armed.

Two security guards were stationed here and they came toward him at a fast pace while gripping the handles of their holstered guns. Dean's absence from the bridge, plus the fact that the ship was stuck in upgrade mode without any way to override it, had clearly generated some red flags. Dean assumed everyone had been alerted, so there was no need to play nice, as far as he was concerned.

"Hold it right there," one of the officers yelled, yet another old friend of Dean's. He and his counterpart were both red hellions, and Dean knew they fully supported the rogue agenda.

Dean held up his left hand in a friendly gesture, signaling that he meant no harm. But as soon as both demons stopped to evaluate his response, he raised his right hand and fired two shots of brilliant white energy, stunning both officers. They fell to the ground, unconscious and lying flat on their backs.

He took a deep breath, feeling relieved and thankful there were no other officers in the shuttle bay. The exterior doors needed to be raised, and with the clock ticking, Dean hurried over to the holographic panel floating in front of the wall. He tapped several buttons, and the safety lock released. Then the nearly one-hundred-foot-long bay door rose.

But then his luck ran out. As he turned around to head toward a shuttle, he came face-to-face with Rhynor, who must have followed him down here from the bathroom.

"I should have killed you on the bridge," Rhynor said. "So much for trusting a friend."

Rhynor quickly punched Dean in the stomach, knocking him back against the wall. The blow caused Dean to drop his gun, and he hunched over, holding his hand over his abdomen, which throbbed in excruciating pain. But Dean was no wimp, despite how hard Rhynor could hit. He had been through plenty of fights before and didn't need a gun to deal with his old friend.

He jumped back up and returned a strong punch to his demon friend, striking the right side of Rhynor's stomach. Dean then turned halfway around and slammed his elbow into the left side of Rhynor's ribcage. Needless to say, Rhynor hunched over in pain.

"*You*, of all people, need to learn that true friends don't stab each other in the back!" Dean said. He slammed his steel-toe boot right between Rhynor's legs, and his old friend instantly fell to the ground, writhing in pain. Rhynor curled into a ball, holding his crotch, crying and groaning in a muffled, agonized tone.

Knowing his time was short, Dean raced over to one of the huge shuttles, entered it, lowered and sealed the door, and then rushed into the cockpit, where he plopped himself down into the pilot's chair. Having plenty of years of piloting experience, he activated the engines easily and then shot out of the bay, racing through space in a triumphant blaze of glory.

His joy was short-lived, though, as the shuttle's proximity sensors beeped with an alert. "You have *got* to be kidding me!" he muttered. The MST ship appeared to be in close pursuit. Someone on the bridge must have overridden the maintenance cycle. "That's the last time I share any of my tips or tricks with those bastards."

He accelerated while trying to gather the coordinates to shift to the Citadel. He quickly moved his hands here and there, swiping holographic controls and pushing glowing green and orange buttons. The ship's database was stuffed with millions of destinations. It would take a minute or two to locate the Field of Gods and then apply the coordinates to the navigation system.

As he glanced through the cockpit window into space, several bright blasts zoomed past the shuttle. Weapons fire. There was no mistaking it. Seconds later, a shot hit the rear of the shuttle, violently shaking Dean in his seat and frightening the hell out of him. The last thing he needed was a hull breach.

"C'mon, c'mon," he fussed while pressing the final button to activate the shifting engines. Beads of sweat rolled down the sides of his head. A few dripped on the console and his hands.

A glittery cloud made of a million sparkles flowed over the shuttle, shimmering and pulsing, pouring over the windshield like heavy rain. Just as the ship began to shift, a second shot hit its rear, causing the navigation systems to flash momentarily. Fortunately, the shifting engines experienced no interruption at all, and within seconds the shuttlecraft appeared high above the Citadel, deep within the Field of Gods.

"Shit!" Dean grabbed hold of the manual controls and steered the ship to avoid crashing into the hundreds of different-size landmasses floating throughout the sky. He had entered the field at a high speed but quickly reduced his momentum with the help of the forward thrusters.

In the distance, dozens of Bear Paw ships surrounded the Citadel. Dean even caught sight of one of the Makers' ring-shaped vessels.

Best to try to contact the bears before they blast the shuttle into pieces, he thought.

He opened up the ship's communication frequencies and broadcast a message: "My name is Dean. I am fleeing from an MST armada. Please, do *not* fire upon my ship. I require immediate assistance and have confidential information of the utmost importance."

His nervous panting turned into absolute terror after a few shots hit the shuttle and sent it into a dive straight down toward one of the Citadel's garden areas.

"What the hell?" Dean stared in shock at the holographic displays above the console. Somehow the MST ship had managed to follow him, and *it* was the one attacking, not the Bear Paw ships.

Two more blasts hit the shuttle, penetrating its shields. The craft collided with a gigantic boulder and several smaller ones floating nearby. The sound of stone raking against steel became deafening. The shots had seriously disrupted the ship's guidance systems, and Dean couldn't maneuver the craft very well anymore. Crashing into the gardens was about to be an unfortunate truth.

As the shuttle plummeted and veered from side to side, Dean caught a quick glimpse of two large Bear Paw ships moving overhead. Hopefully they would deal with the MST vessel.

Thanks to his years of technical expertise and a lot of quick finger action over the console's controls, he managed to level off the shuttle seconds before it would have crashed nose first. He flew over a wide stream and then hit a large area of green grass. The craft tore across the ground for a few hundred feet, tossing him all around the cockpit until the ship abruptly came to a stop.

Copious amounts of black and brown soil covered the shuttle's front window, and the trail of damage across the land resembled a gaping wound, as if the gardens had been maliciously slashed open with a knife.

Before Dean even stood and got his bearings, he heard thunderous pounding against the shuttle's side door. The noise left him feeling nervous and queasy, uncertain of what to expect. *Time to meet the bears, I guess,* he thought.

He pushed a button that released the door's locking mechanism, and the door slowly began to rise. Instantly, huge, furry paws grabbed hold of the door's bottom edge, and the bears outside forced it open faster, growling and grunting in the process.

Four bears, some wearing large leather boots and others barefoot, rushed inside the shuttle and surrounded Dean. Three of them hatefully stared as the a large male grabbed Dean and slung the blue alien over his shoulder like a sack of dirty laundry, striking Dean's head against the steel ceiling in the process. The bear's fur was a mix of woodsy and outdoor odors. The coarse, long hairs scratched against his face.

All four bears immediately turned around and left the shuttlecraft. As soon as they stepped outside, far-off roars and howls erupted from fellow compatriots, all of them delighted to see an MST member in their clutches.

In a daze, beneath the bright afternoon sun, Dean glanced around at the gardens, at the abundance of plants and colorful blooms, at the towers of fur standing everywhere. He gazed at the crash site and managed to turn his head a bit to see that the MST ship that had pursued him had vanished. The Bear Paw must have forced it to flee. Dozens of their vessels now lined the sky. One of the Makers' colossal ships moved through the heavens as well, far in the distance, like a moon on the prowl.

The bear who carried Dean stomped his furry feet, trampling his way through areas of tall grass and shallow puddles of water. Large groups of growda ha'tars followed, all rumbling and snarling in low tones. They were clearly pissed by the sudden and unwelcomed arrival of an MST agent. But who could blame them with all they had been through? They had suffered through ages of being treated like trash.

It took only a few minutes to reach the staircase at the base of the Citadel, but to Dean it seemed like hours. He still felt somewhat dizzy from hitting his head back in the shuttle, but an abrupt stop snapped him out of his daze. While hunched over the bear's broad shoulder, he looked around at the hairy crowd that stood some twenty feet farther back down the trail. Males and females, either partially clothed or fully naked, stared at him with hungry eyes and clutched paws, eager to rip him apart from the looks on their faces.

The bear carrying Dean started up the stone stairs, taking one or sometimes two steps at a time until they passed through the main entrance. They wound their way through the Citadel's massive and ornate hallways, over its ancient marble floors, and beneath high ceilings decorated with painted images of historic tales. Dean had never been inside the Citadel before, so he had no idea where they were headed.

After several minutes, the bear stopped, lifted Dean off his shoulder with both paws, and dropped Dean on his behind in a brightly lit area. Tall arched windows lined the room, and there was a throne positioned at the top of a wide staircase. Large urns overflowed with thick green vines and colorful blooms. The scent had changed from fur to floral in a matter of seconds.

A thick and muscular brown bear approached him. It stopped inches away from his hands and legs. Each furry foot was easily larger than Dean's chest. He had never been so close to a growda ha'tar before.

In a heavy and gruff voice, the bear hatefully growled, "I am Jay E Jay, commander of the Bear Paw. You have two minutes to explain why you've come here before I kill you."

Dean sat up straight and raised his hands in a pleading gesture. He tilted his head back and stared into Jay's dark eyes high above him. "I am here as a friend," he said. "There's a huge MST fleet preparing to attack the Citadel. I came to warn you. I swear. I don't support them."

Jay dropped to a squatted position, aggressively grabbed hold of Dean's shoulders, and pulled him close, so that Dean was just inches away from the bear's snarling face. "Give me one reason why I should believe *anything* that comes out of your mouth."

Dean's entire body shook in fear. His heart raced in terror. He could barely keep his legs still. He was easily less than a fourth the size of Jay. "The ship that followed me," Dean said as he trembled against the floor, "they were trying to kill me. I stole a shuttle after I stunned two troops and knocked out my commanding officer. I can't go back to them. So either *you* kill me here and now, or I wait for them to do it for you."

Jay squinted into Dean's eyes. He let out a disgruntled growl before he stood back up and stepped away, snarling and stomping his huge feet across the marble floor. He seemed aggravated and uncertain.

Dean positioned himself on his knees, figuring it was better not to stand and come off as overly aggressive. "This is no joke," he said. "It's just a matter of time. They want to kill the Keeper of the Citadel because of all that he's done to the MST. They fear their days of ruling are over, and they're determined to go out fighting."

He cleared his throat as Jay shot him a hateful scowl. Both of the bear's paws had tightened into massive fists.

"Please," Dean said. "I don't support the rogue agents or their agenda. I have no desire to see another major war rip the Expanse to shreds. That's why I risked my life to warn you. You can trust me. I swear."

Jay calmed down a bit as he scrutinized the small blue alien from across the room. Morning light poured in through the tall windows surrounding the main chamber. It illuminated them both and reflected off polished areas along the old marble floors and walls. Even Jay's brown fur appeared silkier than moments before.

"Stand up," the bear commander said loudly.

Dean propped himself up on his left hand, braced his right foot flat against the ground, and slowly stood. He felt exhausted, worn out, and incredibly afraid. The furry tower of muscle and anger would either believe his story or not.

"When will they strike?" Jay got right to the point.

Dean shook his head before he said with ample amounts of humility, "I'm not sure. All I know is they were gathering their forces before I escaped. It could be minutes or hours. But they will come. Believe me, they will. You know how the MST operates."

Jay let out a small chuckle. "Lies and deception," he said. "Which is why I never trust anything I hear from your kind."

In a daring move, Dean walked closer to Jay, stopping several feet in front him. There was no doubt in his mind that a single swipe from this powerful bear's arm would send him flying across the room and smashing against a wall of stone. He needed to choose his words wisely.

"Your race has been mistreated for far too long," he told Jay. "I know the volatile history between the MST and the growda ha'tars. It's time for change. Appointing the Bear Paw as the protectors of the Expanse made sense."

Dean took a few steps closer and held his arms out in a humble gesture. He could smell the scent of Jay's fur on the mild breeze passing through the room. It had a tree-bark scent to it.

"Keep me by your side," he proposed to Jay. "Let me join you. I'm a benefit, not a threat. Please."

Both of them stood in silence for a long moment, evaluating each other, uncomfortably making eye contact, letting out frustrated sighs. Jay finally raised his arm and offered a handshake, which Dean hesitantly accepted. As with anyone, the handshake turned into Jay wrapping his massive paw around Dean's entire forearm and even some of his bicep.

After a few seconds, Jay tightened his grip and stared intently into Dean's eyes. "Lie to me," he declared gruffly, "and I'll rip your head from your body."

Dean respectfully nodded before they lowered their arms. Jay licked his black lips along his snout, then turned and made his way over to one of the colossal urns. He reached down and touched several of the large blooms growing along the vines, admiring their beauty, lost in quiet thoughts.

Unfortunately, Jay's peaceful moment turned out to be short-lived. Booming claps of thunder came from outside. The powerful vibrations sent minor tremors racing through the marble floors. Both Jay and Dean hurried over to one of the arched windows and stared out into the sky beyond the floating landmasses of the Field of Gods.

Rouge ships were appearing by the dozens, their shifting engines responsible for all the deafening noise. They blanketed the sky in a variety of shapes and sizes. They had the Field of Gods, as well as the entire Bear Paw fleet, surrounded.

"*Now* do you believe me?" Dean asked, nudging Jay's gigantic arm with his elbow.

Jay let out a hateful, loud growl while pulling his pdPhone out from the pocket of his cargo shorts. He immediately pushed a few buttons on its bright screen.

"Who are you calling?" Dean asked curiously.

"The one person who will shred these bastards to pieces!"

Claps of thunder continued, and massive shadows blanketed the Citadel.

The Bear Paw had become vastly outnumbered in only a matter of seconds.

12

I rolled over and snuggled closer to Doug in bed. I pushed back the sheets so I could slide my arm over his hairy chest. His sculpted pecs felt heavenly. Every hair did too. He was still lightly snoring, comfortable and sound asleep with two pillows propped up behind his head.

A personal delight of mine was draping a slightly bent leg over Doug's thighs. Sometimes I'd bring my leg up a bit higher, so I could feel his morning erection against my inner thigh. Some leg action tended to turn both of us on.

I still felt bad for my sweet man, even though Chuppo had healed him completely. The last thing in the world I ever wanted to see was Doug suffering or being miserable. With all we'd been through lately, he didn't deserve any more headaches.

What he did deserve was lots of love and affection and all kinds of nice things. In fact, a few gift ideas came to mind that I needed to go out and purchase for him. A pair of exotic cowboy boots would definitely put a smile on his face, which in turn would make me happy too. I should get him some new socks too. And maybe some camouflage sleeveless shirts. He loved all that stuff.

"Morning, Little Bear." Doug yawned.

"Good morning, handsome." I snuggled closer so we could exchange a few kisses. His thick beard felt incredible against my face. The coarse hairs tickled the edge of my lips, and I could smell a hint of the scented beard balm he loved to use.

Doug turned a little on his side to face me. With my right hand, I cradled one of his huge, muscular pecs, gliding my fingers through all his wonderful hairs, gently squeezing and massaging his pec just the way he enjoyed it. Doug slowly slid his left hand along my bent leg, brushing through the hairs with his fingertips until he reached my behind. He firmly gripped my right cheek. He then parted my cheeks and worked his fingers deep between them, lovingly poking me a few times.

Unfortunately, our fun time together ended abruptly. Despite the fact that my pdPhone was on silent, it started to buzz and jiggle on the nightstand next to the bed, making a noticeable racket against the hardwood top.

"Sorry," I said to Doug. I was sure I sounded slightly annoyed.

He gave me a quick kiss followed by a satisfied smile. "It's all good, sweetie. It might be important."

I flopped over and grabbed my still-vibrating phone from the nightstand. "It's Jay," I told Doug after glancing at the screen, seconds before answering it. "What's going on, big bear?"

"Keeper," Jay growled, sounding nervous and out of breath, "a huge rogue fleet is here at the Citadel. They've come to destroy it *and* you! One of their agents broke away from their ranks and crashed a small ship in the gardens. He told me everything."

I sat up in a flash and slid my legs over the edge of the bed. Doug could clearly tell the call was important. He sat up and started to rub my back, conveying ample amounts of concern.

"Sit tight, buddy!" I told Jay. "We'll be there in two minutes!"

I ended the call, jumped out of bed in a flash, and raced over to grab my pants and socks from the floor by the dresser.

"Apparently there's a major showdown at the Citadel with a bunch of rogue assholes," I explained to Doug as I fastened the button on my jeans and pulled up the zipper.

He reacted no differently than I had. He flew out of bed and scrambled to get dressed, donning his worn jeans, a tank top, a pair of socks, and his skull-cracking leather boots.

"Just let me get my rifle before we go!" Doug raced through the doorway to go and fetch his beloved gun.

While he did that, I texted a single group message to Bryan, James, Willie, Shake and Finger Pop, and even Chuppo, letting them all know what the hell was happening.

Within seconds, Bryan and James both texted back, "We'll meet you there!"

I heard Doug stomping down the hallway right before he entered the bedroom. He stopped and stood in the doorway, his rifle in hand and a determined-looking scowl on his face. Safe to say, my tough guy looked ready to kick some ass.

"Take us over there, David!"

Before anything, I thought we both needed some simple reassurances. I hurried over to Doug and slung my arms around his muscular body, planting the side of my face against his sculpted chest. The neckline of his tank top left a considerable amount of his chest hair exposed, which I could feel against the side of my forehead and cheek. Doug wrapped his left arm around me and held me tight against his body. He ran his hand over my head soothingly, planted a few kisses on the top of my head, and affectionately brushed the side of his beard over my hair.

"Love you so much," I whispered.

"I love you too, sweetie."

He added one more kiss on top of my head, and I shifted us to the main chamber room at the Citadel.

Jay rushed over as soon as we appeared. A blue alien that I assumed was the former MST member followed close behind. He took turns staring both Doug and me directly in the eye.

"I'm Dean," he said. He smiled happily, but I could sense how incredibly nervous he felt. "I've come here to help."

Jay and Doug wasted no time and headed over to the windows to see what the hell was going on outside. Frequent booms of thunder poured in from all around the room.

"I'm David." I offered a handshake to our guest, and he kindly accepted. "And that's Doug." I pointed, and then we hurried across the marble floor to join Jay and Doug beside the windows.

I leaned half of my body out the windowsill to get the best view of the field and see the hundreds of rogue ships and Bear Paw vessels engaged in combat. The noise was deafening. Blinding blasts of white and blue shots filled the sky, exploding against ships hulls and sending huge chunks of metal spinning wildly out of control throughout the air. Even the Makers' colossal ring ships moved toward the battle.

"Rhynor is the officer behind this attack," Dean explained. "He's determined to destroy you."

From the corner of my eye, I saw Bryan and Seth appear in the main room. Dressed in old jeans, heavy boots, and tight T-shirts that showed off their defined bodies, they came over to our group. I slid off the sill and stood up. The Colt brothers shared a quick brotherly hug while I introduced Dean.

"We need to get the hell out there and shred some ships!" Bryan said, staring out into the field with a hateful look on his face.

"You got that right!" I said with gusto. I then turned and faced Doug. "You and Jay want to stay down here and take care of any freaks who might decide to mess with the Citadel?"

My tough guy smiled proudly as he lifted his rifle several inches into the air and gave it an enthusiastic shake. "You took the words right out of my mouth, Little Bear." Cleary he was more than ready to fire his big weapon.

With a tap of my foot against the marble floor, I rose a few inches into the air and then leaned in to give Doug a kiss. I thought the world of him. He deserved only the best in life. I tenderly brushed the back of my hand down his enticing beard, smiling into his eyes so sweetly. After our kiss, I slowly spun around to see both Bryan and Seth were already floating beside me with eager looks written all over their faces.

In an instant, I shifted the three of us high above the Field of Gods, miles over the Citadel, right along the border of the battle. Bryan and Seth rocketed away like missiles, speeding toward the rogue ships. They encased themselves within eel-type spirits and also summoned swarms of smaller critters that would penetrate the enemy ships and gigantic spirits that would pound the ships from the outside.

I shook my head, feeling utterly annoyed by such a bold invasion by these rogue bastards. It was such a beautiful day at the Citadel. In no way did the Field of Gods deserve such disrespect.

I summoned my favorite type of spirit to shroud myself with—an enormous horned serpent with thick, hard scales covering its lengthy body and fangs as long as my legs. The skin around its neck fanned out, and upon its head lay long spikes angled backward.

Before I took off like a bat out of hell or shifted beside a rogue vessel to rip it apart, I noticed something strange, something I totally hadn't anticipated. All the spirits Bryan and Seth had summoned were being disrupted. Their shapes had become distorted, their features slowly disappearing. In fact, they all resembled clouds of fog and mist.

"A dispersion field," I said hatefully. I knew Ahzoul had been capable of such tricks, but I hadn't known that the rogue agents or the MST had any devices capable of doing the same thing on such a large scale. Maybe that was something else Admiral Rohn had been working on, like the rest of his laboratory tricks.

I shifted beside Bryan and Seth, who had come to a complete stop. The looks on their faces showed confusion and shock.

"They're projecting some sort of dispersion effect," I explained as we floated in space. Even some parts of the spirits surrounding our bodies appeared distorted and vague.

Bryan raised his fist in the air and let out an angry snarl. "Then I guess we're going to fuck them up the old-fashioned way!"

Throughout the Field of Gods, everywhere I looked, Bear Paw ships were engaged against rogue vessels, and all were firing their loud guns at each other, sending blinding shots of energy racing through the skies. Chunks of metal along with explosions and clouds of sparks blanketed the atmosphere. Several smaller rogue spacecrafts were moving deeper into the field, slowly making their way by the huge floating landmasses and knocking many smaller ones out of their way as they headed directly toward the Citadel.

Before the three of us raced away in a furious blaze, a loud clap of thunder sounded above us, followed by many more deafening booms. James's crab-shaped spaceship had appeared, along with dozens of arrowhead-shaped crafts from the Devil Bunnies, who were here to fight beside us. They all flew straight into the chaos with their weapons firing nonstop.

I couldn't believe the scene as I stared ahead—the Citadel at the center of the field, surrounded by all types of landmasses, which in turn were surrounded by hundreds of ships in all makes and sizes. I guessed the truth spoke for itself. The MST and all its affiliations truly needed to be removed from the Expanse. They were not the guardians they claimed to be.

Bryan started to take off, but I grabbed his arm and held him back for a moment. "I can't sense any signatures in the rogue fleet," I explained to him and Seth.

Bryan focused for a moment, attempting to do the same. "You're right," he said with a frustrated grin. He then glanced at Seth, who shook his head and shrugged in agreement. "I guess whatever they're using is masking any signatures."

"Fuckers," Seth mumbled in his accent, which made Bryan laugh.

"We may not be able to shift around either," I explained.

Bryan gave me an aggravated nod of agreement.

The three of us looked at each other for a moment, and then, despite our disadvantage, we rocketed off toward a rogue ship. We could easily punch through its hull and tear the troops apart from the inside out. Our enhanced strength wouldn't be affected most likely.

As we rapidly flew into the battle, we dodged weapons fire. A few shots grazed our bodies, singeing our clothing. All our spirits had completely dispersed, which left us totally vulnerable to getting hit.

"We need to stay together when we land!" I shouted to Bryan.

He gave me a confirming salute before he outstretched his arms and continued to lead the way toward one of the larger rogue vessels.

Backed by bright sunlight and small clouds, ships and floating isles cast shadows all across the Citadel's beautiful gardens down below.

The enemy ship we were approaching was enormous, easily the size of a towering skyscraper turned on its side. However, despite the ship's intimidating size, in my heart I recalled how the goddess Shaye had gifted me the Citadel and appointed me as Keeper. I wasn't about to let this sacred place succumb to any hateful rogue attitudes. Not while I was in charge.

The three of us slammed our booted feet against the ship's hull, sending an explosion of metal chunks twirling and spinning through space like handfuls of tossed coins. Our impact left huge indents upon the dark metal surface and made a shitload of noise too. We had even pushed the ship slightly off course.

I couldn't have been more pleased with Bryan. He had picked the perfect spot to land. We stood no more than twenty feet from a gigantic row of windows that most likely lined a cargo bay of some kind. Easy access, to say the least.

Seth, being the formidable warrior he was, wasted no time and busted his way through the windows, shattering the huge panes of thick glass in a deafening ruckus. Bryan and I followed close behind him. Inside the enormous bay, the three of us floated in the air above a large shuttlecraft shaped like a loaf of bread. Dozens of troops stood all around the huge area, staring at us with terrified and surprised looks on their faces. They were a mixture of alien races, males and females, and all of them were dressed in the signature textured black bodysuits of the MST. Many reached for their holstered handguns as we gazed at them.

Bryan took off like a fired bullet straight toward a group of rogue agents. He landed incredibly hard on his feet and knees and instantly slammed his fist against the hard steel floor. The impact released a massive tremor that knocked all the troops down.

Seth rocketed forward to stand beside his dirty-minded boyfriend. They moved through the bay like wild animals, punching and kicking, using their elbows and fists, knocking out everyone in their path and disarming them too. Seth busted apart several rifles he had taken hold of.

"Get on down here, sweetness!" Bryan flapped his hand at me.

The two massive bay doors were closed, but Bryan and Seth nosily punched through the metal, bending and twisting the doors open in a matter of seconds. We jumped into the corridor and then rose into the air. I followed their lead as we rapidly flew through the ship. Nearby agents fired at us, but their weapons did no harm. I merely watched as Bryan and Seth left each trooper lying unconscious throughout the hallways.

"I'm guessing we need to disable the main power core?" Bryan asked while continuing to fight. He was such a highly skilled man.

"Yeah," I said. "And considering where we entered the ship, engineering should be down several decks. There's probably an elevator around here somewhere."

Seth turned around a corner and zoomed down a long hallway toward four guards, knocking them out with his fists. Sure enough, there were the double-wide doors to the elevator. Bryan and I hurried over the polished silver steel floor of the pristine hallway. Bryan stopped for a brief moment to give Seth an appreciative kiss, along with a firm massage of the shapely bulge in the front of our woodland warrior's jeans. But how could I blame Bryan for showing some love? I would have done the same thing if it had been Doug standing there. I simply gave Seth a smile and a pat on his shoulder as I floated by him.

All three of us gathered in the roomy elevator, and I pushed several holographic buttons to take us down several floors.

I felt I needed to clarify our attack strategy. "Now, we're only going to disable however many cores they have. Okay? I don't think we need to blow up the ship."

Bryan lowered his head and glared at me like I had a screw loose. "Seriously?" he said. "Well, I think we *should* blow up these assholes. They came here to kill you, David. That's fucked up, and you know it. Don't take shit from people. Show them who is in charge." He let out a tiny laugh as he elbowed Seth and said, "After all, a firm hand makes a man groan a lot more than a floppy one does."

He made me laugh. "Since when did you become so philosophical?"

Before Bryan could respond with more of his toilet humor, the elevator doors opened. We rushed out into the shopping mall–size engineering area. Six humongous power cores lay centered in front of us, three on each side. Each one had a clear dome that contained a pulsing blend of white and blue sparkles swirling like a stirred drink. Stairways leading above and below us and dozens of workstations with colorful floating digital controls lined the room. A few frightened crew members stood frozen about the room.

We stopped some twenty feet outside of the elevator. Bryan stepped forward another foot or two and then twisted around a bit so he could stare directly into my eyes. "Let's rock and roll," he said boldly with a clenched fist raised in the air.

In less than a second, Bryan and Seth took off like race cars zooming around a track. They attacked different sides of the room and then stopped beside the power cores just long enough to punch a couple of huge gaping holes in each. Jets of white and blue vapor hissed and spewed out of each opening like sauce pouring out of a broken bottle. The thick, cloudy vapor rolled down into the room, filling the lower space.

I sighed while shaking my head and rolling my eyes. Needless to say, their bold attack would definitely make the cores overload, which would destroy the ship and probably most of the crew.

Alarms sounded, and emergency lights flashed. What crew members had stood about now scurried around like frightened mice. They hurried toward various workstations and pushed buttons and switches in a desperate attempt to prevent an overload.

I rose a few feet into the air as Bryan and Seth flew back over to me. We hovered in a tight-knit circle as sparks burst forth from various panels around the base of each core. Ribbons of visible electricity sizzled and crackled along the massive cylinders.

"What?" Bryan asked with a shrug. He could tell I wasn't entirely thrilled with his decision.

"I know, I know," I told him with my hands raised. "Don't take shit from anyone."

A loud explosion came from down below, some lower level. Through the steel grating of the floor I could see fires spreading throughout the room below. They rolled around like liquid flame, churning and swirling all about the room.

I gave Bryan a firm shove to grab his attention. "We need to get the hell out of here!"

A thunderous boom scared the shit out of us. It sounded like gigantic steel mechanisms unlocking and banging against each other, and it actually shook the grated metal floors. All six cores dropped down several feet. The main lights throughout the room shut off immediately afterward, leaving only several bright spotlights to glow annoyingly in our faces. I could only assume someone had initiated an emergency ejection procedure.

"So much for blowing up the ship," I said.

Bryan shrugged. He looked disappointed.

We all jumped a little as all six cores suddenly dropped a few more feet and then quickly plummeted down beneath the room in a swirling flash of white and blue.

To my surprise, I could vaguely sense signatures again. The ship's dispersion field must have been affected by the ejection of the cores.

"Are you two feeling that?" I asked.

From the captivated looks on Bryan's and Seth's faces, I could tell they were definitely feeling signatures again, though maybe not as clearly as I could.

Bryan smeared his hand all over the top of my head. "Well, shift us the hell out of here, sweetness!"

I focused for a second or two and then moved the three of us back out into space, high above the ship we had just left. We appeared in what I could only describe as a science fiction movie come to life. One of the moon-size ring ships from the Makers was moving along the edge of the Field of Gods. Futuristic-style cities lined its inner edge, with smaller, less prominent structures around its outer rim. What impressed me most about the Makers' ship was how many spacecraft it had disabled. As it moved through space, any rogue vessels that passed through its center opening were instantly disabled, all their power shut down. A number of ships of varying sizes now drifted lifelessly behind the ring ship.

I spotted James's ship, along with a dozen or more ships from the Devil Bunnies. His vessel resembled a crab with long pinchers pointed forward. Blinding bolts of blue energy fired from the tip of each pincher, hitting many rogue ships and inflicting considerable damage. James had many friends who were arms merchants, so I felt confident the guns on his ship were top-notch.

My phone rang and scared the crap out of me. I quickly pulled it out of my pants pocket. It was Doug.

"You guys okay?" I asked him.

"Shit, Little Bear," Doug blurted. "I'm still up in the main chamber room with Jay and Dean, but these rogue fuckers are all over the Citadel's gardens! Bear Paw troops are ripping them to shreds, and I've been shooting at them from the windows up here, but we're kind of outnumbered and could use some help."

"Yeah, we just disabled one of their ships," I told him. "We can't summon spirits or shift around too well. They're using dispersion fields."

Doug sighed.

A round of shots flew right by us, scaring the hell out of me, Bryan, and Seth.

"Okay, I'll fly over to the gardens and help out," I told Doug. "See you in a few!" I slid my phone back inside my pocket and turned back to Bryan and Seth. "Dare I ask if you two can handle these ships?"

They both flapped a hand at me while nodding.

"Piece of cock," Seth said with a wide grin.

I couldn't stop myself from laughing. Clearly Bryan's filthy ways had influenced his warrior boyfriend.

Bryan rested his hand on Seth's shoulder. "He's right, sweetness. We got this. Go take care of the Citadel."

After I gave them both an appreciative smile, I shot off like a rocket down through the Field of Gods, racing through clouds and around floating landmasses. I dodged an assortment of debris, metal of all sizes, chunks and pieces of ships from both sides, plus dozens of mangled bodies. A few rogue vessels targeted me as I raced by, but every shot missed me. In another place and time, I would have felt touched from being so popular, but not today.

I slowed down as I got deeper in the field. The rogue troops had destroyed many of the larger landmasses that floated here in the sky, and seeing so much decimation seriously pissed me off. "Time to take Bryan's advice," I whispered to myself.

I flew over and under vine-encased boulders and around huge chunks of land until I finally made it to the main island, which housed the Citadel. Hordes of rogue troops poured out from small shuttlecrafts lining the edge of the isle and into the Citadel's vast gardens, racing along the flowing river and beautiful clusters of flowering bushes. Obviously the small vessels were coming down from several larger ships hovering along the outskirts of the field.

I sped up and kept flying upon entering the gardens. Straight as an arrow, I rose to about five feet above the ground, altering my altitude here and there as the land changed beneath me. I zoomed around trees, bushes, and towers of fur toting rifles and clenched fists. My goal was to reach the far side of the island, where I would deal with the rogue troops.

Sadly, for as many live bodies I passed there were half as many dead lying on the ground—both bears of all sizes and torn-apart rogue agents. My eyes filled with the beginnings of angry tears. I was so tired of bullshit like this. I wasn't about to let the Citadel become a graveyard for my friends.

Why should I land? I thought. *Just fly through these bastards. Knock them out! Use Bryan's technique.*

I tore through clusters of rogue agents like a guided missile filled with attitude. I knocked them out using punches and kicks. I launched groups of them several feet to the side or straight into the air, and I heard the thuds behind me as they landed on the ground. I probably looked like a wild bull on the loose, running like mad through a crowded street.

A mix of sunshine and shadows covered the gardens as I raced around their thick, rocky ledge. The sound of explosions and weapons fire came from overhead. In the distance a few small rogue shuttles severely damaged by Bear Paw forces crashed against the island's edge, and a few others fell near the gardens. The shuttles exploded in clouds of bold fire and black smoke, launching bits and pieces of metal all around.

Could this day get any worse? I shook my head, utterly disgusted.

A dispersion field still flooded this area. I couldn't sense any signatures or summon any spirits. I thought about James briefly. Hopefully his ship and crew were surviving through all the chaos. I could only imagine how his crew must be scurrying around the bridge. In the few chances I had to glance skyward, I never once saw his ship overhead. However, plenty of Devil Bunnies flew by. They seemed to be doing very well.

I hit the gas and pounded my way through two more groups of rogue agents. They looked overwhelmed and terrified to death as they tried to jump out of the way. I launched many of them over the edge of the island, and with no land below, only sky, each agent would float or drift until rescued. Knowing how the MST didn't value life (members or nonmembers), I doubted they would bother to save any of their troops.

As if to prove my point, some rogue shuttlecrafts pulled away from the edge of the island and headed back up to the main ships, unconcerned with who was left behind. Bears in the distance fired their rifles like mad at the retreating shuttles, filling the air with thin bolts of energy. Maybe these rogue bastards had finally gotten the point. Neither me nor my bear associates were about to let teams of them get inside the Citadel. In fact, a sea of muscle-clad fur surrounded the Citadel's base.

Seconds later, though, my mouth fell open in shock as a huge bolt of energy shot out from a rogue ship and hit the base of the Citadel, directly above the bears throughout the gardens. The first bolt was quickly followed by a second blast from a different direction. A powerful shock wave knocked hundreds of my tough, furry friends to the ground. Just as quickly, they scurried to get back up. All growda ha'tars were hardened warriors. I doubted they would flee from weapons fire of any magnitude.

Not to sound heartless in regard to my many friends, but after the base of the Citadel was hit, my first concern became Doug. I switched direction and rocketed directly toward the Citadel's main tower, to the tall windows lining my throne room.

Loud explosions and crackling gunfire continued to fill the air, not ceasing for a moment. A thick haze of black smoke drifted throughout the field. Ships burned with blazing fires. Metal debris spun wildly through the sky.

Right before I reached the windows, another shot hit the base of the Citadel's tower. Huge clouds of shattered stone, dust, and dirt filled the air. Many of my bear friends raised their rifles and fired shots at the distant rogue ships, but I doubted the gunfire would even scratch the ships.

I slowed down, veered to the right, and flew through one of the windows. I landed on the marble floor of the throne room, and Doug rushed over to me, followed by Jay and Dean.

I tossed my hands in the air, feeling totally pissed. "I can't summon any spirits! They're projecting their fucking dispersion fields everywhere."

Dean nodded repeatedly in agreement. "That's the one thing Rhynor kept going on about. It's a device the MST developed some time ago. He took a lot of pride in knowing he could use it against you."

"Where are Bryan and Seth?" Doug sounded incredibly concerned.

"They're shredding ships the old-fashioned way." I raised my fists and jiggled them in midair, demonstrating Bryan's technique. "The Makers are knocking lots of ships out too. And I saw James and the Devil Bunnies zooming by overhead."

Doug looked even more freaked out after hearing that James was in the midst of the battle. He shook his head and went back over to the window to stare out at all the unfolding chaos.

The three of us followed him, and I stood beside my handsome man, rubbing his back with ample amounts of compassion and understanding. The field was literally packed with spaceships, and the noise from all the weapons fire and explosions was deafening.

A powerful tremor shook the entire room and caught all of us off guard. After glancing at each other with concern, we leaned farther out the wide window and stared off to the left at a huge ball of fire at the far end of the isle.

"A huge ship must have crashed," Doug said. "Hopefully it was a rogue one."

Jay moved in closer against the sill, pushing us to the side. "Look!" he said, pointing into the distance.

I squinted and stared intently but saw nothing for a few moments. Jay's acute bear vision let him see things long before Doug or I could. After a few seconds of looking toward New Cardall floating in the distance, I finally made out a small fleet of ships approaching the field.

"Are those ornighs and humans coming to help us?" I asked, as surprised as I was relieved.

"Kirill and Aldis must have gathered up some troops," Doug said cheerfully. He gently nudged his arm against mine.

Two more gigantic ring ships from the Makers had also appeared and were traveling alongside the small fleet from New Cardall.

I let out a frustrated sigh. "I feel so useless," I mumbled.

Before Doug could give me a sympathetic hug, from the corner of my eye, I saw Sanvean floating in the center of the room. In a dreamlike state, I turned and walked over to her. Never once did she take her eyes away from mine. Dressed in a skirt made of two flowing sheer panels and a top that barely covered her breasts, my spirit goddess raised her arms and invited me toward her.

Time seemed to stand still. My friends, Doug, and even the raging battle outside paused. No noises. No shaking floors.

I stopped in front of Sanvean and inhaled the delightful floral scent of her perfume. She wore a metal circlet that looked like strands of interwoven ivy blended throughout her long cobalt hair, the color of which matched her lips and eye shadow. I took hold of her hand.

Her snow-white skin felt as smooth as silk and warmer than the brightest sunlight on a summer's day.

After a long moment of gazing into each other's eyes, she whispered, "Begin again, David."

Sanvean's messages tended to be vague. Rarely did she clarify her meaning. But from the indications she had made concerning my past lives, I had a good idea what she was referring to. How to recall my past, though, was another issue all to itself.

"You are greater than the sum of *their* parts," she added softly. She tilted her head a bit to the side, smiling sweetly at me. "No technology is stronger than you. No science can put a stop to your determination."

Her hand grew warmer as I held it, and then she floated forward, leading me over to one of the windows.

"You are a child of the Expanse," she said in transit. "You are a creator of life, universes, and so much more." She pulled me closer beside her with more strength than I realized she had and then whispered, "As I have said before, David, trust in yourself. You are more important than you realize... *and* more powerful."

We stopped at the windowsill, and Sanvean nodded toward the field, directing my attention toward the numerous pieces of land floating around the main island. I saw no ships, no battle. It was a perfect summer's day, with a mild breeze; distant stars; and a drawn-out, gentle, rhythmic tone, as if instruments were playing a subtle melody and voices humming softly.

While I continued to stare, I noticed movement around many of the landmasses. Vague yet shapely mists appeared to be growing from each of them, slowly taking the shape of a variety of beasts.

"Spirits?" I shot a questioning gaze into Sanvean's eyes and then stared back out into the field.

She laid her hand against my back before saying in a serious voice, "Keeper of the Citadel, you have felt their pull when they needed you here. *Now*, witness their wrath as they defend what is yours. The Silver Tree will aid you too. Do not forget about its gift."

Chills raced over my shoulders and down my arms. Enormous ghostly creatures had appeared throughout the field—winged beasts on four legs with savage jaws and claws; armored serpents as long and thick as trains; and lengthy aquatic beings from a dark and deep ocean that were covered in thick hides and had limbs that looked strong enough to rip through the thickest steel.

A flash of light caught my attention, and I turned to gaze at the blue stone I'd taken from the winged female at the Silver Tree. Sanvean squeezed my hand, and when I looked back out into the sky, ghostly versions of the Ravages's children had appeared.

Outside, high above the gardens, a huge ocean had appeared with an ethereal image of the Sea Whisperer centered within it. The Silver Tree stood down in the gardens with spirit versions of the winged females flying around it and disabling nearby rogue agents. The Shadow Hunter came forth and slaughtered rogue troops in its sadistic manner. Even the Valley of the Moon had appeared, bestowing its gifts of renewing energy onto our bear forces. And the valley's enormous moon appeared as a ghostly representation high above the Citadel. The sounds of singing voices had become much more prominent, a sign of the moon's influence.

"What about the dispersion fields from the rogue ships?" I wasn't sure how these spirits would be able to appear as long as the dispersion fields were in effect. "Won't they stop the spirits?"

Sanvean stared down at the gardens far below us. Her attention seemed to be fixed on something of significance. I followed her gaze and watched in bewilderment as the largest spirit shape I had ever seen ascended from the center of the island, its form not yet distinct. Its glowing body passed through the pools of water, the small river, and the trees and bushes. It even passed through the image of the Silver Tree and its flying attendants.

"The Field of Gods is aptly named," Sanvean whispered. "Join them, David. Join them, and *be* who you were always meant to be."

The spirit rising from the gardens took shape. It reminded me of the being who had handed me the large spiraled piece of coral far beneath the ocean when Doug and I, and our friends, had visited the Sea Whisperer. Almost as tall as the Citadel's tower, the creature had the torso and face of a man, but instead of legs, lengthy tentacles flowed below its waist, whipping around the gardens in fluid and languid motions, no different than a squid would have done. Perhaps this spirit had come from the image of the Sea Whisperer. I couldn't say.

A larger hand moved over my back with a firm pressure. I turned my head and saw Doug standing beside me, gazing out at the gardens. My vision had abruptly ended, and I was back beside the windowsill with Doug, Jay, and Dean.

"Can you believe what's happening?" Doug sounded astonished.

I looked outside. All the spirits that had appeared during my vision with Sanvean had come forth, including the giant tentacle man. The battle raged on. The fleet from New Cardall had moved closer and were busy firing their weapons at rogue ships. Sanvean had sparked a burst of confidence in me through her touch. I didn't feel as powerless as a while ago. However, I did feel as though I needed to be out there in the battle, making a difference.

I looked up at Doug and tenderly moved my hand over his lower back. He turned his head and gazed into my eyes.

"I love you," I told him with a smile. He meant the world to me.

Doug appeared somewhat caught off guard. My look and tone must have confused him. But after a moment, my sweet man smiled, rubbed my shoulder, and said, "I love you too, Little Bear."

Lowering my arm from his back, I tapped the marble floor with the tip of my boot and rose into the air. Doug's hand gently brushed the side of my leg as I moved forward through the tall window. I quickly drifted away from the Citadel with outstretched arms, rising higher into the air, flying above the humongous half-man spirit. I headed closer to the landmasses of the field, toward the surrounding battle, to my army and the Ravages's children.

The spirits had wasted no time. Against a backdrop of blue skies and summer clouds layered over distant stars, every glowing beast assaulted any rogue ship it could sink its teeth or claws into. Metal had been shredded, and vessels had even exploded by means of violent attacks. I could only imagine how confused and shocked the rogue troops must be. My spirit-calling skills were still suppressed by their dispersion fields, but the Citadel's spirits and the representations of the four pillars were clearly immune to it.

About half a mile in front of me, a small rogue ship shaped like a military jet blew up in flames and plummeted toward the gardens. Bryan and Seth had flown out of the ship shortly before the explosion, and they darted over as soon as they spotted me.

"Sweetness... are those *your* spirits?" Bryan sounded absolutely delighted by their presence. I had not doubt he enjoyed all their hot-blooded actions and seeing so many rogue ships bursting into flames from the attacks.

Several winged females quickly flew by us, each a glowing, ghostly image of the ones we had met in person. Then the giant spirit man moved past us. His chest was bare, revealing a stocky, muscular build. His ghostly tentacles covered the garden area, passing right through groups of bears and the foundation of the Citadel as he moved. Spirits could be as vague as mist or harder than the steel.

I shook my head and gave Bryan and Seth a blank look. "They are the spirits of the field and the children of the Ravages," I explained. "Sanvean pulled me into another vision. She said they would fight for me. She also said I could summon my own spirits despite the dispersion fields, and I'm trying as we speak."

"Is that her?" Seth pointed high into the air behind me.

I spun around in a jiffy and watched as Sanvean rose higher and higher along the Citadel's main tower. Her body appeared translucent, and within seconds she vanished entirely. Never had anyone seen her before expect me. Why now, all of a sudden? Perhaps it was nothing more than her showing support for all of us. I couldn't really say.

"Looks like your spirit calling is working just fine to me." Bryan pointed to my right side.

Not far from us, one of my gigantic serpents had come forth. Its armored skull and lengthy body were outlined in a blue-and-white glow, and its hissing mouth and tree-branch-size fangs were more than ready to strike.

I shot a questioning gaze at Bryan and Seth. "Can you guys summon any spirits?"

They both shook their heads. Then Bryan smiled and patted my shoulder. "Looks like you're the spirit-calling master today."

Several far-off explosions caught our attention, drawing our gaze to raging fires far beyond the field. Safe to say, the rogue fleet was getting its butt kicked.

"What a bunch of assholes," Bryan said, making a jerk-off gesture.

Between the Makers, the Bear Paw, the Devil Bunnies, James, and the small fleet from New Cardall, our forces had proven to be more than a match for the enemy.

The gigantic spirit man, his form transparent and his edges glowing, moved farther away from us. His head could easily have touched our feet if we had floated any lower. Some small pockets of rogue agents were still lurking throughout the gardens, but the spirit man took care of them. He whipped his tentacles throughout the gardens, launching rogue dipshits out into the atmosphere until he essentially cleaned off the Citadel's island. Yet never once did he harm any of the bears still fighting in the gardens. His flailing limbs passed through their furry bodies with the same consistency of a fine mist.

I raised my arm to dismiss my serpent spirit. There was no need for it since the rogue ships were starting to flee. What few remained used their shifting drives to escape. Others floated lifelessly in the field's atmosphere. I imagined the Bear Paw would deal harshly with any survivors, likely shredding them to pieces.

My ability to sense signatures had returned. I could feel Doug, Jay, and James too. My friends were all good. And the Citadel had survived.

13

"What now?" Bryan asked as two of the Makers' colossal ships passed overhead. He still sounded anxious to tear apart some ships. "You know they're going to regroup and come back to finish what they started."

I stared blankly at the damage throughout the gardens far below us and at the few ships that had crashed. Clouds of smoke and debris still lingered around the base of the Citadel from the powerful blasts it had sustained.

Now that the rogue ships were gone, the spirits returned to their specific floating landmasses. The gigantic tentacle man faded as he sank back into the ground of the island, and the images of the four pillars, the Ravages's children, disappeared too.

Bryan had brought up a good point. I felt certain this attack was only the beginning of more to come. I needed to get to the source and stop it.

"Maybe that alien guy can give us some answers," I said.

Bryan and Seth both nodded with raised brows, hungry for answers, like me.

Since we were now able to shift again, I moved the three of us into my throne room, where we appeared right beside Doug.

"Keeper," Jay said with noticeable concern in his deep voice, "how bad is it out there?"

"I really don't know," I said, which left me feeling terrible for not having all the facts.

Bryan stepped up to our bear commander and rubbed his hand over Jay's furry tummy. "Seth and I can take you down there, big guy. Not a problem."

As soon as Jay nodded, the three of them shifted away. I could sense their signatures down in the Citadel's gardens and could feel Jay's distress as bear troops rushed in to relay information to him.

Doug gave me a warm hug, and then we both turned to face the blue alien guy standing nearby.

"Earlier you mentioned a name," I said to Dean. "You claimed he was the mastermind behind this attack."

"Rhynor," Dean said. "I'm sure he was aboard one of their ships, probably the largest one considering how massive his ego is."

Doug rubbed his hand over my back and added a few consoling pats. "I guess you weren't able to get his signature while you were out there?"

I sulked and shook my head. I still felt pissed about those dispersion fields. My tough guy leaned down and gave me a kiss on the top of my head. He could probably tell I was in a bad mood. I leaned back against him. His tender touches always washed away my worries.

"I guess I'll have to consult with Wyler then," I said.

"How is he going to help?" Doug sounded a bit confused.

I turned around to face him, taking a moment to look up into his gorgeous blue eyes as I shrugged. "Well, he's always telling me what a top-notch shifter he is. Plus, he usually has a few tricks up his sleeve he's forgotten to show me. He might be able to locate Rhynor in a snap. It's worth a shot."

Doug smiled and nodded a few times. "Sounds like a plan, sweetie." He then put his hands on my shoulders and turned me to face Dean.

We stared at Dean with raised brows, both of us filled with silent questions.

From the look on his face, he was a smart guy, and he clearly got the gist of our stares, as he held his hands up and said with a smile, "I'm fine with staying here in the Citadel, if you two need to leave. I feel safe here with Jay and his bear friends. Besides, if Rhynor saw me again, he'd kill me for sure for warning you about the attack."

"Well, Doug and I need to head out if we're going to solve this issue," I told him, "so I'll shift you down to Jay."

Dean nodded. He seemed like a respectable guy, though I wasn't entirely trusting of him because of his previous association with the MST. I knew how they liked to lie.

I stepped forward a few inches, focused on Jay's signature, and shifted the three of us to the gardens outside. Columns of thick black smoke still rose into the air where several ships had crashed. It billowed and swirled in the breeze, thinning out the higher it moved above the field.

We had appeared right next to Jay, Bryan, Seth, and a large group of bears. All of them were filled with sadness, mourning the loss of their slain comrades. Large, furry bodies, both male and female, lay dead for as far as I could see.

"I'm so sorry, Jay." I brushed my hand down his forearm in a caring gesture. He didn't flinch or move or sigh at all.

High above, beyond the floating landmasses, James's ship was slowly moving through the atmosphere against a backdrop of clouds and stars. Several arrowhead ships from the Devil Bunnies surrounded his vessel. There were now five of the Makers' ships in a distant orbit, each one sparkling with the many lights of the towering buildings lining its circular shape.

Jay finally let out a loud, miserable-sounding sigh. "My people will take care of the bodies, Keeper. We will also remove the debris and repair the damage to the Citadel and its gardens."

I was sure the expression on my face conveyed confusion and shock. "There's no rush," I told my bear friend, patting his furry arm. "Your fallen troops and their families should come first. Repairing the damage isn't that important. Trust me, it can wait."

"Seth and I can help get rid of all this debris," Bryan added. "Easy fix."

I faintly smiled. "Thanks," I told them both. "Because Doug and I need to go meet with Wyler and see if he can help us locate a signature so we can deal with the asshole who started this."

"Sounds good, sweetness." Bryan rubbed his hand over my head. He was always a delightful goofball.

Jay appeared lost in thought, incredibly devastated from all the loss. I could sense his emotional state, his building tears mixed with a huge amount of anger. Again I moved my hand down the length of his huge arm. "Are you going to be okay?"

Jay nodded a couple of times but never took his eyes away from the aftermath. "I'll be fine, Keeper. Just promise me you will take care of them, that you will eliminate any further threats. My people have suffered too much."

I was sure he meant "take care of them" in the Bear Paw style, which meant going on a killing spree. It was doubtful Doug and I would be doing that. However, this Rhynor guy definitely needed to be taken out.

My tough guy and I gave Bryan and Seth a round of warm hugs, and then Doug leaned back to give Bryan a few behave-yourself looks. His younger brother tended to act first and think later, which wasn't always a bad method, in my opinion.

"Please call me if you guys have any problems," I said to everyone. Bear troops had started to approach Jay, looking to their commander for orders on what to do first.

I focused on Doug's signature and shifted the two of us to our living room, where ample amounts of late-afternoon sunlight poured in through the sheer drapes covering the beautiful windows. I couldn't have asked for a better man in my life. Doug would always be there for me. He'd always take care of me, and I would do the same for him.

I let out a long sigh, feeling exhausted and overwhelmed. "I guess I need to send Wyler a text message."

Doug swooped in and slid his arms around me. He rubbed my back with his strong hands and gave me some kisses on my head. "Maybe you should take a quick break first, sweetie. I worry about you, David. I don't want to see you get all run-down from all this crap."

I rested the side of my face against his chest, then let out a long sigh, though I felt comforted being held in his arms. He hadn't stopped rubbing my back or moving his hands over my shoulders in a caring way. He held me wonderfully close against his body.

"How about I go and send the text, and then I can come back for some cuddle time," I offered. "I'll tell Wyler to swing by in a couple of hours, if he can."

Doug squeezed his arms even tighter around me, adding another kiss on the top of my head. "That would be perfect," he whispered softly.

I pulled away a few inches, then leaned my head back to gaze for a moment into Doug's eyes. He flashed me one of his delightful and sweet crooked smiles before moving in to share a passionate kiss with me. For being a rough-and-tough guy, he sure had such soft lips, and he kissed me so sweetly, nice and slow, moving his mouth with mine while slipping in a few gentle pokes of his tongue. Doug loved to stick his tongue inside me, one way or another. His sweet affections made my heart melt, and his abundant love pushed aside my worries and concerns for the moment, leaving me open for his care, his touch and warmth.

"Okay, sexy butt," I said. "Let me go and send him a text message."

Doug rubbed his hand over the top of my head and gave me a cute and silly smile. "I'll be upstairs in the bedroom when you get back."

I chuckled and then tickled my fingers over his chest and down his tummy. He could be so adorable and funny. "I'll be back in a few minutes."

I took two steps back, focused on Wyler's home in Willow Creek, and then shifted away into a late evening with *very* familiar stars shining above me. Out on Wyler and Josh's tiled patio, I quietly sat down in a cushioned chair near the umbrella table and took a moment for myself to relax and breathe.

Wyler's and Josh's signatures came across to me clearly. They were asleep, cuddled together in bed, Josh holding Wyler in his arms close against his chest. I even sensed both of my dogs, curled up beside each other on the fluffy blanket at the foot of the bed.

I slowly pulled my pdPhone out of my pocket and then typed a message to Wyler, letting him know about Rhynor and what we needed and telling him that there was no immediate rush. "As soon as you can come over, that would be perfect," I wrote.

I sat back in the comfortable lounge chair and took a deep breath. Their patio was such a relaxing place, with the pool nearby, the barbeque pit, and the opened umbrella above the long table I was sitting at. I could have stayed here forever, letting all my problems wash away.

But as soon as I got comfy, the thought of Doug filled my head. I wanted his arms around me, holding me close against his body. The desire to feel his breath, along with his lips, against my neck started to overwhelm me. His signature consumed my concentration.

After about ten minutes of sitting there, I stood up and gazed at the peaceful night all around me, at the countless stars above, listening to the sound of insects in the distance. I felt overjoyed that Wyler and Josh had such a nice home and a wonderful and loving life together. They both deserved happiness, and what better place to find it than with each other, just as Doug and I had done.

I focused on my sexy man's signature, and within a second I appeared upstairs in our new bedroom. Doug was standing right beside the bed, wearing only a snug-fitting pair of very short dark-blue shorts and a pair of gray socks with red heels and toes. He had dimmed the lights in the room and put on some easy-listening instrumental music. His hairy, sculpted thighs, chest, and arms couldn't have welcomed me any more. And his enticing bearded face lured me closer to his lovely blue eyes. I stopped a few feet in front of him and then smiled, my head slightly tilted to the side.

I had a good idea of what he was expecting tonight, but he surprised me as he shook his head and said with a faint chuckle, "No sex." He stepped closer, closing the gap between us, and cupped his hands along my hips. "I thought you might just like to cuddle for a while, talk and stuff, or share a few kisses. At least until Wyler pops in on us."

"That sounds wonderful. You're such a sweet man."

He took hold of my hand and eased me onto the bed. He squatted and pulled off my boots, which he set near the nightstand. He then took a whiff of my socks, inhaling their leather-infused scent. He just couldn't resist, and honestly, I couldn't blame him. I would have done the same to him. He stood and leaned over me, unfastening my belt followed by my pants button. He never stopped grinning as he unzipped my jeans and slowly pulled them off of me. I took the liberty of taking off my own shirt. After all, our hairy chests pressed together was the best way to snuggle.

I scooted across the bed and lay on my right side, getting comfortable against the stack of pillows resting against the headboard. Doug climbed in on the other side of the bed so he could wrap his arms around me from behind. He held me nice and close, the hair on his chest brushing against my upper back and shoulders. It felt heavenly.

With our heads against the pillows, Doug leaned closer and pressed his lips against the side of neck. "I love you more than I can say, Little Bear," he whispered between kisses. "Meeting you was the best thing that ever happened in my life. I'd do anything to make you happy, sweetie."

He rubbed his hands over my chest, sliding his fingers through my hairs and firmly massaging my pecs. He even rubbed my tummy, adding a few gentle pats. I moved my right hand over Doug's hairy thigh. He had such defined muscles.

"I love you too," I happily whispered.

He continued to kiss my neck, then my cheek, and he gently tugged on my ear with his soft lips.

"As soon as Wyler comes for a visit, we'll take care of Rhynor, and all will be better," I said, giving Doug a few pats along his hairy thigh. "After that, we'll have nothing to do but enjoy each other in all kinds of ways. I promise."

Doug snuggled closer against my back. I was in heaven. Little me against big him... nothing felt better. A few times he rubbed his growing erection against my behind. I could feel some dampness against my underwear from his oozing. He had agreed to no sex, but that didn't mean he wouldn't get completely aroused. I gently wiggled my cheeks back and forth against his crotch, making sure my crack lined up perfectly against his whopping piece of meat. I knew it would turn him on even more. I loved teasing him.

Doug gave me a kiss on my ear and sighed in pleasure. "I would love to pump you full of love right now, sweetie. But I know you need to get some rest. We *both* do."

He was right. My eyelids felt like lead weights, and his tender care and light caressing had only relaxed me even more. He was such a wonderful man.

I closed my eyes and wiggled myself into place against his hairy body. He lowered his head and rested the side of his face between my shoulders. It wasn't long before I heard him snoring. After that, I let all my worries slip away, and soon I fell asleep too.

My pdPhone rang and woke both of us up. It was lying on the mahogany nightstand beside the head of the bed. Yes, I could have sat up and grabbed it, but instead, I simply commanded, "Answer."

A notebook-paper-size green-and-yellow holographic image of Wyler's face appeared in midair inches above my phone. He was wearing a nice button-down shirt and tie.

"Uh-oh," Wyler laughed while glancing around my room. "Am I interrupting something?"

I shook my head. "We were taking a nap," I told him. "Where are you?"

"At the Arkenstone Bar with Josh," Wyler said. "Max and Rommie are helping us get our wedding party together."

He surprised me. "When is that?"

"Later tonight," Wyler said. "And don't worry, Davie. I've contacted everyone and let them know about it. Chuppo is bringing a troll band. How cool is that!"

Doug and I glanced at each other with surprised and curious looks on our faces.

"All you two have to do is show up," Wyler said. "Everything else is taken care of. Trust me." He laughed. "So when do you want to meet and discuss this Rhynor guy you mentioned?"

I nodded happily. "Let us get cleaned up and dressed. Then we'll meet you at the bar."

"Okay, sounds good," Wyler said with ample amounts of excitement in his voice. "See you soon."

I passed my hand through the holographic display to end the call. The time flashed right before the screen disappeared.

Yawning, Doug slipped his arms around me and pulled me close against his body again. I squirmed a bit so I could turn over and face my sexy man. I wanted to give him a sweet kiss. I brushed my hand along his sideburn and then down his beard, cradling it, massaging it. Doug loved when I played with his hairy face. It made him smile every time.

"Looks like we slept for about four hours," I told him.

We kissed again. Doug rubbed my back with one hand and my butt with his other.

"So party first, then you'll take care of that rogue piece of shit?" Doug asked.

I lightly pressed my fingers against his soft lips. "Party comes second," I said. "*First...* you and I are taking a shower together."

A huge, crooked grin stretched across Doug's handsome face. I was certain dirty thoughts were tumbling around in his head.

"Sounds like the party will be coming third," he said with a flirty wink before reaching down and massaging my underwear-covered crotch a few times.

I leaned in and gave him a kiss. "My thoughts exactly."

We both jumped out of bed in a flash, stripping off our socks and underwear (or shorts, in his case) while working our way into the bathroom, which was considerably larger than the one in our old house. A huge whirlpool bathtub sat against an even-larger window, and there was an oversize shower off to the side with a tall opaque glass door. There were two generous-size sinks with cabinets below them and wide mirrors mounted on the wall above them. A long and comfortable chaise lounge beside a small wicker table with two matching chairs completed the bathroom's decor. It almost felt too fancy for me and him, but it sure was beautiful.

"Tub or shower?" I asked Doug.

He laughed and then reached down and shook his firm wiener at me. "Let's start with a warm soaking. *Then* we can jump in the shower."

I happily agreed with a smile before firmly smacking Doug's shapely rear as I made my way over to the bathtub. He kept grinning while he fondled himself.

I turned on the water and added a few squirts of bath soap. Five adults could easily have fit in this tub. It was humongous!

Doug moved in close behind me and kept poking me with his hard wiener. I wasn't about to refuse any attention from him. We got in the tub, and I turned off the water after it reached our chests. Heaps of bubbles had spread out along the edges of the tub and reached up to our shoulders.

Surprisingly, Doug went the romantic path. He moved behind me and wrapped his arms around my chest. He spent a long time kissing my neck while slowly rubbing his hands over my stomach.

Beside my ear, he whispered. "It won't take much for me to get off, David."

I laughed. "You're such a sweet talker."

He grabbed hold of my hips and lifted me slightly out of the water. I had a good idea of what was coming next and braced my knees against the bottom of the tub. He expertly guided me back down, slipping his love muscle deep inside me. Lovingly he worked it in and out, raising his hips in a fluid motion, kissing my back and massaging my waist the entire time. I reached down and held on to his strong arms. Soon, he shook and shimmied, and a warm burst of his love filled me from within.

Doug let out a long, pleased-sounding exhale. "Oh, Little Bear, you turn me on so much, baby."

I reached over to one of three buttons near the faucet handles and pushed the one on the far right. "Now it's my turn," I informed him as the tub started to drain.

We both stood up, and an excited smile grew across my sexy man's face. He gave me a kiss before getting down on his knees and leaning his upper body over the edge of the bathtub. Seeing him bent over with his beautiful ass raised and ready got me rock hard in a snap. As the water continued to drain, I moved in and spread his cheeks with both hands, then slowly worked my way inside him. I wasn't as well endowed as Doug was, but he still delightfully moaned with his head hanging low over the edge of the tub.

As the soap bubbles disappeared, I rubbed my hands along Doug's beefy back and shoulders and used the light touch with my fingertips he enjoyed so much. After a couple of minutes, I moved my hands down to his butt cheeks and gave both a few solid squeezes as I sped up and pounded him harder. I spread his cheeks apart even more and then filled him full of love as he had done to me.

"Oh, sweetie," Doug uttered in a long, peaceful breath. "You do that so well." He stood up and turned around to kiss me, slipping his tongue in my mouth, holding me nice and tight. "You're the best, David," he tenderly whispered.

I smiled. My heart melted within his caring embrace. "I think we make a pretty awesome team, wouldn't you say?"

Together we stepped out of the bathtub and hopped in the shower. With plenty of room inside, we soaped each other up with some minimal groping added in, then got out and headed back into the bedroom to get dressed. We both went with dark jeans and square-toed boots, brown for me, black for Doug. And Doug actually put on a pair of underwear today, believe it or not—a pair of snug-fitting briefs with black sides and a red patch over his prominent bulge. They matched his knee-high socks perfectly. I could barely take my eyes off of him; he looked so damn sexy.

I went with a blue theme for socks and underwear, and then we both put on nice long-sleeved button-down shirts before fixing our faces in the bathroom. Doug had a fuller beard than I could ever dream of growing, so he liked to add some balm and then dry it with a hairdryer. His process always put a huge smile on my face. Mr. Shit Kicker, making sure he looked pretty before heading out.

We both stood at the same sink in the bathroom, and I leaned in beside him, slipping my arm around my beautiful man. "Are you all done primping?"

He laughed and playfully reached up to tweak my cheek. "Yep, all ready."

We went downstairs and made sure the front and back doors were locked and then slipped our phones in our pants pockets. Doug stopped right in front of me to give me a few kisses. His cologne smelled so good. It always left my heart swooning.

I took hold of his strong hand while I focused on Wyler's signature. I could sense the bar environment. Max and Rommie were there, along with a dozen or more employees and some patrons hanging out. I sensed a few friends too.

"Here we go," I told Doug.

He smiled and gave me a wink, and then I shifted us to the Arkenstone Bar and Grill.

14

"Wow! This looks incredible." I turned around, taking in the massive amount of decorations. Max and Rommie had really captured the essence of a wedding. Beautiful twirling white streamers had been hung from the ceiling over the tops of all three bars that lined the room. The streamers dipped and rose, with pale-blue and white balloons fastened at the highpoints of each twisted ribbon.

"Look at that." Doug was still holding my hand and gave it a gentle squeeze to draw my attention to the four-tiered wedding cake on a small wooden table off to the side of the room. The cake was stunning with decorative, colorful flowers; fancy edges; and two big red hearts on its top. Josh and Wyler were standing beside the cake, admiring its beauty and size. There would be plenty to feed a huge number of patrons.

The happy couple turned and smiled at us, and the four of us approached each other, meeting in the center of the room. Josh and Wyler both had on nice jeans with tucked-in dress shirts, ties, and black square-toed harness boots. They looked great!

After a round of warm hugs and mild laughs, we stood together as the best of friends, grinning, admiring each other. Some upbeat dance music began to play from the overhead speakers.

"Just to let you both know," Wyler said, "we officially got married yesterday back in town." They both raised their left hands and showed off their matching silver wedding rings. "We didn't want anything huge and fancy on Earth. After all, our best and closest friends are here, on Alemereen. *This* is where the party needs to be."

I gasped in surprise. I felt left out. "You should have told us. Doug and I would have come and stood beside you."

Wyler took hold of my hand. "I'm sorry, Davie. Josh and I decided to get it done as soon as we could. We didn't even dress up or anything. We got our paperwork together, signed some forms, and then made it official."

Staring at them both, I realized how similar they were to Doug and me. Josh was taller, much more burly, and thick, and hairier than Wyler. Josh was a more rugged man like Doug, and both had full beards, while Wyler tended to be more refined and somewhat polished, like me.

My demon buddy let go of my hand, and I smiled. "It's fine," I told him. "Like you said, having the party here will be a lot of fun."

Doug elbowed me and directed my attention to the stage where the band would perform. The instruments were already set up. Guitars leaned against music stands, and the drums looked ready to pound out some hip-shaking rhythms.

"Oh, the performers are already here," Josh said with enthusiasm. "They're a troll band. And from what I've heard, they can get people dancing all around the room!"

I focused on nearby signatures, and sure enough, I sensed quite a few trolls in the bar. Some were upstairs; others explored the downstairs area with the swimming pool and private rooms. But of all the trolls I detected, it didn't take long for me to pinpoint my closest troll friends—Chuppo, Ni, and Ra Wee.

"I invited everyone, Davie, even your reporter friend." Wyler shot me a friendly wink. He had taken care of everything. He was such a sweet and dear friend.

A door opened from behind one of the bars, and Max and Rommie came out along with a few male and female trolls. From the trolls' flamboyant and glitzy attire, I assumed they were members of the band. All of them looked delighted to be here. I was sure they'd put on a fantastic show.

Guests started pouring in through the front doors. A collection of humans, various aliens, and, to my surprise, quite a few huge, furry bears piled in. Each bear had dressed in cargo shorts, and a few wore loose-fitting leather vests.

"So you need my help with a signature?" Wyler asked. He happily smiled at me while holding Josh's hand.

"I do," I told him. "During the attack on the Citadel, the rogue agents saturated the place with dispersion fields, so I couldn't sense anyone. Rhynor is the leader of their gang, and he's determined to kill me. I basically wanted to see if you had any tips or tricks on how to locate him."

Wyler chuckled. "Well, there is a technique to locate unfamiliar signatures. I'll need to touch someone who's been around Rhynor a lot. Then I'll be able to shift to him."

I shook my head, amused by yet another ability Wyler never bothered to teach me.

My demon friend smiled at me. "You'll eventually learn how to pull unfamiliar signatures from people, Davie. It just takes time. But you'll get there. I know you will."

I suddenly sensed a growing desire coming from inside of Wyler, a need for something from me, I gathered. I also detected some apprehension coming from him, some nervousness. It confused me. Why wouldn't he just come out and ask me? We were close friends, after all.

I felt a hand land on my shoulder, and I turned around to see Chuppo had stopped beside me, along with Ni and Ra Wee.

"Little one," he greeted me with a wide smile.

I quickly gave him a warm hug and then did the same for Ni and Ra Wee. They were all so tall. As I hugged Ni, her tusks lightly brushed over the top of my head. Both Chuppo and Ra Wee had really let their beards grow out. Their facial hair was full, thick, and well manicured. I guessed troll beards grew faster than humans' did, because it looked like a month or more growth had occurred. All three had dressed in jeans and T-shirts and textured brown cowboy boots. They all looked great!

I was wondering how they'd all gotten here, and it must have shown on my face, as Ni bobbed her long green finger at Wyler and said, "He brought *all* of us here, including the band."

Before I could thank Wyler for his thoughtfulness, Bryan and Seth shifted inside the bar, appearing less than fifteen feet from us. Seconds later, the front doors swung open, and James and Willie entered, followed by Bray, Woofa, and the three Devil Bunnies, who had apparently joined James's team. The biker-looking maintenance team of Kurt, Reese, and Amp brought up the rear, all dressed in leather jackets, jeans, and tall black biker boots.

Doug waved to them all, inviting them to join us. Most of them did, although the Devil Bunnies and the maintenance team headed straight for the bar. I assumed James must have docked his ship downtown somewhere at one of the many available ports.

Willie tended to be very hands-on, and he went around hugging us or shaking hands and patting backs. Surprisingly, Doug actually wrapped his little brother up in a tight hug, and James slipped his arms around his older brother. For a long moment they both simply held each other.

I quietly laughed to myself, pleased to see James had become less confrontational and more loving. Discreetly, I shot Willie a smile and a wink. From his appreciative nod, he seemed to have understood my silent message. Both of us enjoyed seeing how much James's heart had opened over the past several months. All it had taken was Willie's abundant love.

"Looks like the band is getting together," Bray said.

She and Woofa stood side by side, holding hands, gazing around at all the people filling the bar. There were a lot of trolls here. Chuppo must have invited a ton of his friends. Or maybe they were locals and had come to enjoy the music.

Doug stepped beside me and put his arm over my shoulders. I slid my left arm around his waist and pulled him closer.

"Thank you all for coming," Josh said as he looked around at each of us. "It means a lot to me and my husband." He leaned down and kissed the top of Wyler's head. It warmed my heart to see them both so in love with one another, especially since Josh now knew the truth about who Wyler really was.

"You're most welcome," Woofa said pleasantly. He and Bray then shared a quick kiss.

"So what's the game plan for this shindig?" I asked Josh and Wyler with a twisted smile on my face.

They both laughed. "Drinks and fun," Wyler said with enthusiasm. "We're also going to eat a lot of cake."

Hearing about the cake put a huge smile on Doug's face. He had a weakness for sweets, on occasion.

As the band members took their places on the large stage, Max and Rommie stepped up to the microphone.

"We just wanted to thank everyone for coming out to this celebration," Max said. He raised a bottle of beer to Josh and Wyler. "Congratulations, to both of you. May you share and explore a lifetime of happiness together."

"Congratulations," Rommie said as he leaned in close, his doggy cheek pressing against Max's. Their short brown tails wagged back and forth.

Before anyone could respond, the drummer started with a hip-shaking beat, and two scantly clad female trolls stepped up to their microphones and started humming a tune. They both had tusks, just like Ni, and were dressed alike in knee-high leather boots, short skirts, and loose tops. The other four members of the band were male trolls, and all wore tight-fitting pants, stylish black leather shoes, and dark sleeveless T-shirts. They reminded me of an '80s band, and they sounded like one too.

The bass player strummed his guitar, generating a nice deep rhythm, and the keyboardist tickled his fingers across the keys, sending out some electric grooves. The other two guitarists joined in on the hip-hop rhythm and sung backup to the lead female vocalists, who were dancing in sync, spinning around at the same time and kicking their legs to the side in a dramatic flair.

A variety of individuals and couples piled onto the dance floor in front of the stage. A gigantic disco ball covered in flashing strobe lights spun overhead, and smoke machines billowed out thick white puffs. Doug and I both laughed at some of the bears who were dancing. They raised their huge arms and slowly turned around, shaking their hairy hips and grunting real loud while stepping all around the dance floor.

I wondered if Jay was going to come from the Citadel. Maybe I should call him.

"Well, I'm going to go and dance with my husband," Wyler informed us.

Josh took hold of Wyler's hand and led him out into the crowd. Both of them looked absolutely delighted. Smiles were so abundant.

Doug leaned down beside my ear and whispered, "That'll be you and me someday, sweetie. I promise. We'll get married, and I'll give you everything your heart desires."

I turned and gave my handsome man a sweet kiss on the lips. "You already have, Doug." I could sense the abundant love he had for me, and my eyes filled with a few heartfelt tears. I smiled and patted my hand over his chest. "Dance or mingle?" I asked him.

He let out a tiny laugh and flashed me one of his crooked smiles. "Both," he answered excitedly.

Hand in hand, we moved out onto the dance floor and slowly worked our way around all sorts of people until we found a nice spot below the disco ball. Doug positioned himself behind me with his hands locked on my hips. He rubbed his crotch against my butt, swaying us back and forth and placing kisses all along my neck. Slowly, he moved his hands higher, inch by inch, massaging my stomach and chest. Oh man, Doug really knew how to turn me on. A bulge had grown in my britches, and I could feel his own gigantic bulge pressed against my backside.

Ra Wee was at the bar having some drinks with the maintenance team, and Chuppo and Ni were dancing nearby, moving and holding each other in a very similar manner to Doug and me—him behind her, like my man behind me. Willie and James were also hanging out by the bar. Willie kept busy dancing in place, occasionally bumping his enormous hips against his smaller boyfriend. James did nothing but smile the entire time.

"Okay, Little Bear," Doug said after a kiss on the side of my neck, "let's go mingle."

He led me by the hand through the crowd. The band was so energetic. They had everyone pumped up and moving all about the floor. Smiles and good feelings prevailed.

"Look..." I squeezed Doug's hand and pointed. "There's Fred!"

Our reporter friend was standing beside James, Willie, and the three Devil Bunnies. Quite a few male admirers had gathered around to flirt with the bunnies, who were dressed the same as always, tight bodysuits with their fronts partially opened to show off their cleavage. I guessed that was how bunnies liked to roll.

"Come on over! Don't be shy," Fred said. He set his drink down and took a few steps to give Doug and me some hugs and quick pecks on the lips. He had on jeans and a T-shirt, with a ball cap on his mostly bald head. His wide smile sat below rosy cheeks, as always, and from the look of it he couldn't have been happier to be here at the party.

"How's shifting working out for you?" I asked him.

"Oh, man," Fred said with a laugh. "That is *the* best gift I've ever gotten. I can get around so much easier now. Plus, I can run into the bathroom during those stupid weekly meetings and just shift back to my house to get some work done."

Doug let out a mild laugh. "Or fool around with someone," he added.

Fred acted delightfully surprised, then raised his glass to Doug. "You know it! There's a line of hookers at my front door every night." Our reporter buddy loved to show off his twisted sense of humor.

"And you feel like you have a good grasp on spirit calling?" I wanted to make sure his abilities were all working.

Fred laughed. "That's awesome too! When I'm at home, I put on a frilly dress and summon a tiny pony to ride around inside my house."

Doug and I both shook our heads at his jokes. The bartender handed Doug and me each a bottle of beer. The guy was a human male, about my size, and had waited on us many times before. He always sported a delightful smile on his handsome face.

Fred took another swig of his drink before sitting down on a barstool. "I heard you guys knocked the shit out of those rogue agents at the Citadel."

"I guess word travels fast," I said. As Doug rubbed his hand over my back, I asked Fred, "Have you heard any interesting tidbits about their plans?"

"Mostly rumors, but there are some facts," Fred said. "I've got several people researching their activities. The Kroma M8 have been slaughtering rogue agents by the hundreds. They're on a bloodthirsty rampage. Plus, a lot of those ring ships that orbit the Citadel are appearing throughout the entire universe. It looks like they're permanently disabling any enemy ships they come across." Fred took another drink from his beer. "But something I heard that really grabbed my attention is that a lot of rogue ships are using their shifting engines to leave the Expanse."

"Leave...?" Doug blurted out in a surprised tone. "And go where?"

Fred shrugged. "To other universes where then can be safe, I'm guessing."

A disgusted sigh erupted out of me. "They're never going to stop, are they?"

I had set my hand on the top of the bar, and Fred poked the side of it with his index finger a few times. "You told me the goddess Shaye appointed you with the task of protecting the Expanse," he reminded me. "Well, that's *exactly* what you've done, David. Apparently there aren't many of those assholes left. You could appoint certain individuals to hunt them down before they stir up any more shit."

Fred had made a good point. Any shifter could track the rogue agents, find their ships, and convey their locations to our forces.

Doug leaned in and gave me a sweet kiss on my cheek. "Let's not worry about that right now, Little Bear. I think you deserve some fun. Let your hair down for a change."

Fred almost choked on his drink as he boisterously laughed at Doug's comment about my hair. "Hey now, he doesn't really have much hair to let down," Fred said. "Unless there's some stylish hairdo down inside your pants I don't know about."

I tweaked the side of Fred's belly for being a goofball. He flinched, then giggled in delight with his head titled back. His cheeks had turned even rosier than a moment ago. He was such a charming and entertaining man.

Doug took hold of my hand and lured me back to the dance floor, but the band had come to the end of a song and were taking a short break. Everyone cheered and applauded their energetic performance.

Max and Rommie came back out on stage, and Max walked up to the microphone. "Everyone please take a moment to congratulate our newly married couple, Josh and Wyler." He pointed at the crowd. "And be sure to get some of that delicious cake!"

Rommie said nothing. He only smiled and applauded along with the guests, then leaned in close and gave his hubby a sweet kiss. Again, both wagged their tails. They both had canine features, including pointed ears and short snouts.

A crowd gathered around Josh and Wyler as they got ready to cut their enormous cake. Together, holding a single knife, they sliced into the bottom section, removed a large piece, and placed it on a fancy glass plate. With a fork, Wyler cut a small chunk of cake from the piece, and to my surprise, he didn't shove it in Josh's face. Instead, he fed his husband, and then Josh did the exact same thing for Wyler.

The band played something romantic, a heartwarming and soft melody. It was a mix of subtle piano chords with string instruments layered beneath some humming vocals.

I was so happy for them both.

Doug massaged my back and kissed the side of my neck. "Like I said, sweetie, that'll be you and me someday."

Josh and Wyler cut some more pieces of cake and placed them on glass plates, and the band went right back to playing lively dance music. Both female trolls danced in unison, shaking their hips and swirling their long tusks through the air while moving their arms and bodies all around the stage.

"Hey, look over there!" I nudged Doug's arm and pointed across the room at Kirill and Aldis. They both smiled and waved at us.

"Let's go give some hugs," Doug said. We walked over to our friends from New Cardall and exchanged several warm welcome hugs.

"Wyler brought you both here, didn't he?" I asked.

Kirill nodded with a thrilled grin. My tattooed friend's Mohawk looked particularly tall and spiky tonight. His beard had grown out some more also, which complemented his prominent mustache.

"We were downstairs checking things out," Aldis said. "The swimming pool looks really nice. I haven't splashed around in a pool in years."

Aldis wore a tight-fitting black T-shirt with a large white tattoo-style skull printed on the front of it, a pair of dark blue jeans, and boots. Kirill had dressed similarly to his boyfriend, but his boots were of the cowboy variety. Both boots had pointed toes.

From the looks of it, Kirill and Aldis were fascinated by the band. They kept turning their heads and staring.

"How about a quick dance?" Aldis poked his boyfriend's shoulder.

"Let's do it!" Kirill grabbed one of Aldis's massive green hands, and they headed out into the gyrating crowd.

Doug followed their lead, guiding me out to the dance floor again. Hand in hand, we laughed as we made our way around all sorts of people. My handsome man really enjoyed grinding his crotch against my backside, and I wasn't about to refuse his attention. We danced for a long while, and he kept his body pressed against me the entire time. Holding me in his arms, he moved us together and kissed my neck, my cheeks.

We occasionally stopped to mingle with more guests or have a drink with Fred, who preferred to hang out by the bar. The bartender seemed to have caught his attention. They were both flirting with each other, exchanging glances, some winks, and occasionally brushing their fingers over each other's hands.

Minutes eventually turned into hours. The band had taken a few more breaks, and the wedding cake had all but disappeared. Only a few pieces now remained on the fancy plates. Guests had come and gone, and from the look of it, Josh and Wyler were both slightly drunk. Josh had taken off his shirt, showcasing his hairy and beefy chest and his stylish tattoos, especially the huge one in honor of his little brother that covered his entire back. As for Wyler, he just kept bumping into people while trying to grope and hang all over his husband.

It wasn't long before the party started to dwindle down, and my troll friends came over to say good-bye.

"We had a great time," Chuppo said. He, Ni, and Ra Wee gave Doug and me hugs.

"Where are you guys off to?" I asked.

"Back home," Ni answered happily. She stroked one of her tusks and sighed. "I've got a ton of cookies to bake for another party we have coming up in a couple of days."

"Your cooking should make everybody happy!" Doug laughed at his joke. All of us did, because we knew how the special ingredient in Ni's cookies could cheer up even the most depressed individuals.

Kirill and Aldis walked over to say good-bye too. I looked around for Bryan and Seth and James and Willie but didn't see any of them. Some trolls had brought in a couple of hookahs earlier, so I assumed they were all smoking and telling jokes somewhere.

I tapped Kirill's arm to grab his attention. "You guys should open up a snack food counter at your tattoo parlor," I told him. "Sell some of Ni's cookies or other stuff, and people could get drinks while they wait for their friends to get inked."

Ni smiled at my suggestion and happily told Kirill, "I could keep you well stocked with cookies."

Aldis rested his long green arm across his boyfriend's shoulders. He looked and sounded intrigued. "We could knock out that side wall along the alley and expand a lot more and then put in a counter and some coolers."

Kirill seemed extremely interested in the idea as well. He slid his arm around Aldis's waist as much as he could. "I think that sounds like a great plan."

Ni laughed as she gave them both another round of hugs. "I'll set you up with a bunch of my treats when you get the work all done. Just let me know when."

"We will," Aldis told her.

Our troll friends left the bar. I wasn't sure if they were going to catch a taxi or what. Maybe Bryan and Seth, who had returned to the main bar area, were going to take them back to their ship.

I whispered to Doug, "You think we should take Josh and Wyler home? I think they're drunk and could use some help in that department."

Josh was sitting on a stool in front of the bar, and Wyler was leaning against the counter beside him. Both of them had droopy faces and seemed disoriented. Fred had left about an hour ago, and the bartender he had been flirting with was nowhere to be seen either. I guessed they were out having some fun on their own.

Doug nodded. "That's probably a good idea."

A few of Aldis's people had come over to say good-bye to him and Kirill, so Doug and I took the opportunity to take the happily married couple back home to Earth.

Josh still had his shirt off and was partially leaning over the counter. Doug gently rubbed his hand over Josh's hairy back. "You ready to head out, big man?"

Josh let out a hiccup. "Yeah," he said. "I'm beat."

Doug helped Josh to stand up, holding him around the waist to make sure he didn't fall over. I grabbed Josh's shirt off the bar and then helped Wyler up.

I took a look around and waved good-bye to a few friends who were also leaving. Bryan curiously eyeballed us, and Doug pointed at Josh and then into the air, signaling to his brother that we were taking them home. Bryan understood and gave Doug a thumbs-up. My lovable man sweetly smiled at me with a playful wink tossed in. I then focused on Josh and Wyler's home back on Earth and shifted the four of us into their bedroom.

15

"Let me help you." I supported Wyler while he undressed down to his socks and underwear. Doug did the same for Josh, although Josh wasn't wearing any underwear. He was a lot like Doug and preferred to go commando at times.

Afterward, Doug and I pulled back the bedsheets, and the newlyweds collapsed onto the mattress and passed out in a snap. I pulled the blankets halfway over them so they'd be comfortable and get some good sleep.

"Well, I've got to go pee." Doug gave me a quick kiss on the top of my head.

"I'll go let the dogs out," I told him as he made his way into their bathroom.

In the living room, my doggies raced outside as soon as I opened the patio door. They had never messed inside my house or Wyler's, so I was sure they had been holding it in for some time now.

It was late evening. A star-filled sky twinkled overhead, and the temperature was perfectly comfortable. "Perfect night for a dip in the hot tub," I said to myself.

I headed back inside but left the patio door open. Doug had come out from the bathroom and walked over to me. He gave me a hug and another kiss on my head.

"Think they'd mind if we jumped in their tub?" he asked.

I laughed. "I was just thinking the same thing. It's a perfect night for it. We could go back home and get in our own, but we're already here."

In unison, we pulled off our boots and socks. Doug quickly unbuckled his pants, pushed them down with his undies, and then shuffled his feet out of the pant legs while he took off his shirt. I finished just seconds after he did, and together we stood naked in Josh and Wyler's living room.

Side by side, we grabbed a couple of clean towels from the rack sitting by the door and scurried outside. We removed the cover of the hot tub, and Doug hit the control buttons, turning on the jets and the small blue light down beneath the water. I straddled the edge and slid in the warm water, and then he did the same.

"Oh, this feels incredible." Doug was sitting right in front of several jets that were positioned to run along his spine and lower back.

I stretched my legs out along one of the ledges so that my back and the bottoms of my feet would be massaged at the same time. Small hints of steam rose up from the churning water, and with the solar lights positioned throughout the backyard, there was plenty of light to see both dogs and my sexy man's face. I floated out into the water and moved closer to Doug so I could snuggle against his amazing body.

Just as I laid the side of my face against him, Bryan, Seth, James, and Willie all appeared right beside the tub.

Doug let out a surprised gasp. "What are you guys doing here?" he asked.

Bryan looked at us both like we were crazy. "You two are always ranting and raving about how nice Wyler's tub is, so I figured I'd bring the gang for some fun."

Willie then lifted up a case of beer he was holding and shot us an excited smile.

"Well, there should be room for everybody," I said. The oversize hot tub was roomy enough for several grown adults, and even Willie would probably be able to sit in it and enjoy himself. His fur would get completely soaked, but as long as he had fun with James, that wouldn't be an issue for him, I imagined.

Willie set the case of beer on the widest corner of the tub, and then all four of them took off their clothes and admired each other's naked bodies. Needless to say, being half growda ha'tar, Willie had an absolutely gigantic wiener, and it wasn't even firm. Doug and I chuckled at Bryan and Seth as they gawked and stared with hypnotized looks.

One by one they got in the water. With so many people, the water level rose and poured over the edges. Bryan and Seth made some waves with their arms and lowered the water level back to shoulder height.

Bryan cracked open the cardboard box of beer and handed one to everyone, and then we all snuggled up with our significant others. The beers were nice and cold, a perfect balance to the warm water.

James jabbed his thumb toward the house. "They in there passed out?" he asked.

I nodded. "Yeah, I'm guessing they'll be out for hours."

"Well, the party was fun," Willie said. He had already guzzled down two beers. "The troll band really kicked some ass."

"I didn't even catch their name," James said, lying back against Willie's chest. He and Willie were sitting in the center of the tub, and Willie had wrapped one of his massive, furry arms around his boyfriend.

"Bite Marks is their band's name," I told them, which made sense since trolls passionately loved to leave marks on each other. "They're friends of Chuppo's."

James took a drink from his beer, then asked me, "So is Wyler going to help you locate this rogue guy who wants you dead?"

I nodded and chuckled. "Yeah, just as soon as he's sober again."

"Well, you probably need to kill his hateful ass whenever you find him." James didn't take shit from anybody and tended to be direct and blunt. "Put a stop to all this bullshit once and for all. Trust me, the MST only understands a fist to the face. Being polite gets you nowhere with them. What you did to that Shasa lady a while ago was the right thing to do."

Doug had slipped his arm around me and held me close against his side. He kissed my cheek. "I know you'll make a difference, David. You always do."

"Hey, I just had a thought," Willie blurted out. "When a shifter like Wyler is drunk and dreaming and everything, could he accidentally shift around and not even realize it?"

I had never thought about that. I shrugged as I gave his question some thought.

"I don't think so," Bryan said, shaking his head. He gave a Seth a quick kiss. They were seated beside each other, mingling their legs and feet with mine and Doug's. "Seth and I have been drunk off our butts, and we've never shifted anywhere without actually thinking about it."

Seth laughed with Bryan, and then they shared a passionate kiss, tongues and all.

Doug lowered his hand against my body and rubbed my thigh. He must be feeling somewhat frisky. I leaned my head back and enjoyed the feel of his beard as he brushed it against my face and neck and then over my hair. The stars were so bright, and recognizing familiar constellations comforted me. It was always nice to be back on Earth.

The six of us stayed in the hot tub for a couple of hours and finished off the case of beer. We occasionally switched places, and Willie even sat along the edge a few times, holding James close against his prominent chest.

A round of yawns eventually started, signaling it was probably time for everyone to head home. One by one we got out of the tub. Of course Bryan had to be a buffoon, and he playfully slapped Seth's and Willie's butts the second they started to get out.

Amused by his antics, I shifted over to the patio door and grabbed some more towels from the rack. I then reappeared back by my friends and handed a towel to each of them. Willie needed two towels for all his soaked fur. He eventually gave up trying to dry himself and put on just his underwear. In fact, no one got fully dressed, deciding to carry their clothing home with them instead.

The six of us exchanged some mild teasing and then what hugs we could give with everyone's arms full of clothing.

"Let me know how it goes with you and Wyler," James told me.

"I will," I promised him.

"Don't stay up all night banging each other," Bryan said loudly to Doug and me.

We both shook our heads. It had to be two in the morning, not the best time to make a bunch of noise.

After Bryan's dirty remark, he shifted the four of them away, probably taking James and Willie back to their ship before shifting himself and Seth home to their village.

I slipped on my underwear, but Doug chose to walk around letting it all hang out. I knew he liked flaunting his thick, floppy wiener, either in front of guests or not. He kept teasingly tweaking my sides as we went around turning off the living room lights and making sure the dogs had plenty of water and crunchy food in their bowls. I eventually stopped, turned around, and let out a mischievous laugh while I fondled his meaty man parts.

"You're in a playful mood," I said.

He shrugged and flashed me a twisted grin. "Your hot bubble butt just gets me all excited, sweetie."

I tenderly kissed his hairy chest and then worked in a fast pinch of his nipple. He got a kick out of that, giggling as he flinched and stepped back a bit.

"Okay, ass man," I said jokingly, "you ready to head home?"

He nodded with his eyes wide open. "Oh, yeah," he said. "I'm ready to wrap you up in my arms and snuggle the hell out of you."

I locked the patio door and then turned on the light above the kitchen sink so the dogs could see their food and water. Before we left, I squatted down and gave each one some kisses and rubbed their heads. Their tails wagged the entire time. My sweet babies.

Then I focused on Doug's and my new home, sensing the inside of our bedroom, and within seconds we appeared right beside our bed.

Doug tossed his clothes to the side and pulled back the bedsheets while I turned on some relaxing instrumental music to help us fall asleep. I set it to shut off in thirty minutes.

As much as I wanted to kiss and lick him all over his naked body, I figured it would be better if we got plenty of rest in order to deal with Rhynor as soon as Wyler recovered from his party. There was a velocity to love, and for tonight we would move soft and slow in each other's arms, savoring the feel of simply being together.

I took off my pants and shirt, which I had put back on before leaving Wyler's house, and then slid naked into bed. I cuddled alongside my lovable man, resting the side of my face upon his chest. He wrapped his arm around me and kissed the top of my head.

It wasn't long before Doug started to lightly snore. Barely turning my head, I softly kissed his chest. Two songs played before I finally fell asleep.

Doug and I woke up to some noise coming from downstairs in our kitchen. It sounded like someone was messing with our china dishes.

"Time," I said out loud to my pdPhone. I was turned on my right side with Doug snuggled behind me, his left arm around me. A holographic representation of a digital clock appeared above my phone. We had been asleep for almost eight hours.

I used my remote viewing and discovered Wyler was in the kitchen working on something, messing around with some dishes and utensils.

Doug kissed the back of my neck, then softly brushed his bearded face over my skin. "Good morning, David."

Slowly I turned over so I could kiss him. "Good morning. It's kind of early. Wyler's downstairs doing something."

Although the room was mostly dark, Doug had kept his eyes closed. "I guess he's ready to get the mission started," he said with a smile.

I gave Doug a kiss on his cheek and then moved my fingers down the length of his beard. He had let it grow out a lot more over the past few months, and it looked super sexy on him. He took really good care of it too.

We sluggishly got out of bed, and I turned on the bedside lamp. Doug put on a pair of snug dark-gray athletic shorts with matching socks, and I choose a black T-shirt, camouflage boxer briefs, and a pair of brown socks.

"Hold on," I told Doug. "Let me move us down there."

In a snap, I shifted the two of us down into the kitchen right beside the island. Wyler had some music playing softly in the background, channeled through the few speakers sitting around the kitchen. Each blended in with the stylish decor. A few large landscape paintings hung framed on the walls, and plants in decorative pots sat on the plentiful counters. We definitely had a lot of space in our kitchen.

Wyler shrugged and held up a large china platter in his hands. He was dressed in a plain dark T-shirt, an old pair of jeans, and brown work boots. "Thought I'd surprise you two with a nice breakfast, since you made sure Josh and I got home safe last night."

Sitting on the island were several Styrofoam boxes printed with the name of a local restaurant, a place that specialized in breakfast food.

"You didn't have to do all this." I gave him a questioning but playful stare.

Wyler laughed as he set the platter on the marble countertop. "Well, you both deserve a nice treat," he said. "Plus, we're going to need full bellies before dealing with those rogue agents. There's plenty for all three of us, so dig in!"

I patted my demon buddy on the shoulder as I walked by him to grab some plates out of the cabinet. Doug opened a drawer and pulled out enough silverware for all of us.

The containers were filled with a mound of scrambled eggs with pieces of ham mixed in, biscuits and gravy, sausage patties, and long strips of bacon. Wyler had even brought breakfast burritos and some kind of rice mixture that looked and smelled amazing.

There were three barstools on both sides of the island, and we all sat together on one side, Doug to my right and Wyler to my left. We filled our plates. Wyler had also brought apple and orange juice, and he poured some for me and Doug.

"So how exactly are you going to get Rhynor's signature?" I asked my demon buddy.

He finished chewing his mouthful of eggs and then swallowed before answering me. "I just need to touch someone who's been around him. An experienced shifter can pull unfamiliar signatures from anyone." He gave me a lighthearted nudge with a smile to match. "I'll teach you how to do it, Davie. It'll be a piece of cake, considering who you once were."

I gave him a scrutinizing stare. Doug and Wyler had both heard all the stories Sanvean had told me, about how I was the first shifter who had left the Expanse ages ago. Doug smiled and winked at me. It warmed my heart knowing he would support me no matter what.

Wyler continued, "You are the answer, Davie. Without you the Expanse would have never survived, and its inhabitants would have known only suffering and death. Sanvean was correct in defining you as the catalyst of change. You are the Keeper of the Citadel, the protector of the innocent, the last remaining god hunter. You are the embodiment of hope and dreams for all of the Expanse's citizens. Everyone has a story to tell. Everyone has a gift to give. Your story and gifts will continue on throughout all of history, changing all who come to learn about the great things you've done for us. And your gift-giving ability will help people you don't even know."

I stared straight ahead as I digested his words while chewing on a bite of biscuit. The last thing I wanted was to be labeled a hero. I didn't want crowds of people rushing around me, pawing at me, thanking me, and so forth. The fact that I could help people was reward enough for me. Having a big heart had always been a part of my life. It had always been a part of *me*.

"So how do you plan on stopping them?" Doug asked Wyler. He was on his second plate of food. My bottomless pit. Always hungry. "You need me to take my fancy rifle?"

Wyler stood up and moved to the other side of the island. He held out his upturned hands and, using his demon skills, brought forth a thick and long cloud of dark smoke in front of him. A frighteningly recognizable weapon materialized as the smoke disappeared.

"That's the dagger of attunement." My mouth had fallen open in shock. It was the weapon another demon had used to slice open Doug back in his apartment shortly after I'd first come into the Expanse. That same demon had then used mind control on me, and I'd almost plunged the dagger into my own heart. Luckily James had come to our rescue before that.

Doug looked completely caught off guard and somewhat unsettled. He paused in cleaning his plate, his eyes fixed on the weapon. The dagger's long crafted handle of polished wood and steel was topped with a shiny steel blade at least twenty inches in length. The blade was bisected down the center, with a noticeable gap from tip to base.

"I plan on finishing this the way it started," Wyler said. He held up the dagger, rotating it in midair, admiring its design, its pointy tips.

"How did you get that?" I asked.

Wyler chuckled but then quickly sighed with a hint of regret. "I've always kept a close watch on you, Davie. Some things were meant to be, and I apologize for that. But the goddess Shaye steered me in the best possible direction. She always intended to give you her position. She saw a perfect future for you and Doug, so I wasn't too unsettled in knowing what would come from this weapon's use."

Doug and I both sat in silence. I wasn't sure what to say. We simply watched Wyler as he continued to stare at the dagger.

"Admiral Rohn has been killed," Wyler said. "Commander Shasa Vierlenn also. So much for being protectors of life. They all should be killed, Davie. And I will make sure each one of them is eliminated in order to keep you on your appointed path."

I still sat speechless.

"I've been doing this for millions of years," Wyler said. He then produced a fast puff of dark smoke that consumed the dagger and made it disappear. "When we find Rhynor, I will end his life. You are the protector, Davie. Allow me to be the slayer. I do this not only to protect your future with Doug but to protect *all* who value each other, *all* who understand the meaning of love, which includes me and Josh."

Doug tenderly rubbed his hand over my back, comforting me while Wyler moved around the island and sat back on his stool.

My demon buddy went right back to eating as if nothing had ever happened, shoveling forkfuls of scrambled eggs into his mouth.

"Speaking of Josh," Doug said, "is he not coming along?"

Wyler shook his head. "He and a buddy were hired to take down a huge tree today on someone's property. It should keep them busy all day. They have to chainsaw the entire thing."

"Does he know what we're planning?" I asked.

Wyler nodded with a wide smile. "My husband knows how I roll. I told you Josh has even seen me in my demon form." He laughed. "Hell, we've already had sex several times with me in my demon form." Wyler turned his head and looked at me and Doug. "So with that in mind, let me ask you this, Davie. Knowing how Josh has a short life span in comparison to mine, would you mind giving him a gift of longevity the next time you see him? I would greatly appreciate it, and I'd be forever in your debt."

I reached over and patted the back of his hand. "I'd be happy to do that for him... for both of you."

Doug pushed his plate aside and drank his glass of juice. "I guess we need to get ready, sweetie." He smiled at me and rubbed his hand along my arm affectionately.

"Well, there's no crazy rush," Wyler said. "Take your time. I'll clean up the dishes and put the leftovers away." He stood and picked up two of the containers of food.

"C'mon, Little Bear." Doug gently wrapped his hand around my wrist and guided me out of the kitchen.

As Doug walked ahead of me, I took some time to admire his shapely rear inside those snug shorts. His muscular, hairy thighs looked amazing too. I could have shifted both of us upstairs, but I wanted to walk up our grand staircase with him. The stairs turned a little as they rose farther up, and I ran my hand along the wooden banister, feeling its lightly carved detail. As we walked down our stylish broad hallway, I admired the decorative panels that ran along the seams between the ceiling and walls. Everything was so fancy and ornate. I couldn't thank Doug enough for finding such a beautiful home for us to live in.

In our bedroom Doug stooped over a bit to give me a warm hug. He held me close against his bare chest for a long moment. "Are you okay with what Wyler is about to do?" he asked. He cared so much about me.

We separated and went around the bedroom gathering up some clothes to put on after taking a shower.

"Well," I said quietly, "I don't agree with more bloodshed, but I do agree with stopping Rhynor and his entourage of freaks. The Expanse needs to be a safe place to live. It's so magical and beautiful. Everyone deserves to have a good life. You know what I mean?"

Doug already had his rifle in hand. He gave it a quick shake in midair, admiring its size, its power. "I know exactly what you mean."

We laid out our clothes on the bed along with his rifle and then took a quick shower together. Since we were headed into battle, we both dressed in older clothes. After we each zipped up our jeans, we put on some long white tube socks and then slipped our feet inside our favorite pairs of steel-toed boots. Sleeveless T-shirts completed both our outfits, although Doug's sculpted arms looked a million times better than mine.

Doug grabbed his rifle, and we met Wyler back downstairs in the kitchen. As promised, the clean dishes were drying in the drainer, and all the leftovers had been packed away.

Wyler stared happily at us with his hands locked on his waist. "You two look like you're ready to kick some serious butt."

Doug chuckled as he laid his rifle on the island. "Did you say *lick* some butt?" He playfully grabbed hold of me and tickled his fingers along my armpits, sides, and chest. "Because David here is a pro at doing that!"

"Okay, okay!" I laughed and tried to get away from his tickling. I stepped to the side and smiled at him. All of us got a kick out of Doug's playfulness. I shook my finger at him. "You're going to get some serious payback if you don't behave, silly man."

His eyes opened wide with want, and I could tell he was thinking of something dirty. "Ooh, what do you have in mind, Little Bear?"

"That'll come later," I reassured him. "In fact, we both will." We all found my play on words funny. I moved beside Doug and patted his chest. "Let's focus on the mission, sexy man. Then we can play around."

He leaned down and gave me a kiss. "I'm looking forward to that," he whispered.

"Me too." I patted the side of his face, and he giggled and stepped back a bit.

"Are you two ready?" Wyler asked. "Because all this lovey-dovey playfulness has me missing my husband."

"Yeah, yeah," I answered happily. "Let's go to the Citadel and get Rhynor's signature."

Doug picked up his rifle and then took hold of my hand and tenderly gave it a firm squeeze. I focused on his and Wyler's signatures, added the Citadel's and Jay's too, and then shifted the three of us to the Citadel's main room. We appeared beside the tall windows, where we got a nice view of the Field of Gods.

16

"Keeper," Jay said after Doug, Wyler, and I appeared beside him. He sounded somewhat exhausted and worn out, and his fur looked kind of rough and matted. He had on cargo shorts, nothing more.

Doug and I walked over to a nearby window while holding hands, and I was pleasantly surprised by the amount of work Jay and his bear associates had done. Throughout the gardens below, all the crashed spaceships had been removed and the land mostly repaired, leaving only minor issues like broken trees or winding, deep grooves across the grasses. The sun always shone to some degree at the Citadel, and I could clearly see tiny specks of individuals moving about, keeping busy with various tasks.

"Wow," I said. "You've really cleaned things up fast."

Doug appeared completely surprised and amazed too.

"My people can't take all the credit," Jay said, slowly walking over to Doug and me. "A lot of ornighs and humans helped from New Cardall. Your friends Aldis and Kirill are outstanding individuals. I would love to get a tattoo from Kirill, but nobody would ever see it under all my fur." He laughed at his own comment.

"Where's our little blue friend at?" I asked Jay. I had looked around, but Dean wasn't in the main chamber room.

Jay let out an agreeable-sounding growl. "Believe it or not, he's actually outside. He's down there helping to fix what damage he can."

"Sounds like a decent guy," Doug said.

I agreed with my tough guy. It was very nice of Dean to jump in and lend a hand. That pretty much proved he was here to help us and not to hurt us.

"Well, Wyler here needs to meet with Dean to get a signature from him," I explained to Jay. "But you look extremely tired. We can go down and find him. You should go and get some rest."

"I haven't slept for a long time," Jay said. "My room isn't far from here, down a few flights."

I glided my hand along Jay's silky arm. "We'll only be here for a few minutes," I reassured him. "I'll tell your troops you need a break." I smiled. "They won't argue with the Keeper of the Citadel."

Wyler enjoyed my remark. "That's for sure, Davie."

"What's with the rifle?" Jay asked.

"We're going to eliminate that piece of shit who commanded the attack against the Citadel." Wyler sounded hungry for bloodshed. "And Doug brought his gun to work in a few shots as payback."

Jay's eyes opened wide. Wyler's explanation seemed to get his blood pumping. "Do you need my help?" he asked.

I shook my head. "I appreciate your offer, and I know you would shred them to pieces with those claws of yours. But the three of us will handle it. I'd feel better if you got some sleep."

He slowly nodded. "As you wish, Keeper." He didn't sound disappointed in any way, only tired and ready for bed.

I reached up and patted the side of his furry arm again. "Okay, you go jump in the sack, and we'll go find Rhynor."

The three of us headed across the marble floor to the large doorway on the other side of the chamber room, and Jay followed us on his bare feet. I could sense Wyler's mood had changed from a desire to kill to a more at-ease state of mind. I imagined he was recalling memories of being in the Citadel many times before with the goddess Shaye. They had known each other for countless lifetimes. Theirs was a very lengthy and close friendship.

I understood his emotional state. The pristine marble hallways and grand stone staircases were always a delight to see. The magical lights that glowed brilliantly from above were always a wonder to behold too.

After moving down two flights of stairs, Jay headed through a doorway that would take him toward his room. I had never seen where he stayed or what items he had brought with him. But I certainly hoped he was comfortable staying here.

"I'll call you later," I told him.

He nodded respectfully and then headed down the corridor, a tower of dark-brown fur sloshing his tired feet over the marble floors.

We moved down several more flights of stairs until we reached the vast reception hall and then made our way through the grand foyer toward the main entrance. I could tell Jay's bear friends had been repairing small areas in here too. Sections of the floor that had been fractured or broken into rubble had been fixed after centuries of being neglected.

Doug held my hand as we stood in the wide and towering arched front entrance. We gazed out across the gardens at the many individuals moving around, all of them working hard to make things better. It warmed my heart to see such support and care.

We headed down the entrance staircase and stopped on the large deck halfway down. A female bear saw the three of us standing there and approached. I recognized her as one of Jay's assistants and also a commander of a Bear Paw spacecraft.

"Keeper," she said with a courteous bow of her head. She was a stocky brown bear, maybe ten and a half feet tall, and wore only a pair of khaki cargo shorts. The fur on her chest was thick and full, completely covering her large breasts. Her snout was short and wide, and her ears stood close against her furry head.

"You're Jor'johno Kess?" I asked.

She nodded politely. "Jay called me a moment ago and asked me to help you locate Dean."

"That would be perfect." I smiled into her brown eyes.

She turned and pointed down into the gardens. "He's over there with several bears. They're restacking the stones along the riverbank."

Sure enough, I spotted Dean right away. He was squatted along the edge of the water busily moving rocks around, making sure they were all tightly packed together.

"Thank you," I told Jor'johno.

She bowed again and then stepped aside so the three of us could pass by and continue down to the grounds. Commander Kess had a bit of a tummy, but almost all the bears did. It was a signature trait among them.

Dean must have heard others welcoming us, because he turned his head and watched as we came closer to him. He quickly stood and walked across a short stretch of grass to greet us.

The sun shone brightly, illuminating every tiny detail. I could tell a lot of work had been done in a short amount of time. Several of the Makers' ring ships orbited high above the field, along with Bear Paw crafts and vessels from New Cardall.

"Good to see you again," Dean said to me as we all stopped and stood together. His blue hands were covered with wet soil, and there were noticeable smears on the front of his shirt.

"Nice to see you too," I said. "This is my friend Wyler. He's a shifter, like me."

Wyler held out his hand, and Dean shook it. Wyler's face lit up with a twisted smile, and he gave me a quick confirming wink. With his exceptional skills, he'd probably grabbed Rhynor's signature instantly upon contact with Dean.

"Looks like you've been busy," Doug said. He nudged me, and I got the hint that he was quickly changing the subject in case Dean suspected something from Wyler's grin.

Luckily, our blue alien friend turned to look around at the gardens, his hands on his waist. "Yeah, it's coming along nicely," Dean said. "Did you guys come back to help?" He stared happily at all three of us, a polite and nice guy, so different from other MST agents I'd dealt with.

I shook my head. "No, we have some business we need to take care of. I just wanted to stop by and make sure everything was going okay."

"The bears have been very welcoming to me," Dean said, "especially considering my former affiliations." He let out a small chuckle.

"I'm glad to hear that," I said.

"We should probably get going." Wyler softly elbowed me.

"Sure, go take care of your stuff." Dean raised his hand a bit and waved to us. "We've got this under control."

"Thank you," I told him.

He nodded politely and then went back to arranging the stones along the edge of the river. A really nice guy.

Wyler wasted no time, and in a bold move he shifted the three of us back up into the main chamber room of the Citadel. We appeared within a dissipating dark cloud of smoke, a signature trait of his demon kind.

"Here. Take my hand," Wyler said. "Try to sense Rhynor's signature."

We held hands, and I tried to clear my mind and concentrate.

"Think of Dean's traits and then dig deeper," Wyler instructed me. "Expand your remote viewing and let *his* memories and experiences flow into you. It might be more difficult without actually touching him, but you should be able to pull them from me."

I took a deep breath, closed my eyes, focused, and found myself in an utterly relaxed frame of mind. In my dreamlike state, vague images of friends and acquaintances of Wyler's popped into my head, along with their specific signatures. He guided me throughout this exchange and then focused solely on Rhynor's specific traits. Signatures could be different for each shifter, but Wyler managed to send me the one that I needed. In my head, I saw a cloudy and vague outline of the man in question. His horns stood out and also his large, burly body. Chills raced over my shoulders and down my arms as I caught hold of the rogue demon's signature.

I opened my eyes to stare directly into Wyler's.

He smiled at me. "Good job, Davie. You are a top-notch shifter." He tenderly patted my cheek.

Doug then moved in and gave me a hug, slipping in a few sweet kisses as well in celebration of my achievement.

Wyler tapped my shoulder, getting my attention. "I think the best way to approach our mission is for you and Doug to shift over to him first. Then I'll show up with dagger in hand and surprise him." He let out a mildly sinister laugh. I had no doubt Wyler was looking forward to eliminating these rogue agents in the bloodiest way possible.

Wyler stepped back from Doug and me, and a swirling dark mass of smoke consumed him. Within seconds it dissipated, and he now stood before us in his demon form. I shook my head a bit in surprise. I hadn't seen him like this for a long time. He was shirtless, showcasing his red skin and chest, and spiraled black horns grew out of his skull right above both temples. He also held the dagger in his left hand, more than ready to strike.

He smiled at me. "This should freak them the fuck out, huh, Davie?"

All I could do was chuckle and smile, though I couldn't stop staring at him. Doug did the same, both of us somewhat startled yet captivated by Wyler's sudden change of appearance. In fact, I wasn't sure if Doug had ever seen Wyler in his true form before. I couldn't remember.

Wyler slashed the dagger back and forth through the air a couple of times. "Sometimes a slice and dice is the best way to get your point across. And since Rhynor is from a demon race, he'll understand my point."

"I'll summon some spirits when we arrive," I told him. "Maybe use one to encase me and sexy butt here." I playfully elbowed Doug.

"That's a great idea," Wyler said with a nod. "And *please* don't hold back. Feel free to summon a shitstorm of creatures to shred that place to pieces, if you feel like it."

Doug stepped closer to me and stood straight as an arrow with his hand wrapped around his rifle just above its trigger. "Are we ready to get this show on the road?" My tough guy sounded serious.

Wyler stared at us with a thin smile. "Lead the way, Davie. I'll be right behind you."

I focused on Rhynor's signature and used my remote viewing to get a feel for the environment. I could tell that he was in a large conference hall and was surrounded by twenty or more people, all kept busy with work-related tasks.

I shifted Doug and myself to Rhynor. We appeared at the far end of the room, our backs against a marble wall. Enormous fluted stone columns supported a massive and elaborate ceiling covered in etched designs and paintings of historic moments. The floor was also marble with swirls of white and gray throughout its surface. Large windows lined the room, revealing a sunny afternoon sky outside on some unfamiliar world.

After a few moments of us standing there, a pinkish alien female with long, dark hair finally noticed us. She hurried around the hovering holographic displays of her workstation, pointed at us, and shouted, "Look!"

Everyone turned around, including the head honcho, who immediately walked away from his terminal and headed straight for us. Rhynor was an oversize demon, to say the least. Large brown horns with a whopping attitude, I sensed. He was dressed in one of the MST's signature black bodysuits but with no sleeves, and he'd left the front unzipped down to his belly button. He stopped and looked at us with his hands locked on his waist. His arms were a lot more defined and muscular than Doug's.

"Keeper of the Citadel," he said in a hateful tone, with a scowl to match, "I'm glad you've come here, because killing you in person will be so much easier than gathering an army to deal with you and your worthless friends."

"You're a real piece of shit, you know that?" Doug blurted out. "The Expanse will be better off without you *and* your fucked-up followers."

Rhynor shook his head and laughed before lowering his arms. "Perhaps," he said. "But for right now, I promise you and your boyfriend are going to die slowly and painfully."

After hearing his threat, I instantly summoned a huge four-legged winged beast to shroud Doug and me. Although translucent, its outer edges glowed with a blue-white light that delineated its scaled body, long snout with sharp fangs, leathery wings, clawed feet, and thrashing tail.

Rhynor chuckled. "You realize I can contact the ships in orbit and have this room flooded with a dispersion field. Your spirit-calling skills will be as useless as you are."

Doug flipped off the smart-ass demon. I wasn't sure if Rhynor understood the gesture, but he immediately pulled his pdPhone out of his pocket. However, before he could make any calls, a tall cloud of thick, dark smoke appeared behind him. Wyler boldly jumped out of the cloud with his long dagger in hand. He quickly sliced through Rhynor's hand that was holding the phone.

Rhynor fell to his knees on the ground, crying out in pain. He held his bleeding limb with his other hand as he stared down in shock at the pieces of his four fingers lying on the ground.

All the other troops reacted without any hesitation. They pulled their handguns from their holsters and aimed at Wyler, firing bolts of deadly energy throughout the room. But my demon buddy wasted no time either. In his true red-skinned and barefoot form, wearing only black shorts, he swiftly shifted around the room, appearing in columns of black smoke. He reached out from the smoke and sliced rogue agents' stomachs open, spilling their intestines. He hacked off their arms and cut deeply along their thighs. From one side of the room to the other, he shifted back and forth, keeping everyone confused as he swung the dagger of attunement, hacking away at all of them with no mercy. They screamed. They panicked. Some ran to the doorways in hopes of fleeing from the massacre, but Wyler shifted close behind them and ran his dagger through their bodies as easily as a sharp knife through a stick of warm butter. Blood glistened on the sunlit floors. Splashes and sprays of it coated the pristine marble walls.

Still gripping his injured hand, Rhynor gazed around in horror at his fallen comrades. Severed limbs lay upon the ground in thick pools of blood. Some men and women struggled to take their final breaths, while others had met their end quickly after Wyler had sliced off their heads.

In a puff of smoke, Wyler appeared behind his main target. He grabbed hold of one of Rhynor's thick horns and yanked the brawny demon's head back. A look of sheer terror blanketed Rhynor's face. Even his charcoal skin appeared somewhat pale.

"Your days are over," Wyler said in a superior tone with a slight snarl. "And as soon as I'm done with you, I'm going to kill every rogue agent on those ships in orbit."

Before Rhynor could respond, Wyler stabbed the dagger into his back and straight through his heart. The long double blades jutted out of his chest. The dagger was coated in bits of flesh, and blood dripped from its double tips. Rhynor's mouth fell open. His face had gone blank, and both eyes had rolled back in his head. Wyler then let go of his horn, and the smart-ass demon fell onto his face, oozing blood that pooled all around him.

Wyler hurried over to Doug and me as I dismissed my protective spirit. His bare red chest was covered in streams and droplets of blood, and he had a look of utter satisfaction. I stared at him in shock and wonder, confused by his actions.

"I had no idea you could be such a heartless killer," I said to him. Witnessing what he had done left me feeling somewhat queasy in my stomach. I was sure Doug was just as startled.

Wyler raised his left hand and tapped the side of the soaked dagger blades against his opened palm. "Demon skills," he explained happily. "I wouldn't have made it this far in life, Davie, if I didn't play the killing role sometimes. Like I said, I'm here to protect the Expanse, to protect you and everyone else I care about."

He tilted his head back a bit, gazing toward the ceiling. Both of his black horns glistened in the sunlight. I could sense him using his remote viewing to get a feel for the crews aboard the rogue ships. He was planning his attack.

Wyler sweetly winked at me and then said, "I think the best course of action is for you two to head back home and let *me* finish the job."

Poor Doug hadn't even gotten to fire his gun.

"Are you sure?" I stared at Wyler with ample amounts of concern. "I can summon some spirits to help you."

He shook his head and then briefly laid his hand on my shoulder. "I've got this, Davie. Trust me. Let me do what I was born to do."

Born to do...? I wasn't sure I understood him. Somehow I doubted he was a cold-blooded killer at heart. That wasn't the friend I knew and definitely not the loving boyfriend I had dated long ago.

"Okay," I said. "We'll go home and wait for you to let us know how things went." I gave my demon buddy a loose hug, trying not to get blood on my shirt.

Doug took a few steps forward and patted Wyler's bald red head and then ran his fingers along one of Wyler's black horns. I guessed Doug was curious about them. After all, how many demon horns would you get to touch in life?

Wyler backed away from us and then disappeared in a swirling mass of dark smoke.

I turned around, and Doug wrapped his arm around me, giving me as much of a hug as he could while holding his rifle. I pressed the side of my face against his chest while staring at Rhynor's body. His signature had changed. It had become muffled and clouded much like my dearest bear friend Pahma's had when she'd died beside me.

"I guess you can take us home, sweetie." Doug gave me a kiss on the top of my head.

His phone rang just as I was about to shift us home, and he took a second to answer it. "Hey, how's it going, Ellet?" He listened a moment. "Oh, really... Yeah, David and I can swing by. What time is good for you and Nheyja?" He paused for a moment and tickled his fingers over my scruffy beard. "Okay. That sounds good. See you two in a little bit."

I glanced at Doug with raised brows. "What did they want?"

He shrugged. "Not really sure. Ellet just said that Nheyja wants to see you and me."

"So she can cut me down again. Tell me how much of a problem I am instead of a solution."

Doug gave me another one-armed hug. He held me close, my face pressed against his chest. "I'm sure it's nothing like that, Little Bear." He gave me another kiss on my head. "Maybe she wants to congratulate you for all the hard work you've been doing."

I laughed out loud. "You're a funny, funny man." I reached around and smacked his butt. "You know she's never really cared for me."

"Well, let's not jump to conclusions." Doug rubbed his hand over my back and shoulders. "Let's just go and see what she has to say. Okay?"

I patted his side before I shifted us back to our bedroom. He went into his closet to put his gun away, placing it horizontal in the wooden gun rack mounted to the wall.

"Anything we need to do before we go?" I asked.

"There's only one thing I can think of," he answered. A smile stretched across his face as he came over and stopped in front of me. He slipped his hands around my waist, then leaned down and pressed his lips tenderly against mine while massaging me above my hips.

He whispered between our kisses, "I know I've said this before, but you are everything I've ever wanted in a man. I can't imagine my life without you in it."

His heartfelt words left me teary-eyed. We mashed our tongues together in that wonderful sloppy way we both loved to do.

"I feel the same way about you, Doug," I said. "You're so good-looking and strong and kind. You are such a wonderful lover too. You make me feel so good in so many ways."

We shared a few more kisses.

"You're in my heart, sweetie," he told me. "I'll never let you go. Plus, the fact that you and I enjoy the same fetishes really turns me on. You're a sexy man, David. Nothing would make me happier right now than making love to you."

He made me smile. "I know. I love that about us too. But we probably need to get to Nheyja's and see what the heck is going on. Hopefully it's nothing bad."

He gave me a warm hug and held me tight against his body as he planted some kisses on my head. "I hate that you had to see so much bloodshed from Wyler. I wish things weren't so messed up all the time."

"It's okay," I mumbled with the side of my face pressed against his chest. "Like Wyler said, that's who he is. I just hope Josh never has to see that side of him."

"You and me both, sweetie."

I concentrated on Nheyja's signature and used my skills to get a feel for the environment. She and Ellet were inside her main chamber room, the one with the pool and the balcony that overlooked the lower levels of the city.

Doug and I appeared beside the knee-high stone wall that surrounded the pool. Streams of water gently rained down onto the pool's surface from the decorative tiered fountain in the center. The sun was starting to go down here, and the balcony provided a great view of the gorgeous sunset.

"Welcome, Doug," Nheyja said. She was dressed in a sheer pale-blue top that barely covered her breasts and a loose matching skirt that was slightly angled around her hips. "I welcome you too, David."

Ellet stood beside her. Both of them were barefoot, and Ellet wore his usual minimal attire of a short, tight pale-blue sarong wrapped around his waist, showcasing most of his thin, hairy thighs.

"Your place is looking a lot better." Doug glanced around at all the repairs that had been done since the last time we had been here.

"Yes, it is," she said. "A team of repairmen have been very diligent toward fixing everything." Nheyja approached us with Ellet right behind her, but they stopped maybe ten feet from us. "I wanted to say thank you for all that you've done," she said to Doug. "And I feel I need to apologize for my feelings toward you, David. I see now that the MST and its rogue agents can't be trusted. They've been more of an obstacle than a benefit to all life throughout the Expanse."

She'd caught me off guard. Doug looked surprised too.

"What made you change your mind about me?" I asked, curious.

Nheyja smiled and hesitated for a moment before she said, "Your reporter friend came to visit us here. He had many questions to ask me, plus many good things to say about you and Doug."

"Fred...?" Doug sounded slightly surprised. "He shifted here? Did he call first?"

My lovable man's questions left me laughing.

"Yes," Nheyja said. "He contacted Ellet, and I invited him over to talk. After meeting with him, several things became clear to me, especially that you, David, are needed and are not here to harm anyone, only to bring balance and support."

She stepped closer and offered me her right hand. I moved forward to meet her, and we joined hands. With her left hand, she covered our clasped hands and stared into my eyes. "I apologize for the way I treated you," she said humbly. "I am happy that you and Doug are together. With your combined determination and courage, you both will surely topple any forces who would challenge you as a team."

I nodded, and we let got of each other's hands as Doug stepped closer. He laid his hand on my shoulder, giving me a tender massage.

"If there's anything you ever need, Nheyja," Doug said, "please don't hesitate to ask either of us. You have been my friend for many, many years. David and I will always be there for you, no matter what."

She smiled. "You two are perfect for each other."

I gazed at the metal circlet she wore around her head. Its sculpted leaves and vines blended in perfectly with her dark-silver hair.

"Would you both like to join us for dinner sometime?" Doug asked. "We could even do something tonight."

To my surprise, Nheyja gave each of us a friendly hug. I nudged Doug's arm, and he followed me over to Ellet to give him some hugs too.

"Thank you for the offer," Nheyja said. "But I would like to get some rest tonight. I haven't had much sleep lately, being so worried about you two and many other people I care about."

"No problem," Doug said. "Just give me a buzz when you two want to hang out. We can be here in a snap."

The four of us exchanged some final friendly looks and good-byes, and I shifted Doug and myself back home to our bedroom.

He gave me a playful smack across my rear. "You know what we should do, Little Bear?"

He could always make me laugh. I stared at him with a single brow raised, curious about what he had in mind. However, I was pretty sure he was itching for some sex. "What would you like to do?" I asked.

He reached out and lightly tweaked my cheek. "You should shift us over to that pool in the Shards, and we could get naked and take a dip in it again. How's that sound?"

I scrunched up my face, turned my head a bit to the side, and gave him a questioning stare. "Me... get naked with you?" I even raised my hand in mock surprise at his suggestion.

He shot me a silly grin. "Real funny, smart-ass. You know you'd like to take a swim. Besides, I think we could both use a quick getaway... please."

Without hesitation and before he could say anything else, I shifted both of us to the edge of the pool. We stood on the uneven stones along the path leading right up to the water's edge. Above us floated the dozens of gigantic ghostly flowers that resembled my spirits. They hovered in the air at different heights, each a full bloom that looked similar to an opened rose.

"Hurry up!" Doug sat down along the edge of the stone wall and pulled off his boots and socks. He then quickly stood up, took off his shirt, undid his pants (no underwear, of course), and jumped naked into the middle of the water, well beyond the submerged ledge.

I tried my best to shed my clothes super fast. When I was done, I jumped right into the warm pool as he had, making a huge splash right next to my tough guy.

Doug sank lower than me in the water, and I took the opportunity to straddle his thighs and wrap my legs around his sides. He massaged my chest, squeezing my small pecs, and I glided my hands back and forth over his enticing beard.

The night sky was filled with twinkling stars, and a nearby nebula shone brightly through the tall trees with its swirling hues of green and blue along the horizon.

Doug smiled while kissing me a few times. "See, I told you this would be relaxing."

He was right. It was, and apparently arousing too. I felt his hard, meaty mammoth poking me between my legs. He reached down and pushed it farther down so he could slide it between my tight cheeks. I shook my head with a tiny chuckle before we shared a sloppy kiss.

"We don't have to make love or do anything like that," he said. "I'm having a shitload of fun just holding you in my arms. That's the best part of being with you."

I brushed the side of my face against his beard and whispered, "Same for me, handsome."

I could have sat here forever and enjoyed kissing my sexy man, but I had to admit I did enjoy his rock-hard erection teasing me. He added some hip motion, sliding his firm manhood in and out along my crack, which turned me on even more than his hairy chest had done.

"So what's the game plan?" Doug kissed my cheek, then gazed into my eyes.

I took a moment to give his question some thought and then answered, "Well, I think we need to meet up with Wyler and make sure he's okay. Then we should probably find some MST council members and verify with them that their forces have been disbanded. I'm not going to tolerate any more lying, like Admiral Rohn did to me."

"And if they haven't disbanded yet?" Doug asked.

I smiled and gave him a sweet kiss. "Then I'll let Wyler deal with them. He might even have some demon friends who'd be happy to help him."

Doug grabbed hold of my butt. He spread it open even more than it was with my legs wrapped around him and teased me with the tip of his wiener.

I grinned happily. "You're a dirty man," I told him. "You know that?"

"Well, it's your fault," Doug said. "If you weren't so damn sexy, I wouldn't be trying to poke you all the time."

I slipped in another kiss. "You can poke me anytime, Doug."

We took some time to swim through the pools, exploring, turning corners beneath the glowing flowers until the water deepened and the pool area widened. Doug found a small, comfortable nook, and we took a break there. He encouraged me to float on my back so he could savor my feet. I rested my head against the edge of the stone wall while he ran his tongue along the bottoms of my feet. He planted a ton of kisses over my feet, slid his tongue between my toes, and sucked on my big toes. If felt amazing. And afterward, I did the same to him as he floated on his back, although his feet were hairier than mine and much larger. But that just meant there was more for me to enjoy. I absolutely loved gliding my fingers along his muscular legs and thick feet. My big sexy man!

We spent about an hour in the pools before we got out and put our clothes back on. I used my remote viewing to sense Wyler's whereabouts. Oddly enough, he was still in the Expanse. In fact, he was on board James's ship with James and his crew. I told Doug.

"That's kind of weird," he said. "I wonder what's going on."

"Let's go find out," I said. "Or do you need to go home first for anything?"

Doug shook his head, then reached out real quick and tweaked my nipple beneath my shirt. With my durability, it would take more than that to make me flinch.

We exchanged some delightful grins for a brief moment before I shifted us to Wyler's location.

17

"Hey there!" Wyler greeted Doug and me after we'd appeared on the bridge of James's ship. He was back in his human disguise and dressed in clean clothes, jeans and a T-shirt. The dagger was nowhere to be seen, but with his demon skills I was sure he could produce it on a moment's notice.

All three Devil Bunnies stood near a workstation tapping buttons, and Bray and Woofa were at a nearby terminal. Willie stood next to James beside the enormous holographic display that floated between the two decks of the bridge. And to my surprise, Shake and Finger Pop were here too, right beside Dean, our dark-blue alien friend.

I looked around at everyone. I was curious and confused. Why would Dean be here?

"What's going on?" I asked.

James stepped away from the hologram with Willie following close behind him. "Well," James explained as he tapped a few controls on the screen of his phone, "you know a ton of the rogue agents are leaving the Expanse. They're making use of shifting engines to travel to other realms, to other universes. Your buddy Wyler thought we could use help in finding out where exactly they are going."

I glanced at Wyler. "With remote viewing?" I asked.

He shook his head. "With your buddy there." He bobbed a pointed finger a few times at Dean.

I shrugged. "I don't understand."

Wyler headed over our way and stopped beside James and Willie. "When I touched Dean at the Citadel," Wyler said, "I picked up on the fact that he is an expert at hacking computer systems, *especially* MST computer systems. With his help, James and his crew are going to know exactly where those rogue agents are headed to."

"Yeah, but what do you plan on doing once you know where they're going?" Doug sounded as confused as I did.

"We're going to eliminate them," Willie said boldly. "There's no sense in letting them spread chaos into other universes or planets. That's just crazy."

Shake—a sentient android in the shape of a black bodysuit with a helmet on—communicated something in his mechanical voice. Finger Pop knew we wouldn't understand him, so he stepped up to translate for us.

"My boy," Finger Pop said, dramatically flapping his hand through the air, "with the upgrades that we've installed on James's ship, he will be able to track down those freaks with very little trouble." He sounded like a laidback southern-belle drag queen addressing an audience, but instead of a ball gown he was wearing a brown sleeveless vest with matching boots and dark-green pants. "Plus, with Dean's skills we will be able to hack their systems and find out who is doing what and where they are all located."

Shake uttered a quick robotic phrase.

Finger Pop chuckled. "Exactly," he responded to Shake. "A piece of cake indeed."

Doug asked James, "So you contacted Wyler?"

James shook his head. "Actually, he came here to tell us about your mission... the one where you took out that oversize smart-ass demon." James slowly sliced his finger across his throat with an added choking sound.

Wyler laughed. "I thought they'd enjoy hearing about all the rogue agents I took care of."

Willie rubbed his huge, furry hand over Wyler's head and then patted his back. "And we greatly appreciate what you did, my friend." He sounded so delighted.

Doug put his hands on his hips. "So what do you plan on doing? Follow these agents and track them down?"

"Exactly," James said. He then walked away to push some holographic controls at a nearby workstation.

"We've taken the ship out of the Expanse before," Bray politely reminded us. "We shouldn't have any problems." She wore her usual attire of crimson pants tucked into tall matching red boots and a long-sleeved vest with a tank top beneath it.

Woofa turned his head and smiled into her eyes. The love they shared for each other was unmistakable. He had on an opened brown vest that showcased his furry chest. Jeans and boots completed his attire.

"Well, do you need us to come with you?" I thought I'd offer to help.

James shook his head and gave Doug and me an appreciative glance. "We'll be fine. Shake and Finger Pop and Wyler are heading out shortly, but the rest of us will handle them."

Doug seemed incredibly concerned. I could sense fear building inside of him and worry about James's safety. He headed over to James and said softly, "Hey, come here, little brother."

Surprisingly, James stepped right up to Doug, and they wrapped their arms around each other, swaying slightly from side to side. I had a feeling both of them had longed for a brotherly bonding moment like this. All three brothers were the epitome of a close-knit family. They'd do anything for each other.

"Just promise me you'll be safe," Doug said as they ended their hug.

"We'll behave," James said in a reassuring tone. He then let out a tiny laugh. "Besides, I've got the best crew in the galaxy, not to mention the biggest and baddest boyfriend in any universe!"

Willie smiled at the compliment, hurried over to James, and picked him up so they could share some passionate kisses. There was at least a three-foot difference between their heights. Seeing them both so happy together made me smile. So much for James being reserved about expressing his loving side in front of others.

"So when are you guys heading out?" Doug asked after he'd come back over to stand beside me.

"I think we're about ready," Woofa said with a positive attitude. "We have a ton of coordinates programmed into the ship's navigation system, so it shouldn't be too difficult to find some rogue ships."

Doug rested his hand on my shoulder, and I looked up at him. He seemed lost in thought. I could sense he felt left out of the situation.

"Well," Wyler announced, "I'm going to head home to see how my hubby is doing."

He walked around the bridge saying good-bye to everyone. He shook hands with James and Willie, exchanged hugs with Bray and Woofa, and simply waved to the Devil Bunnies and Shake and Finger Pop.

"Tell Josh hi for me," I told Wyler as he stopped to give me and Doug a friendly embrace.

"Don't forget to stop by and work your magic," Wyler quietly reminded me with a wink.

That was right. I still needed to give Josh some longevity upgrades. I didn't mind Wyler asking for some gifts from me. In fact, I planned on giving Josh a little bit more than Wyler had asked for. But I'd keep that bit of information to myself for now.

"I guess I should give Fred a call," I mentioned to Doug.

"For what?"

"To find out who's in charge of the MST," I explained. "With all his contacts, I'm sure he knows a lot more than I do."

Wyler waved to everyone once more. "Okay, I'm out of here! Best of luck, James. Show no mercy to those assholes!" He then shifted away in a puff of black smoke.

Everyone on the bridge continued working at their stations. Shake and Finger Pop met with James and seemed to be discussing some last-minute details about their mission.

"Well," Doug announced loudly, "I guess me and David will head out too. We've got some people to meet and things to get done."

"Sounds good," Willie said.

"I'll keep in touch with you guys and let you know about our progress," James told us. He sounded incredibly determined. I hoped it would all go well.

I glanced around the bridge one final time. I couldn't have asked for better friends in my life. Like James had said, his crew had proven to be outstanding in many ways. I knew within my heart they'd always come out on top.

"Ready, handsome?" I asked Doug.

He confirmed his eagerness to leave with a swift yet soft pat against my back. "Take us home, sweetie."

We appeared in our new living room. I was still in awe of all the details and the sheer size of it. Doug had really gone overboard on our new home, but it made me happy having him with me and having a place to call our own.

I pulled my phone out from my pocket and called Fred.

"Hey there!" He said. "How are you doing?"

"I'm doing great," I told my reporter friend. "I thought you might know who's in charge of the MST. I'd like to discuss a few things with them."

Doug massaged his hand over my shoulder and quietly mouthed he was heading into the kitchen to grab something to drink.

"I do," Fred answered. "Would you like to swing by later and I can tell you all about them."

"Sure," I told Fred. "We can stop by tonight. I can actually grab their signatures from you."

He laughed into his phone. "And how will you be able to do that?" he asked, sounding confused yet highly intrigued.

"You'll be able to do the same thing someday," I said. "It'll just take some practice. It's a skill all shifters have."

After I hung up, I sent a text message to Kirill just to touch base. He responded right away and said Doug and I should come over to check out the new work they'd started at the tattoo shop. I then went into the kitchen and sat beside Doug on one of the barstools along the kitchen island. To my surprise, he had filled a bowl with some vanilla ice cream with caramel and toffee bits, definitely one of my favorite flavors.

"We're meeting Fred later tonight," I told my tough guy.

He nodded in acknowledgment and offered me a spoonful of ice cream. I opened my mouth to let him feed me. "Damn, that is good stuff!"

"I know," he said. He flashed a smile my way and then shoved a giant spoonful in his mouth. "What about the rest of the gang... Chuppo and Ni, Aldis and Kirill? Should we get with them to see how things are going?"

"I actually just sent Kirill a text message. He invited us over to check out the new work they've started in the tattoo parlor."

Doug laughed. "Are they putting in the counter to feed waiting guests?"

"That's the impression I got." I nudged his arm with my shoulder. "Guess we'll see when we get there."

We finished the bowl of ice cream and then freshened up a little. Doug put on a sleeveless red plaid button-down, and I chose a dark-blue polo. We kept our jeans and boots on. No need to change those. I brushed my teeth and watched while Doug worked some conditioner through his beard. He liked to keep it styled.

After about thirty minutes we headed over to Kirill's tattoo parlor. He and Aldis were talking to a maintenance team of large and muscular ornighs along with a few humans. Some '80s-sounding dance music played softly in the background. Hearing that types of music always made me smile.

Kirill and Aldis came over to greet us right away.

"Hey, the new construction is looking great," I told them. A long wooden counter had been added to one side of the waiting room area, and I could already imagine food and beverages being served there. It looked like there'd be room for barstools in front of the counter too. Decorative wooden cabinets had also been installed along the outside wall. The work crew was doing a really nice job, and the smell of freshly cut wood filled the air.

"Thanks." Kirill shook my hand while tapping my arm with his free hand and then repeated the greeting with Doug. "We decided not to waste any time. Figured it'd draw in more clients. People always enjoy eating and drinking."

Aldis rubbed his stomach and laughed. "I sure do!"

Aldis crossed his green arms over his prominent chest. He had on a black tank top and khaki shorts. "So what do you guys have planned for today? Or are you two just being nosy?" he asked with a chuckle. He kept glancing back and forth between the construction people and us.

"Well," I said, "we just wanted to check up on a few friends, and then hopefully I'm going to meet with an MST representative later this evening."

Kirill and Aldis both looked disgusted by that last bit.

"Why even bother," Kirill said in a hateful tone. "Let them all die. They don't care about any of us, so why should you give a shit about them, David?"

"Well, I just want to make sure they're following my demands about disbanding." I looked directly into Kirill's eyes. "And I'll use my shifting skills to tell if any of them are lying."

Aldis laughed. "They're the MST; they *always* lie."

I let out a long sigh. "I know, I know. But I guess I'll find out for sure tonight."

"Plus, the Kroma M8 are on our side now," Doug reminded them. "The MST doesn't have a lot of options left. They'll have to do what David says, or else."

"So when do you plan on serving food?" I asked. I imagined it wouldn't be too long.

"In a few days," Kirill said. He turned and faced the crew, who hadn't stopped working this whole time. "We'll have different kinds of drinks and some quick-serve foods like deli sandwiches and snacks, plus a huge stack of Ni's cookies. I'm thinking it should be a nice addition."

Aldis stepped closer to wrap his muscular green arms around his tiny boyfriend. They reminded me of James and Willie with their difference in size.

My phone chirped with a text message from Chuppo: "You and Doug stop by when you have time. Ni just made a fresh batch of feel-good cookies! Come and grab some! We're in our kitchen on the ship."

Kirill's face lit up the minute I read the message out loud. "Oh, make sure she sends me a bunch of them. I'll be happy to split the profits with her."

I nodded happily and then texted Chuppo back to let him know we'd be right there.

The four of us exchanged some hugs, and Aldis and Doug fist-bumped. It always made me laugh to see them acting like badass thugs.

I focused on Chuppo's signature, and Doug and I appeared inside his kitchen. Our three troll friends were sitting on fluffy pillows smoking from the golden hookah in the center of the room.

"Little one!" Ni jumped up in a flash and came over to give us hugs. "It's so good to see you. I've got a ton of cookies for you and Kirill." She stepped back. A wide smile stretched between her tusks. "People are going to snatch them up nice and fast!"

A noticeable scent of the magic flower filled the air. It was their favorite product to smoke. I wasn't sure where they got it from, but there was always plenty of it on their ship. All of them were barefoot and wearing shorts and T-shirts.

"How's everything going?" I walked around and shook hands with Chuppo and Ra Wee.

"Real good," Chuppo said. "Grab a pillow and join us."

They knew I didn't smoke, but Doug would probably take a puff or two. And sure enough, he did. As soon as my handsome man sat down on one of the many pillows, Ra Wee passed the hose and mouthpiece to him. Doug took a deep inhale from the decorative metal pipe, held the smoke in for a few seconds, and then slowly blew it out in a large cloud.

"Kirill and Aldis have a crew installing the food section of their parlor," I informed them. "I imagine you're going to make a nice chunk of change from selling cookies."

Ni batted her hand through the air and surprisingly passed me a cold bottle of beer. "I'm just happy to help them out. You've got really nice friends."

"I do indeed." I tipped the bottle toward her in an appreciative gesture.

"So you guys got any plans or maybe something fun going on?" Doug asked and then took another hit from the hookah.

Chuppo took a sip from his beer and said, "The three of us are heading over to the Gelis system, to the planet Orfem. There's another monthlong festival soon. It should be a lot like the one you two visited."

"That's why I made so many cookies!" Ni sounded so excited to get her treats out to the public.

"You both should swing by the festival," Ra Wee said. He then took a hit from the hookah pipe.

Doug and I both nodded.

"That sounds like fun," I said.

"We definitely will come and visit." Doug smiled with anticipation. He and I had enjoyed the last troll celebration we'd attended, especially the food and the bands.

We stayed for about two hours, spending much of that time listening to stories from our friends. I eventually told them about my meeting later tonight with the MST representative. They all shook their heads and sounded just as doubtful as Kirill and Aldis had.

Doug tried his best to stay away from smoking any more magic flower, but whenever Ni or Ra Wee dangled the hose and mouthpiece in front of his face, he just couldn't resist. He already looked a little disoriented.

"Okay," I told everyone finally. "It's time for us to head out. I've got to meet with Fred and get the info I need for the meeting."

Ni, Ra Wee, and Chuppo stood up with ease to give us hugs, but Doug wobbled a bit as he tried to stand. I think the smoke in the air had affected me a bit too, as my head felt sort of cloudy.

"Don't forget to call me," Chuppo said as we hugged.

"I will," I promised him.

Ni's and Ra Wee's tusks actually bumped the top of my head when we said our good-byes. They were both more careful when embracing Doug since he was so much taller.

Doug slung his left arm over my shoulders, leaning against me for support. He could probably use a nap, I figured.

I waved good-bye to our green friends and then shifted us home to our living room. My handsome man flopped down on the longest part of the sectional and let his head fall back against the cushions.

"Here, let me help you." I leaned down and pulled off his boots so he could wiggle his toes and get comfortable.

"Thanks, sweetie." He fell to the side and stretched out along the couch. He patted the sofa, inviting me to join him.

I took off my boots and snuggled beside him with my back against his body. We mingled our feet together, as always, and Doug slipped his arm around me to hold me nice and close against his chest.

"I feel like I have loved you for a thousand lifetimes," I whispered quietly.

Doug let out a deep breath. "Who knows... maybe we've been together before?"

He gave me a couple of kisses on my neck, but it didn't take long before he was out and snoring. Good thing I hadn't taken any hits from the hookah, or I'd be wiped out too. But I wasn't about to deny myself some cuddle time with my sexy man. No way! I rested my head along his outstretched arm and made myself comfortable. The feel of his arm around me, of his sculpted chest pressed against my back, and of his breath upon my skin soon soothed me to sleep.

As I dozed, my beloved spirit guide pulled me into another vision. Sanvean and I stood on the edge of a high cliff, looking out upon a bright and gorgeous sunrise above an endless green valley. Barefoot, she hovered a few inches above the ground. She was wearing her usual attire: long, flowing sheer panels, one in front and one in back, that dangled from her thin metallic belt and a loose-fitting top that looked similar to a bra. Her pale skin stood out in the sunlight, and her lengthy cobalt hair gently swayed from left to right in the mild breeze. Her favorite silver circlet of ivy and leaves had been woven throughout her hair.

"Where are we?" I asked. "Usually you bring me to the Citadel. This place actually reminds me of a location in South America that Wyler and I visited when he was teaching me how to shift."

"We are still in the Expanse," she said. "We are on Alemereen, where you and Doug will share a long and wonderful life beneath an ancient sun." She raised her arm and pointed ahead. "There... *there* is your future."

I stared straight out into the orange-and-red sky, at the rising sun. "The horizon?" I asked in puzzlement.

In a soft, sweet voice she said, "Two hearts as one, hand in hand, you and Doug will be together forever, where the land meets the sky."

"So you're saying our future will be good?"

"You have fulfilled your destiny, David, in many ways. As I have said, from past to present you have influenced how the Expanse has developed. Your silent footsteps are now being heard. And even though you have reached your journey's end, you will continue on as a god hunter, gifting powers upon those in need, securing their futures in ways they could at one time have only imagined. You are the rising sun, David, the wind that guides them, the dawn of a new day that brings hope to all who embrace your gifts. Gaze toward the horizon, for that is where you are headed."

I was somewhat confused. "But with the MST gone, why would people be in need of my help?"

She briefly held my hand. Her skin felt silky smooth.

"A gathering storm can either be large or small," she explained. "Problems will arise in many shapes and sizes. You are the Keeper of the Citadel, the protector of life. Even the smallest of individuals will need your guidance, your gifts."

"But how will I know who to help and where I should go?"

"They will call to you in their time of need," Sanvean said, "no different than they did to me. They live beneath a night without stars, in shadows and echoes of despair. You will feel their struggles and understand what it is they need. Look toward the sky, David, and hear their voices within you."

"And I'll have their signatures? I'll be able to shift to them?"

Sanvean nodded. "Wyler did the same for me. Together we traveled to numerous worlds, in hundreds of different universes, changing the lives of all who reached out for my hand."

I let out an easygoing laugh. "Sounds like I'm going to have a busy schedule."

Sanvean smiled a bit and then turned her head for a moment to face me. She was so beautiful, so flawless in her appearance.

"You and Doug can work together. Both of you can change people's lives," she said. "He will never abandon you, David. Nor you, him. You once asked for love, but you were never without it. Your two hearts have always been and *will* always be as one, forever."

Her words moved me deeply and left me somewhat teary-eyed. She had touched my heart.

I thought of Doug as I stared at the rising sun. I recalled making love with him and simply cuddling in bed. I smiled as I thought about his corny jokes and how he'd shake his butt in front of me while doing a silly dance. Doug meant the world to me, and I couldn't have been more grateful for having him in my life.

"Are you still going to be around to help me if I have any questions?" I asked, unsure whether this would be our final shared dream or not.

Her fingertips brushed along the side of my hand, and then we gazed into each other's eyes.

"In time, you and I shall meet again, David."

She smiled at me, and in a bold move I gave her a heartfelt hug, which she returned, wrapping her arms gently around me.

"I can't thank you enough for all that you've done for me." I lowered my arms and stepped back from her. She was still floating a few inches above the rocky ground.

"And the entire Expanse is grateful for having you, David."

We stood beside each other for several minutes and simply enjoyed the sunrise. I concentrated and focused on our location, this mountain range and the edge of the cliff. In the back of my mind, I imagined bringing Doug to this very spot sometime soon so we could bask in the warmth of the beautiful morning light and enjoy some private time together.

I woke up and opened my eyes. Doug's arms were still around me, and I felt his chest rise and fall against my back as he breathed. I had no idea how long we had been here on the couch. Inside Sanvean's visions minutes always turned into hours. I pulled my pdPhone out of my pants pocket and checked the time. Wow! Four and a half hours had passed. I needed to get my butt moving and meet with Fred.

I carefully turned over to face Doug. With my hand, I followed the outline of his beard. It felt so full yet incredibly soft. He slowly woke up as I lay there admiring how handsome he looked.

"We need to get going, sweetie." I told him how long we had slept.

He nodded while yawning. "I could use a shower first to get this magic-flower smell off of me."

I gave my tough guy a kiss. "I'm sure Fred wouldn't mind a little whiff, but I understand what you're saying."

Doug smiled and reached behind me to rub my back. We both stood up, and I shifted us upstairs, where we took a shower together. I worked our dark-blue pouf over his body, covering him in soap, and then moved my hands down lower to his impressive wiener. It got rock hard the second I touched it, so I stroked him a few times, which put a smile on his face. He then returned the favor after covering me with the same fragrant bodywash.

Out in our bedroom, I stood naked beside him at his walk-in closet. "Oh, no," I told him as he held up a crisp button-down. "I don't think you need to wear a fancy shirt. Just jeans, boots, and maybe something to show off your awesome bulging biceps. You know, something to remind the MST that we *do* kick ass."

Doug laughed. "I would seriously hope they'd know that by now!"

He put one of his favorite sleeveless red plaid shirts with faded jeans that fit nice and snug in all the right spots, followed by a pair of white tube socks and steel-toed brown boots. I sort of mimicked his outfit but opted for a dark-green T-shirt. And, of course, I wore underwear.

I called Fred. "Are you ready for me and Doug to stop by?"

"Sure," he said in an excited tone. "I'm at the office dealing with some developing crap. Anytime you guys are ready, come on by. I could use a break."

"Okay, we'll be there in a few minutes."

I wrapped my hands around Doug's waist. He had left his shirt unbuttoned a bit, so I gave his hairy chest a kiss.

"Let's fly," I told my handsome man.

18

Doug and I appeared on the far side of Fred's office, next to three cushioned chairs positioned around a round glass tabletop supported by a brass frame. A brown carpet covered the floors, and hanging on the white walls were numerous framed articles, pictures, and awards. He also had two tall potted plants in heavy-looking decorative ceramic pots.

"Hey there!" Fred jumped out of his chair and hurried around his desk to give us some hugs.

He had a spacious office. I was impressed. Several small holographic displays floated above his oversize desk, and through a tall row of windows I saw nearby sections of the city outside, complete with flying vehicles zooming through the sky.

"So how's it going?" I asked. "How did your office survive the attack? Is this the same building?"

He appeared sort of frazzled despite his nice attire of slacks, button-down shirt, tie, and great-looking brown shoes.

"Oh, I'm sure you know how it is," he said with a twisted grin. "Everybody wants a piece of you in one way or another. And no, this is another building we use. I work out of three different offices around the city because I never know where I'm going to be or how soon we'll need to get a story published."

"Speaking of pieces," Doug said, "how's it going with the bartender from the Arkenstone? You two *are* seeing each other, right?"

Fred gasped and acted shocked. His rosy cheeks blushed. "Well, I wouldn't exactly call it *seeing each other*. Both our schedules are kind of hectic. But now that I'm a shifter, I can pop into his house and get busy with a lot of hot sex real fast. He's pretty versatile too. Oh, and did I tell you he's hung like a horse and can pound my ass like a pro!"

I held my hand up and laughed. "Okay, too much information there."

Fred shrugged. "Well, it's true. And he eats ass like he's got a college degree in it."

Doug and I both sighed while shaking our heads. My tough guy then elbowed the side of my arm. We needed to get to the point of our visit.

"So you've met with this MST commander?" I asked Fred.

He nodded and walked over to a picture hanging on his wall. "Here she is." He pointed at an alien female standing with several other MST officers and a few reporters. Her skin was a smoky orange color, and her long brown hair fell over her shoulders in subtle curls.

"Her name is Locklynn," Fred said. "She holds the rank of admiral, like Rohn did. Not a bad lady. But she definitely likes to speak her mind. She and I have had a few minor arguments in the past. Honestly, though, I think she only tolerates me because of the newspaper. Otherwise I don't think she'd even deal with me."

"Well, I hope she doesn't get offended by anything I'm going to ask her," I said, but honestly, I couldn't have cared less if she was bothered by my questions. At this point in time, I had lost all respect for the MST. They could all disappear today, and I wouldn't care. In fact, it'd probably put a huge smile on my face.

Fred stared at me with his hands on his waist. He looked curious. "So how are you going to get Locklynn's signature from me?"

I bobbed my finger at him. "A trick Wyler showed me. Hopefully, it'll work."

Fred shrugged. "If not, I can give her a call."

I shook my head and then stepped closer and offered him my hand. He took hold of it. I closed my eyes and did exactly what Wyler had taught me. I focused on the signatures within Fred, digging through his experiences, his encounters. I came across his bartender friend right away, along with several coworkers and various other people. Fortunately, it didn't take me long before I found Locklynn's signature. Her silhouette and image became part of my own repertoire. I could now shift to her.

After I released Fred's hand, he asked, "Did you get it?"

"Yes."

He smiled at me. "*That* is a pretty cool ability. You're going to have to teach me how to pull signatures from people and pry into their memories. It'll be a lot more resourceful than just reporting what people tell us."

I chuckled. "I'll get around to showing you sometime. But first we need to go and talk to her. I want to make sure they've done what I asked them to do."

Fred's face lit up. "Hey, I could come with you! And no, I don't mean that kind of come." We all laughed at his perverted joke. "If I show up with you, then Locklynn might be less of a hassle. In fact," he said, "you should show up floating above them, encased in a huge menacing spirit! That would freak the hell out of them all and show her you aren't playing any games."

Doug rubbed his hand over my back. "I kind of like that idea. You should do it, Little Bear."

"Seriously...?" I asked them both.

"Sure. Why not?" Doug shot me one of his adorable twisted smiles. "Remind them that you're dead serious and not going to take any more of their bullshit and lies."

"You don't have to demolish the place," Fred added. "At least not yet. It'll be a minor show of force on your part. I imagine you like it forced in. Doesn't he, Doug?"

My tough guy slid his arm around me and laughed while he squeezed me against his body a few times. "I *always* enjoy forcing it in."

"My kind of man!" Fred blurted with gusto.

I held up my hands and stopped them both. "Okay, guys. Let's focus. I'll show up and remind them how serious I am. Fred, would you like to shift there with Doug after I appear? Can you do that?"

He nodded, looking sure of himself. "Yeah, I can bring him along. I've already shifted three people at one time. And I promise I won't leave his clothes behind."

I smiled. Fred couldn't resist slipping in some kind of dirty comment. He reminded me so much of Bryan.

I rose about six feet into the air, and Doug moved aside to stand beside Fred. I liked the idea of shifting with a spirit already called, but a huge, overwhelming spirit wasn't really what I wanted to go for. Instead, I thought a ravaging swarm of microwave-size winged creatures would be more intimidating. Yeah, I liked that idea much better.

I raised my arms, brought them close against my chest, and then summoned a horde of ghostly critters with four broad wings and thick, long stinging tails. Their bulbous heads contained rows of jagged teeth, and their six legs were tipped with razor-sharp claws. My summoned pets had translucent bodies, but they shimmered with outlined hues of blue and white.

I glanced down at Doug, then at Fred. Both stared at me with looks of wonder. My choice for a swarm versus one gigantic spirit had turned out to be a great decision.

With my remote viewing, I sensed Locklynn was seated in a type of conference room with several other MST individuals. It had to be a large place since their signatures weren't positioned close to one another.

"Follow me," I said in a loud voice to my spirits right before I shifted to her.

I appeared floating above one of many desks positioned around a large, circular hall with marble floors and walls. Tall, decorative windows and lots of tall flowering trees potted inside massive ceramic urns surrounded the room.

Locklynn instantly stood up and backed away with a look of sheer terror on her face. In fact, all her associates rose, and some even gasped. My spirits noisily flew around me. They certainly had gotten everyone's attention.

Doug and Fred appeared seconds later and stood close to me. My summoned spirits circled them, and some even passed through them as if they were as thin as air.

"Keeper of the Citadel," Locklynn said with a hint of detestation, "I see you like to show up unannounced instead of properly asking for an invitation. And you even brought the editor from the *Transgalactic Press* with you. Imagine that."

"Well, with how things are going lately," Fred said in a snarky tone, "we never know what sort of trouble the MST is going to stir up next. I've got to stay on top of any stories."

She glared at Fred. Her expression changed from dislike to hatred in a snap.

All of Locklynn's associates wore black MST bodysuits with matching over-the-calf boots, but hers was a white version. A large red symbol of some kind decorated her chest, but she had left her suit partially unzipped, so the image was split in half.

"But the MST is no more," Locklynn said.

"And that's why we're here," I said bluntly. "I'd like to know what's going on and what your organization is now doing. Admiral Rohn turned out to be a lying sack of shit, so I'm just making sure you aren't too."

She moved back to her workstation. Small holographic images of planets and rolling streams of data hovered above its console.

I continued to float in the air, my boots dangling inches away from the top of Doug's head. I commanded my spirits to move throughout the room. Some flew around high above us, while others crawled along the marble walls and decorative ceiling. Somehow I felt it would probably be safer to make all the MST men and women feel intimidated instead of relaxed.

Locklynn leaned her head back and looked up at me. "We have done *everything* you asked of us. Our warships are being docked at various ports throughout the galaxy, and our troops have been informed that their services are no longer needed. I, along with my council members, will continue to oversee our disbanding until it is complete."

"Why are your ships being docked and not dismantled?" Doug had brought up a good point.

She sighed and sounded aggravated, then crossed her arms in front of her chest. "Because we don't know if any other organizations will try to take control of the Expanse. It's better to be safe than sorry. Wouldn't you agree?"

"If any race tried to do that," Fred said, "we all know David would take care of them. Plus the Bear Paw are overseeing things now. There shouldn't be any pending threats."

I stared straight down into her eyes with only one thought on my mind. "I think the Bear Paw should take possession of your ships. They've definitely earned a major upgrade."

She looked confused and a bit irritated by my suggestion, and after a short pause she rolled her eyes. "That wouldn't be a wise decision. The Bear Paw would interpret that as nothing more than a means to dominate all races and create havoc throughout the Expanse."

"So basically they'd become the MST." I wasn't going to be polite. "Is that what you're afraid of? The Bear Paw are working with me to restore order and let everyone live freely, like they should always have been able to do."

Locklynn barely shook her head as she laughed. "You're a fool if you think any group will obey your every word. Give the Bear Paw ultimate power, and they will turn against you. I've seen it happen many times before. They desire only conflict."

"Kind of sounds like the MST," Fred pointed out.

She continued giving him hateful looks. Good thing I'd made Fred a shifter and a spirit caller. He'd be able to outrun her on his tiny pony if she ever wanted to smack the shit out of him for his comments.

I shook my head and floated closer toward her, descending several inches. "Let me make this clear," I said. "I'm not asking you. I'm *telling* you to give the Bear Paw access to those ships. And if you piss me off, I'm going to make your life a living hell. You understand me?"

I could sense an overwhelming feeling of satisfaction coming from Doug. A noticeable smile had popped up on his face. Apparently he enjoyed my boldness.

"And don't forget about the Kroma M8," Fred added under his breath with a small chuckle. "From what I've heard, they don't like you very much either. But that's what you get for treating people like shit."

She stood in place, but I felt a lot of hateful feelings tumbling around inside of her. "Fine," she said in an aggravated tone before heading back around to her desk. "Since you're in charge and want to run everything, I'll give you complete access to our ships. But don't come crying to me when you find yourself outnumbered and disrespected by those furry twits."

Doug let out a hiccup of a laugh. "Well, we've gotten to know the Bear Paw much better than it sounds like you ever did. They're honorable and decent, and they respect David."

She sighed. "Whatever," she said, sounding irritated with all of us. "I'll send word to our remaining troops at the shipyards and inform them that all vessels are to be left fully accessible. Will that make you all happy?"

Fred pursed his lips and then put his hands on his hips. "Well, I'd be even happier if I could get a box of chocolates too."

I wanted to laugh but stopped myself.

Locklynn pulled out her pdPhone and typed a message. "There," she said and then tossed her phone down on top of the desk. "It's done. The Bear Paw will have complete access to all former MST ships. Is there anything *else* I can do for you?"

"You could put an end to all the rogue-agent bullshit," Fred said. "They're actually worse than when they were part of your organization."

She smiled faintly. I think a small part of her enjoyed the back-and-forth exchange of insults. "As you probably already know," she said, "the rogue agents are acting on their own accord. We have nothing to do with them. If you want them dead, then you're going to have to see to that yourself. Or you could publish a scandalous article to turn everyone against them." She gave Fred a sinister scowl. "I'm sure you're familiar with how to do that, right?"

Fred shrugged. "If scandalous is equal to the truth, then yeah. Stay tuned for a juicy article."

I glanced around the impressive room before making eye contact with Locklynn again. "We have our forces dealing with the rogue agents. But don't go behind my back and help them out. If you do, you're going to get an up-close experience of what my spirits can do. You understand me? Admiral Rohn didn't listen to me, and you've heard what happened to him."

She nodded courteously to me. "We have every intention of staying as far away from you *and* your Citadel as we possibly can."

"Where are your troops going to go?" Doug asked.

"As I said," she answered, "they will disband and go their own ways. Most likely many will return to their home worlds and seek out new careers. The Expanse is a large place. It shouldn't be too hard for them to find new paths."

"Good," I said. "I only came here to confirm things that Admiral Rohn had promised. I only want what's best for everyone, and that includes you and your friends."

Locklynn gave me another courteous nod, but I sensed she was tired of me talking to her. "I understand," she said.

"Guess it's time to get going," Doug said. He sounded ready to leave.

"If you need anything from me," I told Locklynn, "feel free to contact me or Jay E Jay. He's stationed at the Citadel. I'll try to help out as much as I can."

"Thank you," she answered. She then sat back down at her desk and got right back to whatever she had been working on before I'd appeared.

I glanced at Fred, dismissed my spirits, and then shifted the three of us back to his office.

"So are you going to write a story about all of that?" I figured he probably would, but he shook his head and batted his hand through the air.

"It's not worth it," he said. "There's more important stuff to publish than all the crap she mentioned. Besides, I don't want to give any lingering rogue agents a heads-up on what the Bear Paw plan on doing."

"Sounds like a smart approach," I said.

"You guys want to grab a bite to eat?" Fred asked. "There are some really good places right down the street."

"Actually," I told him, "I need to meet up with Wyler and Josh. I've got a little gift to give them both. I also need to talk to Jay. Could we take a rain check?"

Fred pretended to pout, putting his hands on his waist. "Oh fine, just blow me off like I don't matter." We all laughed at his joke. "I know you have a busy schedule, so whenever you guys have time, that'll be fine. We'll go out and have some fun."

"Maybe see if your bartender buddy can come along with us," Doug said.

"Austin... oh, he would *love* to hang out with you two," Fred said in delight. "He's a really nice guy. And did I mention he's absolutely huge down there?"

"Yes, you did," I told Fred with a smile. I gave him a hug and a quick kiss on the lips. Doug did the same right after me.

"Thanks for all your help," I told him.

Fred giggled and pointed his finger at me. "Now don't forget: the next time we meet, you need to show me how to pull signatures from people. A skill like that will come in handy. And I swear it won't inflate my ego any more than it already is!" He could be such a joker.

"I promise I'll show you," I reassured him.

"Okay," he said with a pat for each of us on the shoulder. "Get the hell out of here and keep saving the universe."

"I'm on it!" I focused on the Citadel and shifted Doug and me to its main chamber room.

It was early evening, and Jay was staring out a window into the Field of Gods with his furry hands locked together behind his back. I sensed feelings of contentment coming from my bear friend.

"Hey, buddy," I said as Doug and I walked over to him. "How's it going?"

Jay turned his head and smiled. With his acute hearing, he'd certainly heard our footsteps on the marble floor. "Keeper," he said, "I'm simply thinking about how far my race has come over the years. I am grateful for your continued help and support. We couldn't have made it this far without you."

I stopped beside my tower of fur and gently brushed my hand along his arm. His brown fur felt silky smooth. He wore only a pair of knee-length shorts.

"I'm glad the growda ha'tars are finally seeing better days," I said. "No one deserves to be oppressed like you have been."

"We have some good news for you," Doug said.

Jay let out a deep chuckle. "Let me guess—the MST and all rogue agents have been wiped out?"

"Well, not exactly," I answered with a small laugh. "I just met with Admiral Locklynn, and she agreed to release all former MST spaceships into Bear Paw custody. So you'll have an improved fleet while overseeing order throughout the Expanse."

Jay growled a bit and turned around to face both of us. "And what terms did she demand?" he asked.

I shook my head. "None. In fact, I told her if she didn't cooperate with me then she'd see up close and personal what my summoned spirits could do."

Jay growled again, but this time it sounded more happy than suspicious.

"Do you know where the MST shipyards are located?" I figured Jay did, since the growda ha'tars had been affiliated with the MST for so long.

Jay nodded.

"I'm guessing troops will be there to facilitate your possession of them," I said.

"They will be," Jay said without any doubt in his gruff voice. "And I'm sure the transfers will be uncomfortable for both sides."

"But despite any tensions," Doug said, "you'll be the ones in charge. If they start any trouble, then remind them what David will do."

"Demanding those ships was a bold move on your part, Keeper." Jay looked at me with a proud smile along his long snout. "But it was also a generous and kind act. My people and I will be grateful to you forever."

I patted his huge, furry arm. "You deserve it," I told him. "Just let me know how it goes when you get there."

"I will, Keeper." He turned his head to gaze out into the field again. I could sense he was in a contemplative mood, his heart filled with good feelings and lots of ambitious ideas tumbling around in his head.

"Okay," I told Jay. "Doug and I need to take off. We've got some stuff to take care of."

My towering bear friend turned around. Without stooping down, he wrapped his arm around me and pulled me close against the bottom of his belly. He did the same with Doug, who got more of Jay's rounded stomach pressed against his face than I had since he was taller than me. Jay was silky smooth, as always, with a faint aroma of woodsy outdoors rolling off of him.

"Thank you, again, Keeper." He emitted such hopeful feelings. I was glad to see him with a much more positive attitude than usual.

I held my hand up like a phone, extending my thumb and pinky. "Call me," I reminded him.

He nodded, still smiling, and then turned back to gaze outside, dreaming about what the future would hold for his race.

19

I shifted Doug and myself into our living room. I then shifted alone to Earth for a moment so I could send Wyler a text message. I appeared out in the woods not far from his house, sent the message, and returned, all in the span of maybe two minutes.

When I came back home, Doug was standing in the kitchen enjoying a cold drink. He loved orange juice, and we always kept a large pitcher in the fridge. He set his glass down, and I moved in for a hug. I slid my arms around him, weaving my fingers together behind his lower back and planting the side of my face upon his chest. Nothing felt better than his strong arms holding me close. Doug gave me a sweet kiss on top of my head.

"You doing okay, sweetie?" he asked me. "You look kind of tired."

"Actually, I've got this weird sort of feeling inside of me. I can't explain it."

Doug rubbed his hand over my back. I could sense how immediately worried he had become. I probably should have explained myself better.

I straightened up and leaned my head back a few inches so I could look into his eyes.

"What exactly are you feeling?" he asked, sounding concerned and nervous.

I stared out at our yard through the tall kitchen windows and patio door. It was a clear day, full of sunshine, with small puffs of clouds moving across the beautiful blue sky. Sanvean's words came to me again, her suggestion about looking toward the sky and hearing the voices of those who required my help. Perhaps this was yet another part of my role as Keeper of the Citadel.

"I feel like a signature is pulling me toward it," I explained to Doug. "It's getting stronger. Sanvean told me this would happen occasionally, that I would sense people's need for help and then go to them."

Doug dropped both of his hands on my shoulders with a firm grip. "Don't you *dare* shift away without taking me with you, okay? We're in this together, David, and I want to be there with you. I want to watch as you change people's lives, when they see what you've become."

"I love you," I said while gazing at Doug's handsome face.

My focus wavered, but I managed to keep hold of his signature as feelings of conflict and strife overpowered me. I sensed death and despair.

"It's happening!" I blurted.

Together, we shifted into a nightmarish scene of smoldering fires, slain individuals in armor and chainmail, and ancient weaponry scattered throughout a vast field on some unfamiliar planet. Many leafless trees had fallen over, and others stood at precarious angles. Clouds of smoke billowed high into the evening sky across the green land, and jagged mountains sat in the distance. Spiked posts carved from the thickest of trunks had been assembled into a barrier nearby. Everywhere I looked hundreds of alien bodies lay slaughtered all around us with axes and swords and helmets scattered about. The scene resembled the battlefield between two primitive warring parties.

I immediately rose into the air and summoned an enormous winged spirit to encase me, a sort of dragon-looking beast with long arms, a massive tail, and clawed paws. Its outline glowed intensely in shimmering hues of blue and white. I called a somewhat-smaller four-legged bear spirit to surround Doug and protect him.

The smell of death filled the air. Pools of blood and spilled intestines left us cringing. The ground was covered in both, along with severed heads lying here and there. Wooden posts stood throughout the field with one or two bodies dangling from thick, long ropes wrapped tightly around their necks.

The signature that had pulled me here lay straight ahead. I could sense his presence.

A young alien male had collapsed upon the ground, cushioned by his fallen comrades. His helmet had been lost, and his dark leather armor had been torn and sliced apart from countless slashes. His skin tone bore a resemblance to mine but with a noticeable tint of rusty orange. He had a thick brown beard and short shaved hair.

"Is that him?" Doug pointed as his bear spirit followed mine over to the guy. We stood and stared at him for a moment.

The alien male raised his head and gazed at us. I could sense fear, wonder, and confusion coming from him. The sudden appearance of such enormous and bright spirits with individuals encased within must have been quite a shock, especially in a primitive culture like his.

The guy gasped as my ghostly dragon reached out and scooped him up in its clawed paws. It held him directly in front of me so that our faces were less than a foot away from each other. Beads of sweat rolled down his terrified and young bearded face. He breathed in panicked bursts, and I sensed he was in severe pain. Along his right side copious amounts of blood oozed from a deep gash caused by some sort of sharp blade.

I pushed my arms through the scaled chest of my spirit and cradled the alien's face with both of my hands. From his surprised look, I knew he felt the heat pouring off of me. It was the source of my imbuing gifts. It didn't take long before his expression changed to awe as we gazed into each other's eyes, for not only was I giving him abilities but also the knowledge of how to use them too.

I spoke quietly, gifting him with four unique powers that would alter the history of his world and forever change how his race would perceive him. "From the sky you will observe and learn from what lies beyond the clouds," I said in a low voice. "Your touch will heal others in need. No weapon will ever harm you again, and you will live a long and meaningful life."

He slowly nodded with his eyes wide opened. He understood my words because the fourth gift I'd given him was the ability to understand all languages from outsiders.

As he began to shed a few pleasurable tears, I pulled his name from his signature and memories—Torven.

Torven leaned forward through my spirit dragon and gave me a hug. He held on to me for the longest time, his arms tight around me, and I could feel his powers taking hold.

I ordered my dragon to let go of him, and he hovered in midair before slowly floating several feet away.

I watched with pride as he rose into the air. He outstretched his arms and called forth a familiar healing spell, one I had seen Chuppo use many times before. He cast traveler's wind so his spell could be used to heal many individuals at one time. An intense point of light had appeared high above Torven, and it quickly burst forth and covered the land with a rain of bright glowing flakes that would not only heal him but his people too.

The deadly wound along his side healed before my eyes. Blood no longer flowed from it. As Torven turned around high above his people, many of the folks who'd had minor injuries carefully stood and checked their wounds. Each of them seemed surprised and gazed around in wonder. Unfortunately, many could not be saved. But those who were healed would stand tall from Torven's curing gifts.

Doug's bear spirit pawed at my dragon's leg, and I turned to face my handsome man.

"I think we should go, sweetie," he whispered. "You've done your job."

I smiled at him and happily nodded. I took one final look at Torven before we left. He was still hovering in the sky, casting his spell over the masses of individuals who had been wounded.

Then, off to my side, maybe several hundred feet away, I saw Sanvean floating in the air. The long, flowing panels of her gray skirt gently flapped in the wind. She gave me a heartfelt smile with a courteous nod, and I knew today would be the beginning of many times like this to come. My role as a god hunter had officially begun.

Sanvean vanished before I could say anything to Doug. I then focused on home, taking the two of us back to our comfort zone. We appeared in our living room without our spirits. We flopped down on our long couch, feeling amazed and overwhelmed, pleased and satisfied.

"What do you think will happen to them?" Doug asked.

I shrugged. "Their lives will change for the better. Just like ours have." I couldn't resist pushing Doug to the side and then lying on top of him. I wanted to give him a lot of kisses. "Thank you for coming along."

He wrapped his arms around me, licking my lips before he slipped his tongue in my mouth. "I'll always be there for you, David. Having you in my life is the greatest gift of all."

"I feel the same way, sexy butt."

Doug pulled my shirt up and over my head and tossed it on the floor near the coffee table.

"What's on your mind?" I asked him with a grin.

He merely smiled, leaned in, and gave me two more sloppy kisses. "Making love to you is what's on my mind."

We took our time getting naked, helping each other pull off our boots but keeping our socks on. With our backs pressed against opposite ends of the couch, I raised Doug's foot and sniffed his socks. They smelled like fresh leather, with a hint of warm dampness. My sexy man had such big, delicious, hairy feet.

He did the same to me, kissing the bottoms of my socked feet and then running his tongue along them. "Damn, you taste so good," he mumbled. "I need to lick some other spots on you too."

My sweet talker always made me laugh.

Doug sat up on his knees, grabbed hold of my ankles, and helped me raise my thighs toward my chest. I knew exactly where my hairy, muscular stud was headed. He moved in gently, placing tender kisses all along my hairy cheeks, my inner thighs, and finally my tender spot he loved so much. He shoved his tongue in as far as he could and savored my taste. He took his time and drowned me in exquisite ecstasy. I let my head fall back against the pillows. I felt wonderfully dizzy.

Using his spit and wet lips, Doug left me nice and wet and opened enough for him to do what he did best. He sat up and scooted forward on his knees, close enough to insert his thick and lengthy piece of meat with ease. He moved slowly, taking his time so both of us could savor the feel. He braced his hands against my knees and pushed my legs open wider. He leaned over and pressed his face and beard against me, kissing my chest, my stomach. He sucked on my nipples as he pleasantly rolled his hips, moving in and out of me.

I cradled his head, rubbing my fingers over his short hair and then brushing them along the sides of his breathtaking beard. A strong whiff of his intoxicating cologne hit me, carrying me higher into a state of sheer bliss.

Doug straightened up so he could give me some kisses, then smashed the side of his face against my chest once more. I could tell he was close to getting off. He started to grunt and moan and speed up his movement. Within a few seconds he jerked and shivered for a long moment as he pumped me full of his scrumptious, warm love. Afterward, he collapsed against me, beads of sweat rolling down the side of his face and brow. He took deep breaths.

"Okay, Little Bear," he said. "Your turn, sweetie."

After Doug moved a few inches to the side, I happily began to stroke myself, but he grabbed hold of my hand and stopped me.

"No," he said. "I don't want you to do any work. I'm going to make you feel good."

We gave each other amused smiles. I wasn't about to argue with him. He could really send me over the edge every time, keeping me filled with joy.

Doug slid down the length of my body. He took hold of my erection and stroked it with languid twists of his hand as he covered my boys with lots of kindhearted kisses and moist licks.

"Oh, yeah," I whispered in delight. "Do it just like that."

With all of Doug's up-close and personal attention, it didn't take me long to get off. As I began to come, he quickly shoved his mouth down the length of my shaft and swallowed every warm shot I had to offer.

"Yummy," he said, licking his lips. He had kept his hand wrapped around my erection and ran his tongue along the length of my boys once more. He then added some kisses along the inside of my thighs.

I couldn't have asked for a better lover or man. Doug would always please me.

He lay down behind me, wrapping one arm around me and holding me close.

"Did you like that?" He laughed a little and rubbed his bearded face on my neck.

"You really know how to make me feel good," I answered. "Which reminds me, there's a place here on Alemereen I'd like to take you after we're done with Josh and Wyler. I think you'll love it. Sanvean showed it to me during one of my visions."

In between nibbling on my earlobe, he softly said, "Sounds like a date, sweetie."

My pdPhone chirped with a text message, and I recognized the familiar tone assigned to Wyler's number. My pants weren't far away, so I reached down and grabbed my phone out of my pocket.

"What'd he say?" Doug asked.

"He and Josh are ready to have us over. They're cooking dinner, so we can grab some food while we're there." I laughed. "Wyler even made one of his famous cheesecakes."

Doug gave me a firm squeeze. "I *love* cheesecake!"

"Then I guess you're going to get your fill of even more delicious treats than my scrumptious goo."

Doug burst out in laughter and tickled me along my sides and under my armpits. I wiggled and tried desperately to get away, but he had me pinned down pretty good.

"Okay!" I shouted. "You're going to make me piss all over the couch if you don't quit."

Doug stopped and gave me a kiss along my neck with a firm tweak of my left nipple. "I love you so much, David."

"I love you too, silly." I turned my head so we could kiss. "Let's go jump in the shower and then head out."

"Sounds like a plan."

We pulled off each other's socks, and Doug gave mine one final sniff. He was such a sweetheart. We then ran upstairs with our clothes piled in our arms, took a shower together, and got dressed. Doug put on his sexy brown textured cowboy boots and a pair of tight blue jeans that left little to the imagination in both front and back. He left his red plaid sleeveless shirt more than halfway unbuttoned, showcasing his hairy, muscular chest. I came close to drooling from his appearance, he seemed just as aroused by my look. I had slipped on a pair of jeans and square-toed brown boots, and I'd left my dark-blue short-sleeved shirt halfway unbuttoned too.

Doug slipped his hand inside my shirt and rubbed my chest. "Damn, you look so freakin' hot," he told me.

I pressed my body against his and slipped my arm behind him, giving his butt a few firm squeezes. "And you really know how to fill out a pair of jeans."

We kissed and shared a few gropes.

"Ready?" I asked.

Doug gave me an energetic smack across my rear. "Let's go get some cheesecake!"

I sighed and laughed, shaking my head, and then shifted us to Wyler's backyard.

20

"Howdy, boys!" Wyler was standing beside the grill, busy cooking some delicious-smelling steaks. The entire patio was infused with their intoxicating scent. He must have marinated them.

Immediately, I felt Doug and I had overdressed. The sun was just starting to set, but Wyler had dressed in a pair of dark-blue swimming trunks, brown sandals, and a light-gray tank top.

I leaned close to Doug and whispered, "I think we've got too many clothes on."

He laughed at me. "Well, we can easily fix that after we eat."

Good point.

The patio door slid open, and Josh let both dogs out. They immediately ran over to Doug and me. We both squatted to pat their heads and let them lick our hands.

Josh was wearing even less than Wyler. He had on a pair of red swimming trunks with matching sandals and no shirt. He was the hairiest man here, for sure. Even his back and shoulders were covered in hair. His muscular chest and bit of belly looked nice. I was glad Wyler had found such a caring and comforting man to share his life with.

The dogs ran off to bark at whatever critters were playing on the other side of the fence, and Doug and I stood to give Josh some hugs.

"How's it going?" I asked Josh.

"Better, now that you two are here." He smiled and quickly bounced his eyebrows up and down. Such a sweet talker. "Hope you guys are hungry," he added. "My hubby made a shit ton of food for us."

Doug licked his lips and patted his stomach. "I'm always ready for a feast!"

The three of us laughed. Then Doug and I followed Josh over to the patio table, where we all sat down in the cushioned chairs. The table was all set with plates, silverware, and napkins. I glanced over at the swimming pool. It looked inviting. I was pretty sure we'd be taking a dip in it later on tonight.

"Made a pitcher of sweet tea," Josh said. "Let me go and grab two glasses for you both."

He jumped up and headed back inside the house. A big puff of smoke rose up from the grill as Wyler flipped the steaks.

"So when are you going to gift Josh with some added abilities?" Doug asked. He sounded a bit excited.

I sighed and gave that some thought. "Probably after we eat. I'm not even sure Wyler told him about it yet. But I'm sure Josh won't mind some extra enhancements. Who wouldn't?"

Josh came back outside with two huge glasses of sweet tea, each with a lemon wedge hanging along its edge.

"Thanks." I took a sip. "Wow, this is awesome! Is that a hint of raspberry I taste?"

Josh nodded cheerfully. "Made it myself. My own special recipe."

Doug gulped down almost half of his glass in one single shot. "Good stuff, Josh. I'm a huge fan of all kinds of tea. But I'm really here for that cheesecake Wyler made. I think I need a giant slice of that right now!"

Josh and I laughed.

"It's tucked away in the refrigerator," Josh told us. "And trust me, no one is laying a hand on that cake until *after* Wyler serves us dinner."

"Steaks are done!" Wyler shouted out to us from the grill.

Josh gave a few confirming nods to his husband, then jumped out of his seat. "You two sit here while we bring out all the goodies."

Wyler carried over a huge platter piled with steaks.

"Looks like we'll be getting our fill of meat tonight," I said to Doug.

He laughed and massaged my leg under the table. "You know how much I love a nice piece of meat."

Wyler and Josh had to make two trips to bring out all the food. They had made a pasta dish, several baked potatoes, and one of those delicious green bean casseroles with the mushroom soup and French fried onions as toppings. They also brought out cheese bread and a sliced-fruit platter. And then there were the steaks. I swear each piece of meat was about the size of one of Doug's boots. Josh set down two pitchers, one filled with sweet tea and the other with apple juice. Wyler adjusted every item on the table, making sure everything looked perfect. He even had an abundant bouquet of flowers in a crystal vase as centerpiece.

They both took their seats, sitting side by side.

"Dig in!" Wyler told us. A huge smiled stretched across his face as he stabbed his fork into a steak.

All of us filled our plates and gobbled up as much as we could. Wyler and Josh were excellent cooks. Everything had left my mouth drooling for more.

"So how's married life treating you both?" I asked them.

Wyler and Josh smiled, then glanced at each other.

"It's wonderful," Josh said. He reached across the table and held Wyler's hand for a moment. "I couldn't ask for a better man to share my life with."

"Me too," Wyler said.

The memory of Wyler's recent murderous rampage suddenly popped into my head, but I didn't recall the incident in a bad or doubtful way in regard to their relationship. It actually reassured me. It proved that Wyler would do whatever it took to ensure Josh's happiness. I knew my demon buddy would give his husband nothing less than the purest of love, just as Doug and I gave each other.

We chatted and stuffed ourselves for about an hour before Wyler shifted inside the kitchen and reappeared with his humongous cheesecake and two buckets of toppings, a chunky strawberry sauce and a chocolate sauce.

Doug's eyes opened wide with want. He even drooled a little.

"Looks like somebody is ready for dessert!" Wyler smiled at Doug and then set the cake on the table and handed Doug a knife to cut it.

"I've been thinking about this since David mentioned it," Doug admitted. He sliced four big pieces and scooped them out on white china plates.

My sexy man and I opted for the strawberry topping. Wyler went without, and Josh elected for the chocolate sauce. As Josh shoved spoonfuls of cheesecake in his mouth, he got chocolate all over his beard. We all laughed at him, and Wyler leaned in and gave him several kisses and licks to help clean off his face.

I hoped good times like this would never end. My friends provided a much-needed escape for me.

It wasn't long before the sun disappeared below the horizon and very familiar constellations and stars started to twinkle above us.

Wyler suddenly stood up and pulled off his tank top, kicked off his sandals, and pushed his shorts and underwear down. "Don't worry about the dishes. Everyone get naked and get your butts in the pool!"

Josh, Doug, and I all jumped up and pulled off our clothes. Big and small wieners flopped from left to right as the four of us raced over to pool. We held our breath and jumped in, plunging beneath the surface with huge splashes. We then floated in warm embraces with our hearts' desires. Doug held me close as we shared passionate kisses. I wrapped my hands around his wet head and savored the feel of his soft lips and tongue against mine.

Beside his ear, I whispered, "I'm ready."

He understood my intentions, nodded, and then gave me a firm squeeze. "Work your magic, Little Bear," he said quietly before releasing me.

I made eye contact with Wyler, and from the look on my face, my demon buddy knew it was time for the Keeper of the Citadel to act. As he and Josh held each other and kissed, Wyler carefully and quietly moved them closer to the shallow end of the pool. I joined them, the water stopping at my belly button.

"Okay, guys," I said, raising my hands just above the surface of the water. "I need you both to take hold of my hands."

Josh seemed surprised, yet he smiled at my request.

Wyler tapped his finger against the tip of his husband's nose a few times. "We have a surprise for you," Wyler told him.

I could sense confusion mixed with intrigue building inside of Josh. He had no idea what I was about to do.

The three of us held hands, forming a circle with our outstretched arms, and Doug came and stood behind me. He placed his hands along my waist and rested his chin over my shoulder.

I glanced at Wyler and then stared into Josh's eyes. From the look of wonder on his face, he must be feeling the heat coming from my hands, the flow of my gifts into his body.

I took a deep breath, then let it out. In my head, Sanvean's words came to me from long ago. "Your touch will convey your will. Speak, and you will make them strong," she had said to me.

I gently squeezed Wyler's and Josh's hands and then took a moment to gather my words. "Over unbroken roads and age-old stones, the two of you will travel throughout this universe and many more as you explore life together beneath ancient suns. From out of the cold so long ago, you now stand together around a fire built upon your love. Distant horizons will welcome you. Time will be gentle to you both. City gates will stand open, inviting you within. And there will never be a night without stars. Your journey together will be blissful. You will walk hand in hand, for all times."

I released their hands and then lowered my arms below the water so I could rub my fingers over the front of Doug's hairy thighs.

My sexy man kissed the side of my neck and whispered into my ear, "I love you, sweetie."

Josh leaned his head back and stared straight up into the night sky with a blank look on his face. I had given them both improved longevity. They would be immune to corrosive spells, magic, and weapons of any kind. But more importantly, Josh could now shift along with his husband, which explained his bedazzled expression. I could definitely appreciate his reaction to the flow of signatures now rushing into his body and mind.

"Thank you, Davie," Wyler said. A few happy tears ran down his cheeks.

"You're welcome," I said happily.

Doug took hold of my chin and turned my head a bit so we could kiss.

Josh and Wyler wrapped one another in a warm embrace, kissing and happily crying, cradling each other's face in their hands. Wyler worked his fingers through Josh's beard and then brushed his lips over it. I felt an overwhelming amount of love pouring off of them both.

"Well," Doug announced in a loud and cheerful voice, "I feel like I could use another piece of cheesecake!"

I spun around, shaking my head, and reached up and tweaked one of his nipples. "Your tummy isn't full from the huge dinner?"

My handsome man shrugged. "That cheesecake tasted really good." He tapped my butt. "You know I can never get enough of a good thing."

While laughing, Wyler shifted over to the patio and grabbed the dessert dish and a fork. He then reappeared beside us in the water with a small splash. "Here you go, muscle man. Service with a smile." He handed Doug what was left of the cheesecake.

Doug happily accepted the dish and fork. He gave Wyler a quick, loud smooch on the side of his head. "Thanks, buddy."

The four of us moved into deeper water while Doug gobbled up the cheesecake. He actually offered a few bites to me, and I happily sucked them off the tip of his fork.

Wyler gave Josh a few tips and tricks in regard to shifting, and then our new recruit tried his ability for the first time. It took a few minutes, but Josh finally got the swing of it. He moved in and out of the pool, managing his skills nicely, and I could tell he would make an excellent shifter. A bedazzled expression never left his face. I felt so happy for him.

"So what are you two going to do now that the MST is abolished?" Wyler asked. He had slid his arms around Josh from behind so he could massage his husband's hairy chest.

I glanced at Doug and smiled happily. "I think we'll make some time for ourselves—enjoy our new house, visit with friends, and so forth." I grabbed hold of my tough guy's manly hand, raised it to my face, and kissed the back of it. "I'm sure Jay E Jay and the Bear Paw will handle things real well. Plus, Doug and I could use a break, which I'm sure you can relate to."

My demon buddy nodded with a sigh of relief and a look of gratefulness on his face. All the years he and the goddess Shaye had spent working behind the MST's back must have been exhausting. But they'd finally accomplished what they had set out to do. It warmed my heart knowing that Wyler could now sit back and enjoy life with Josh.

We played in the pool for about an hour. Facing Doug, I wrapped my legs around his waist while he held me in his arms. He got turned on from all my sloppy kissing and slid his meaty erection along the crack of my behind. From the looks of it, Josh and Wyler were doing much the same as Doug and I.

Soon we climbed out, and Doug and I put our clothes back on beside the patio table.

"We'll take care of the dishes," Wyler told us. "You two go and have some fun."

Josh and Wyler both pulled on their trunks. Then Josh gave me and Doug a warm hug with a kiss on the cheek. "Thank you for everything," he said to me. "You both are charming and beautiful guys."

"You're welcome, furry man." I tickled my fingers over Josh's hairy chest.

I then squatted to say good-bye to my dogs, Sian and Zoe, who were sniffing the edge of the table looking for handouts. There were a few pieces of steak lying on a plate, so I gave them both a few treats. Doug leaned down and rubbed their heads. The friendliest of pets, they loved each of us so much. Doug's affectionate gesture made me smile. My sexy man looked so good in jeans and cowboy boots.

Wyler had taken some dishes inside to the kitchen and came back out to us. "Come and visit anytime you two feel like it," he said. The three of us exchanged some tight embraces. He and Doug had developed a much better feel for each other. Good friends now, for sure.

"Go," he told us, tapping the side of our thighs. "Have some fun! You've earned it."

Doug wrapped his arms around me from behind and whispered in my ear, "Didn't you say there was some spot on Alemereen you wanted to take me to?"

I kissed his cheek. "Yeah," I said. "You want to go now?"

His reciprocating kiss against my cheek answered my question with a definite yes.

We waved good-bye to Josh and Wyler, and they returned the gesture as I focused on the signature I'd gotten from Sanvean. I shifted Doug and me to the mountain cliff.

"Wow," he said, dropping his arms from around me and taking a few steps to the side. "This is beautiful, David."

It was still early in the morning here. The sun had just begun to rise above the blue-and-pink horizon. Plenty of stars still shone high above us too. We had a good view of the mountains in the distance as well as the valley below us. There were several small bushes filled with blooms nearby, and the morning songs of birds filled the air. Below our booted feet lay chunky stones, tiny pebbles, and a small amount of sand. It was a gorgeous view of our world.

Doug sat down on the ground near the ledge, and I sat down between his legs and leaned back against his powerful chest. I took in a whiff of his intoxicating cologne as he held me within his arms. He gave me kisses on the side of my head and along my neck as we watched the sun rise.

"Are you happy with the way things turned out?" I asked him. I figured he was, but I wanted to hear it from him.

He let out a small chuckle. "I am, sweetie. You've dismantled the MST and helped the Bear Paw take their rightful place. You've given a better future to Kirill and Aldis. I've never seen James happier than he is with Willie. Bryan's content and getting his fill of sex with Seth. Hell, even Nheyja is proud to be your friend."

Doug kissed the side of my head again. "I'd say everybody is very pleased with how things have turned out, sweetie. But are *you* happy with what's going on? Are you okay with being the Keeper of the Citadel and taking care of people who call out for your help?"

I rubbed my hands along his outstretched legs. His jeans fit so tightly that I got a good feel of his muscular thighs. The sight of his boots excited me also, since we both shared the joy of sniffing each other's socks, especially when they had an enticing leather scent.

I leaned back more against my handsome man, wiggling my body against his, getting myself comfy against his sexiness.

"Yeah," I told him. "I'm happy with being the Keeper. I actually enjoy helping those people who need me. I'm an official god hunter. It feels good gifting powers to them. I'm looking forward to seeing who else will need my help."

Doug massaged his hands over my stomach and then moved lower, fondling my crotch and legs. "I love you so much, David. Thank you for bringing us here. It's really beautiful."

I laughed a little. "I love you too, sexy man. I knew this would be a good spot to take a break. It's very relaxing, isn't it?"

"It is. The breeze feels nice. Maybe we should build a log cabin or some kind of getaway house up here. Having a retreat might come in handy."

"I like the sound of that! You know so many construction guys who could build it for us." I brushed my hands along his hairy arms. Touching Doug pleased me in ways I couldn't even begin to explain. I absolutely loved his hairy body, the way he made love to me, and how appealing he always looked and smelled.

The sun had risen higher and now filled the sky with a bright-orange color. Very few clouds had moved by as we'd sat on the ledge overlooking the vast green valley below.

"So what do you see in our future?" I asked him.

Doug kissed my cheek. "Oh, I am going to make you the happiest man on the planet. That's my goal." He gave me a firm hug. "I want to see you smiling every day and full of laughs all the time. I hope we can go to a lot of new places and see some really great stuff throughout the Expanse."

I leaned the side of my head against his shoulder. It felt so good just sitting here with him and enjoying the sunrise together. So many other places that we could have gone to popped into my head, but this one seemed fitting for the moment.

"So what do you see in our future?" he asked me.

As I snuggled against him, wrapped up in his strong arms, I recalled my vision with Sanvean along this cliff. I finally understood her reference about the horizon and its unending reach and potential. What she had said about how Doug and I would explore and grow with each other throughout all of time now made sense.

I pointed at the sunrise, out at the horizon. "There," I said. "That's where I see us."

"Are you going to take us flying into the sun?" Doug asked, sounding confused.

"No, silly!"

We both laughed, and I tickled my fingers along his side. He gave me another kiss on my cheek. I twisted in his arms so I could look up into his beautiful blue eyes, and we kissed. I slipped my tongue in his mouth, and he sighed in pleasure. He tightened his arms around me and took a deep, satisfying breath. I could sense his desire to make love to me had grown on the inside as well as the outside of his body. I stroked his thick beard and brushed the back of my fingers down his cheek. My eyes pooled with tears a bit while touching my beautiful man. The tiniest of happy tears ran down my face, and Doug was quick to wipe them away with his thumbs.

"You okay, sweetie?" he asked. It seemed he could tell they were tears of joy, though, because he was smiling at me.

Nothing pleased me more than being with Doug. My heart eased into a state of happiness and joy. I could have sat here forever, knowing moments like this would never end for us. I gave a confirming nod to his question. I added a kiss on his lips, then snuggled against my sexy man.

"Sanvean was right," I whispered to him. "She told me what she saw in our future, and I see the exact same thing. I see you and me, our hearts together forever, hand in hand for all time as we share our lives with each other. How's that sound?"

Doug tenderly kissed my cheek. "That sounds perfect, David, absolutely perfect. You're the greatest part of my life, sweetie. I'm never letting go of you."

"Then I guess it's a date!"

We both laughed, and Doug gave me a heartfelt squeeze and kissed the top of my head again.

"You've made the Expanse a better place," he whispered happily. "I can't wait to see how many more lives you change. I love you, David. I have loved you for a thousand lifetimes."

"I love you too, handsome." I sighed with an abundance of delight. "I think I'm addicted to you, Mr. Colt."

He tenderly rubbed my hands while squeezing his legs around both of mine. Then he brushed his beard along my cheek, making me feel so incredibly loved and wanted. My heart couldn't have been more satisfied in this moment. I had found the love of my life, and I would do anything to keep him happy. I would never stop loving him. I would never stop pleasing him in all ways possible.

Doug rested the side of his face against my head, and I sank against his enticing body as we entwined our fingers. Together, two as one, we stared at the rising sun, its brilliant orange light, the valley down below the cliff's edge, and what few clouds drifted above. A few birds flew overhead singing their early-morning songs of joy.

"You know what sounds really good right about now?" I asked.

"What's on your mind?" Doug sounded a bit intrigued.

"I think we should get a ton of cheesecake, followed by a dip in *our* hot tub, and then some slow and sensual sex!" I said bluntly. "Would you be up for that? I could shift us to a grocery store, and then we could head home." I giggled. "We could probably squeeze in some foot and sock appreciation too. After all we both have leather boots on." I wiggled my boots, drawing his attention to them.

My lovable man laughed and wrapped me up in a warm, affectionate hug. He kissed the top of my head, then nuzzled his thick beard against the side of my face. "Little Bear," Doug whispered, "you just made me the happiest man in the entire Expanse."

"That makes two of us," I told him.

I sighed in pleasure before gently leaning back some more against his muscular torso. Doug held me for the longest time, supporting my entire weight and giving me many sweet kisses. I gazed out onto the sunrise feeling incredibly relaxed. I snuggled against my sexy man, using him like a hairy pillow made of muscles. I closed my eyes as he rubbed his hands over my back and sides. Nothing felt better than Doug's attention and tender care for me.

Sanvean was right. Doug and I would be the protectors of the Expanse... in love and together forever.

About the Author

M ark Reed is an award-winning visual artist in figure drawing and design and is experienced in both traditional and digital media. Numerous works of his art have sold to collectors in the United States, Europe, and Australia. His literary work brings to life many of the characters and exciting places seen throughout his artwork.

Printed in the United States
By Bookmasters